The Goldilocks Zone

The Goldilocks Zone

A Novel

DAVID D. LUXTON

MYSTERIOUS LIGHT *PRESS*
www.mysteriouslightpress.com

ISBN: 978-1-7348248-4-1

www.mysteriouslightpress.com

Printed in the United States of America

For those with the courage to seek and know the truth, regardless of what it may be or how it may change them.

"The first principle is that you must not fool yourself and you are the easiest person to fool."

—Richard Feynman

1

LIGHTS IN THE SKY

Any investigative journalist worth their salt will tell you that a good bullshit detector is a must. And for me, whenever someone claims to have special knowledge about mystical experiences and makes you pay for it, my detector needles up, big time.

I was headed to a place called The Valley of the Moon, just outside of Missoula, Montana, to interview Daniel Byrne. Byrne's a Harvard lawyer turned professional UFO researcher, public speaker, and co-founder of the Proxima Foundation, a not-for-profit focused on advancing contact with extraterrestrials. My plan was to attend one of his "contact events" where, according to the promotional videos on their website, he and his assistants would point lasers into the night sky, play New Age music, and have attendees meditate on happy thoughts until glowing objects appeared in the firmament. Byrne was charging three grand, and with nearly a million followers on social media and endorsements from celebrity talent and at least one former NASA astronaut, he had to be raking in some serious dough. Sure, he had his dissenters and skeptics, but the devotees far outnumbered the haters.

While I was suspicious of Daniel Byrne and his group, I

must admit I was excited to be doing the story. I've had an interest in UFOs since I was a kid and even saw one back in the late winter of '97 when I was ten. I was on a Cub Scout camping trip near Prescott, Arizona when seven amber lights in a V formation floated silently by in the night sky. My best friend Jonathan Mahue saw it, too, and so did about ten thousand other people between Prescott and Tucson. You may have heard about it; the incident became known as the Phoenix Lights.

To tell you the truth, I have no idea what I saw that night, or whether I believe that aliens have ever visited our planet. What I do know is that it's a big universe, and according to the Drake Equation, millions of planets out there could support life. Besides, scientists have confirmed the existence of more than four thousand exoplanets, some of which are in the Goldilocks Zone, neither too hot nor too cold to sustain organic matter. The problem is that any habitable planet with intelligent life, if there are any, is just too distant for anyone out there to get here, even if they wanted to.

Something else had me even more pumped about the assignment. A week earlier, the police had found a woman's body on a ranch not far from where Byrne holds his viewing events. All I knew about the deceased was that she was a *Montana Morning Magazine* investigative reporter named Sally Jensen. She was in her late-thirties, brunette, mother of two, and from the news clips I saw, took her job seriously. I phoned the Missoula County Sheriff's Department before I left Seattle to see what information I could get, but they were tight-lipped, saying only that it was an "active murder investigation." Could there be a link to the Proxima Foundation? It would give the story more legs, if so. I'd inquire about the case while I was out there.

I arrived at the Missoula airport around 5 p.m., got an economy rental car, and found a Motel 6 just half a mile out of town off Interstate 93 near Clinton. I checked in, brought my suitcase to my room, took a piss, and checked my restaurant app. Ramblin' Joe's with three stars was right next door. Outside, it looked like an old saloon with wood slab siding and a large porch, and the inside was ridiculously eclectic, with animal heads on the walls, dark red carpet, dozens of old photographs everywhere, and one of those toy-filled claw machines by the front door.

It was mostly vacant, and with no one greeting me, I sat in a booth near the bar. A waitress popped out from the double swinging doors in the back—tall, thin, in her late twenties. Her hair was dark brown, almost black, and long and curly but pulled back in a ponytail. The tag on her shirt said "Brenda," and her big dark brown eyes under perfect eyebrows made her drop-dead gorgeous. No ring on her finger. I smiled when she approached, expecting one in return, but all she did was drop off a menu. Maybe her standoffishness was to keep the local yahoos and out-of-town slick dicks from hitting on her. I examined the menu. When she returned with water, I smiled, hoping my crush wasn't too obvious.

"Here for the UFOs?" she asked, setting the water down.

"How could you tell?" I asked, surprised she wanted to start a conversation.

She gave me a snarky look. "Hope it's worth the three thousand dollars."

"Actually, I'm a journalist. I'm doing a story on the Proxima Foundation."

Her eyes lit up a bit. "Yeah? What paper?"

"*Hot Reports*, an online magazine based in Seattle. Heard of it?"

"Nope, should I have?"

"I did a big story on nuclear waste cleanup at the Hanford Nuclear Reservation in Washington. Maybe you saw it."

"What's your name?"

"Ben Davenport."

She shook her head. "Nope, never heard of you. Sorry."

Bummer. I thought about pulling the article up on my smartphone to show her. I'd spent nearly two years investigating the construction of a new facility, west of

Yakima, Washington, part of a multibillion-dollar cleanup operation. *The most toxic place in America.* My exposure of the construction delays, cost overruns, and cover-up of contracting shenanigans by the Federal and State governments got me a Pulitzer nomination.

"Do you want to order something?"

I glanced at the menu. "I'll have the Rancher's Burger, medium-well, sweet potato fries, and a Big Sky IPA."

She grabbed the menu.

"Is it always so quiet in here?" I asked, looking around.

"It's not happy hour yet," she said, before disappearing through the double swinging doors.

I liked her sassy attitude and good looks, but it wasn't like I was going to do anything about it. I'd been with Jennifer back in Seattle for almost three years. Lately, she'd been giving me a hard time for drinking too much, and she wanted me to find a better paying job. I told her I had one as a Pulitzer-nominated investigative journalist, but she reminded me that being a nominated writer is not the same as an award-winning writer. I took her digs because I loved her and was hoping we'd have a future together, maybe marriage and kids.

Brenda dropped off my beer and returned a few minutes later with my food. "Anything else?" she asked.

"Know anything about that TV woman who was found dead out here last week?"

Her eyes narrowed. "Yeah, she was my aunt."

"Seriously?"

"Yes, Sally Jensen was my mother's sister. She was doing a story on the UFO culties."

"Gosh—my condolences. Would you be willing to answer a few questions about your aunt?"

"Now's not a good time. I've got to get back to work."

"Of course," I said to her back, wondering if I came off too aggressive.

I dug into my burger and checked my emails. Brenda breezed by and dropped my check on the table and was gone.

After my last French fry, I handed my AMEX card to Brenda at the cash register. She ran it and handed it back.

"If you want to talk," I said, handing her my business card.

"I'll think about it."

"Okay. Have a good evening." I grabbed a toothpick from a jar on the counter.

"Don't get abducted."

"What?" I queried, her comment not registering.

She pointed her index finger upwards, smirked, and raised those perfect eyebrows.

I smiled. "Right."

After a quick stop in my motel room, I checked my directions and headed east on I-93 toward Byrne's property. The sun was just starting to set in a perfectly clear late April sky. A feeling of nervous anticipation came over me. I was looking forward to a little night stroll, but I was also well aware that I needed to stay focused. I wasn't sure how cooperative Byrne was going to be. You have to be careful with investigative interviews, especially with someone as sharp as Byrne. The trick is to appear interested and neutral. If you don't, your interviewee may shut down on you.

I headed up into the hills and made the turn onto Valley of the Moon Road, passed through an open cattle gate reading *PRIVATE PROPERTY*. Three hundred yards later, the road turned to gravel and threaded through fencing on both sides. Two miles further, I came to a dozen or so parked vehicles and twenty, maybe thirty people standing about, putting on their daypacks, some with folding lawn chairs in hand. I turned my car around, stirring up dust in the twilight, and parked in a spot behind a minivan, then headed over to a group of people congregating at the trailhead signpost.

Daniel Byrne was standing by a white GMC Yukon. Early 50s, tall, and a full head of coppery hair. The casual vibe of his khakis offset the jolt of his jacket with that Proxima Foundation logo—a hexagon with a circle over each corner blaring bright green and black. Byrne was giving orders to a young man in a baseball cap pulling large military-style black boxes out of the GMC Yukon. *Camera and laser equipment*, I figured.

"Welcome," Daniel said, casting a wide smile and hand once I approached.

"I'm Ben Davenport with *Hot Reports*."

"I know who you are. Glad you could make it."

Releasing his grip, he glanced up at the sky. "We're lucky. No clouds, no moon. Perfect conditions for an eventful night. I can feel it."

I glanced at the equipment on the ground. "Can I help carry anything?"

"No, thanks, we've got it," he said. His helper cast a suspicious glance. That's when I spotted the handgun holstered on his hip under his OD commando sweater. Was he Daniel's security? Why did he need it? I introduced myself to him. He stood up straight and squeezed my hand,

"Mike," he said simply before returning to his duties.

At 7:30 sharp, Daniel and Mike did a quick headcount, then led the group single file onto a narrow trail winding up a tall grassy slope. Several had flashlights. In fifteen minutes, we were cresting the top.

"Here's the spot, everyone," Byrne announced. "Find a place, semi-circle facing north."

Mike went to work setting up the equipment.

"Why north?" I asked Mike.

"That's where they come in from," he said, his East Coast accent coming through.

I nodded. *We'll see*, I thought.

Mike took another device out of the box and fixed it to a tripod.

"What's that?" I asked.

"Special equipment," Mike said.

"It's a magnetometer. It will beep at us when they're here," Daniel offered, coming up behind me, then turning to address the crowd. "Remember, everyone, all phones silenced and in airplane mode, or turn them off."

"Should I turn mine off?" I asked, still watching Mike set

up the video equipment.

"Airplane mode is fine. We do this because the interference will mess with our equipment. I'll let you know when it's okay to turn it on."

I sat in a lawn chair and scanned the folks—everyday men and women, mostly middle-aged, some younger. Mike was going around with an electronic device in his hand.

"That's an electromagnetic field sensor," Daniel informed me. "We want to make sure no one is forgetting the protocol."

His gadget would pick up my phone anyway, so I kept it on just in case I wanted to pull it out for a photo.

A light breeze rose from the northwest, and the air temperature was dropping fast. A chill rippled through me. The Milky Way was becoming more visible by the minute.

"Okay, everyone, let's meditate," Daniel said quietly. "Remember what we learned today in the workshop. Wish to meet with them. Invite them to us. Send them your good will."

Soft music began to play, a Native American flute and rattle with arpeggio beeps and blips of synthesizers. *Oh, here we go*, I thought. I hope he's not going to have us all hold hands.

Just then my phone chimed with a text message, startling me. I reached into my pocket and hit the power switch.

"Whoever has a cell phone on, please turn it off," Daniel commanded, and flashing his laser pointer toward the northern sky, its thin red beam disappearing into the dark. Someone in the crowd spotted a faint white object moving across the sky almost directly overhead. It grew brighter, then vanished.

"Whoa, did you see that?" the man next to me said.

"Just an Iridium satellite," Daniel explained, "they have large solar panels reflecting the sun. It's not them. Keep your minds focused, think good thoughts."

The meditation continued until the stillness was broken by a woman in the group. "Look over there!" she yelled. "Over there!"

She was pointing northwest. A third of the way up from the horizon we saw three amber lights, bigger than the brightest star or planet in the night sky. Gasps and shouts of ecstasy. "Holy sweet Jesus!" the woman in front of me cried. Daniel, now sitting in his chair, nodded, "It's them, they're here. Oh, this is something, everyone, look! Keep thinking positive thoughts. Invite them into our atmosphere with positive thoughts. Mike, are you filming this?"

Mike was looking into the digital viewfinder display. "Yes, I've got it."

"Zoom in if you can."

"I'm trying, can't seem to get it to focus. Wait, here we go—Damn it!"

"Come on, Mike, get it," Daniel pushed impatiently.

The lights were similar to what I'd seen in '97, minus the geometric formation. They appeared to be stationary, yet looked as though they were moving. Suddenly, the three lights became six. What could they be? Flares from Air National Guard F16s out of Great Falls? Spotlights from Army Black Hawks? They were too far apart to be on the same object. My heart began to beat faster.

"This is an event, everyone," said Daniel. "Keep wishing them good will. Invite them to come closer, there's nothing to worry about." His voice was calm and mesmerizing, his laser pointer still cutting through the night sky.

Everyone had their eyes on the lights. I started to reach for my smartphone when Byrne reminded everyone to keep them turned off. In less than a minute, the lights began to move lower in the sky, seemingly away from us. After another minute, they disappeared.

"Did they go behind a ridge or something?" I asked.

"Nope, no ridge," Daniel said. "They do that sometimes. Crossing the trans-dimensional boundary."

We all stared at the horizon. The air temperature had dropped another few degrees.

Byrne turned to Mike. "Did we clock it?"

"Got it, three minutes, eight seconds. Got it all on film. Just wish they had gotten closer."

"Yeah, well," Daniel shrugged. He stood up and addressed the awestruck group. "Okay, everyone, that's all for tonight. Gather up your things and head back to the parking lot for hot chocolate."

We trekked down the ridge. When we got back to the vehicles, Mike began pouring hot chocolate into Styrofoam cups for any takers.

I went over to Daniel. "What was that?" I asked.

"It was them," he said simply, "our intra-dimensional friends. Who did you think it was?"

"What exactly do you mean by 'intra-dimensional?'"

"They visit Earth often; you just can't see them. It's our meditation that allows them to show themselves."

"What caused them to disappear so quickly?"

"They get spooked easily, maybe an aircraft in the area, military or commercial. But tonight, I think it was someone in our group, someone just was not on the right wavelength. They were sensitive to it."

"Do you think it was me?" I asked.

He looked at me and smiled. "Well if it was you, I'd be worried."

"What do you mean by, worried?"

He put his hand on my shoulder. "The more you learn, the better. We can discuss it at brunch tomorrow at the ranch. I can explain more then, and you can ask questions for your story. My wife Nadine is looking forward to meeting you. Where are you staying?"

"The Motel 6 in Clinton."

He nodded. "Nice place." We shook hands. "Goodnight, Ben."

On my way down the valley, I kept glancing up. The urge still gripped me at the Motel 6 parking lot. Back in the room, I checked to see if the local news station was reporting anything. Nothing. I checked the Internet. Nothing. I shot out a tweet. "Lights in the sky tonight. UFO maybe.

#Lightsinthesky #UFO."

I called Jennifer. I knew that I'd wake her up, but I needed to tell her about what I had seen.

"We saw something," I said.

"Yeah? What was it?" Her voice was groggy and muffled.

"Lights in the sky, Jennifer. I don't think they were airplanes. I don't know what they were."

She yawned. "Probably a drone or something. What time is it?"

"I don't know." I looked at my smartwatch. "Eleven."

"Can we talk about this later? I've got work in the morning."

"I know. I just wanted to tell you."

The line was quiet for a moment, and then she pressed, "You'll be back tomorrow night, right? We've got to shop for Gabriella's baby shower on Sunday. Don't forget."

"Yes, I know. I've got an interview in the morning, then I'll be catching my flight. Love you."

"Text me when your flight lands and you're on your way," she said, and then hung up.

I got undressed and into bed, still thinking about what we'd seen that night. Before I hit the light, I checked my phone for news. Nothing. Social media feeds had nothing. What was it? Had to have been a hoax. Flares, Japanese lanterns. Whatever it was, I couldn't wait for the interview in the morning.

2

PROXIMA B

The Proxima Foundation grounds stretched down a long dirt road of flat valley terrain, about 20 miles east of Missoula. Finding the entry gate open, I drove in, raising a cloud of dry dust. The surrounding hills were a peachy orange and blanketed by a fast-disappearing mist. I noticed a massive white tent off to the left and more than a dozen metal shipping containers with residential doors and windows around the back part of the property.

Byrne's house was farther down the road beyond a bluff of trees—a big ranch-style two-story with a wrap-around screened porch, a red-walled barn and large horse corral off to one side. Nadine Byrne greeted me at the front door. She was in her late forties with cornsilk hair, indigo eyes, and a warm and welcoming face. I had learned earlier at the Proxima Foundation website that she was a Harvard lawyer and the Chief Financial Officer.

"Good morning, you must be Ben," she said, smiling broadly. "You're younger than I was expecting." She held my hand for just a few seconds longer than a normal handshake. Was she trying to get a psychic energy read on me or just flirting? I found myself wondering what the Byrne marriage was like.

She led me through the house to the back porch where Daniel and Mike were sitting at a round table with a gas patio heater radiating overhead.

"'Morning, Ben, welcome to our humble abode," Daniel said, raising a smile. A small blue light flashed from the Bluetooth receiver planted in his left ear. Large plate of pancakes, steaming scrambled eggs, and glistening vegan substitute bacon beckoned from the bamboo Lazy Susan.

"So, what did you think of the sighting last night, Ben?" Nadine quizzed, filling my earthenware coffee mug.

"I'm still… in awe, I guess. I wasn't expecting to see anything like that."

She smiled. "That's the response we always get when people have their first experience at one of Daniel's events. They are life-changing for so many. Have you ever had an extraterrestrial experience before?"

"Actually, yes. I was witness to the Phoenix Lights in 1997."

Daniel's and Nadine's eyes widened. "Lots of controversy about those lights. What do you think you saw?" Nadine asked, passing the sugar to me.

"I don't know yet. I mean, I know I saw something, like last night, but I'm not really sure what."

"Well, you are in the right place to learn more. Dig in everyone." She gestured to the bamboo centerpiece. I was hungry and loaded my plate.

"I read your story on the Hanford nuclear facility," Nadine added. "Very impressive writing. And to be nominated for a Pulitzer already at your age. Your parents must be proud of you."

I smiled, equally impressed that she'd read my article.

She still had her eyes on me. "So how long have you been with *Hot Reports*?"

"I've been freelance writing for them for about three years now."

"Do you come up with your own story ideas?"

Plainly, she was sizing up my angle for the UFO piece. I

needed to play it cool and shift the attention back on her and Daniel.

"My editor assigned this story, but the Hanford one was my idea. I spent two years on it. I like to thoroughly understand things before I write. I have a few questions for you, is that okay?" I took out a small notepad.

"Shoot," Daniel said, chewing

"Tell me about how you all got into UFOs." I narrowed in on Daniel first.

"I had a life-changing event when I was in law school," he began. "Some of us from my class went to Newfound Lake in New Hampshire, about seven or eight of us. We stayed in a cabin. I was teaching my friends how to meditate when we saw lights descending over the lake. They sparkled and grew brighter, hovering over the surface of the water. Some went outside to look at the spectacle, but I kept meditating. My eyes were half open when I saw an EBE."

"EBE?"

"Extraterrestrial biological entity. We don't call them ETs anymore," Byrne clarified. "It raised a three-fingered hand, and our minds directly connected for a minute. The EBE told me that my destiny was not to be a lawyer but a teacher of humanity."

"But you continued with law school and went into practice?" I remembered that from his bio.

"Oh yes, family pressure. No complaints, though. I went to work at a law firm in Chicago. That's where I met Nadine." He glanced at her, nodding. "We'd spend hours meditating together, talking about mysteries, didn't we, honey?"

She nodded, sipping her coffee.

"We were on the same wavelength, if you know what I mean," Daniel continued. "After a few years, we both realized that corporate law was not for us. She convinced me to leave."

"So whose idea was it to start the Proxima Foundation?"

Byrne tapped his chest. "It was my idea to focus on alien

contact, and Nadine is the business end. I don't know what I would do without her."

"We all have our special talents," Nadine said, looking softly at Daniel.

I turned toward Mike. "What about you, Mike? What got you into all of this?"

"I was in the Navy, a boatswain's mate on the USS Enterprise. One night I was on watch out in the middle of the Pacific, and we saw some lights trailing after us under the water. It wasn't bioluminescence but an EBE craft. Eventually, it shot out of the water at an angle into the sky and disappeared. It was small, rainbow colors. A bunch of us saw it."

"Wow," I said. "Is there a record of this event? I'd love to see it."

Mike looked me in the eyes. "We were commanded to keep our mouths shut."

"Typical military," Byrne added.

That was when I noticed that all three of them had the Proxima Foundation symbol stitched somewhere on their clothing.

"Proxima. Is that where the aliens are coming from?"

"Yes, it is," said Daniel. "Proxima Centauri b is the closest planetary system to Earth that's in the habitable Goldilocks Zone—just under four and a quarter light-years from Earth."

I was skeptical to say the least. "Wow, four light-years is pretty close. And how do you know that's where they are from?"

"They told me. Ever had a psychic download, Ben?" Daniel asked.

"I don't think so. What's a psychic download?" *Bullshit and more bullshit*, I thought.

"It's when you are telepathically given a download of information." He and Mike shared a knowledgeable smile.

"Wish I'd had one for graduate school," I grinned.

Daniel returned the grin. "You'd know it if you had one."

"Are you open to experience, Ben?" Nadine asked, reading

my skepticism.

"I think so." I assumed she was referring to openness as a personality trait.

"That's important. People who aren't receptive will never wrap their minds around this."

I turned my attention back to Daniel. "So, you've had one of these downloads from the aliens?"

"Yes, I have, several times. They told me about their visits here, and that our meditation protocol is their preferred way for interacting with us. You can't fake intentions through meditation. We invite them to appear in peace, and they know that is exactly what we want and what we expect in return. Peaceful communication with open hearts."

"You mentioned that they're multidimensional. What does that mean exactly? Are they coming from another dimension? Bending time and space?"

"As I mentioned to you last night, the EBEs communicate and travel on a different dimensional wavelength than ours." He reached over and pinched the skin on my forearm. "This physical realm is but one of many layers of dimension in the universe. I explain it all in my books and my workshop. You should have come earlier yesterday."

"Why do you think the ETs, I mean EBEs, don't just appear to everybody so it's more obvious that they are here? Why not land on the White House lawn or something?"

"If I had a nickel for every time I've been asked that. They're not making a diplomatic visit. Maybe they don't trust government. They're subtle in how they interface with us. As I said before, they trust the way we communicate with them."

I struggled. "It just seems like they could do something to make their presence more known, assuming that it's important for them to be known. Why are they so elusive?"

"They're not that elusive. You saw them last night, didn't you?" said Nadine.

"They want to be known but in a calculated way," said Daniel. "They are as curious about us as we are about them. They've been coming here for a long time and know to be careful."

I sipped my medium roast. "So how long have they been coming to Earth? I've watched some of those documentaries on ancient aliens, and you hear all kinds of hypotheses."

"Routinely, for the last seventy years, but of course there's evidence that they've been interacting with humans for thousands of years."

"Could you ask them?" I said, trying not to smirk.

Nadine saw straight through me. "Ben, they don't have to provide evidence of their presence or justify it. They don't have to answer to us."

I took another tack. "So what do the EBEs look like? Are we dealing with the grays? The ones with the large slanted eyes?"

"The types of grays you see in the movies and TV are fake. The species that have been coming here have gray skin, but no pointy chins or oversized eyes. Their eyes are larger than ours, though, to let more light in."

Mike pulled out his smartphone and showed me a fuzzy, pixelated photo of an EBE, a humanoid gray figure with a large forehead and obsidian eyes.

"Is that real?" I asked, silently considering the wonders of Photoshop.

"Yep," he said. "I took this during an event at Mount Shasta last year."

"We have other photos, too," Nadine added.

"Did it walk up to you? You talk to it?" I asked Mike.

"We were all meditating, and I saw a flash of greenish-blue light. A moment later I saw him peeking from behind a bush. I asked if it was okay to take the photo, and he told me yes."

"Wow," I said, "he spoke English? You must have been freaked out."

Mike put his phone back in his pocket. "Telepathy, and not at all."

I addressed everyone. "So let me make sure I'm getting this. You're saying that they've been coming here for a long time, and the government knows but is keeping it secret, but the government also has fakes to scare people. Is that right?"

"Almost, Ben," Daniel said, replenishing everyone's caffeine reserves and drizzling molasses in his own. "Let's be concise. I was personally told by a very high-ranking Cabinet official in the previous administration, whom I cannot name, that part of the shadow government controlled by the globalist oligarchy, has been collecting recovered EBE technology and will do anything to keep it secret. You see, the EBEs understand energy technology that will revolutionize how we power the world. No more fossil fuels. The rest of the government is kept in the dark and fed misinformation about the UFO phenomena to keep their technology secret. The fakes are coverups and distraction."

"So, the shadow government has retrieved alien craft and presumably reverse-engineered it. Roswell…"

"Not Roswell: that was a weather balloon. But there are others, and the cover-up is real. We've collected mountains of evidence," Daniel said, sipping his coffee.

Mike's eyes were on me.

Daniel continued. "We estimate that about 80 percent of UFO sightings are either hoaxes or natural phenomena. Twenty percent of them are the real deal."

"It's pretty easy to fake a sighting with special effects these days, isn't it?" I asked.

"Sure, some are fakes created by people, and some are ginned up by the shadow government. We have an archive of more than two thousand videos of alien craft, all verified by science like radar evidence, independent eyewitness testimony, and more."

"With so much evidence, why can't you convince the President or Congress to just come out and admit that we are not alone?"

"The government and mainstream media love to make contactees seem like tin-foil-hat fools, complete idiots, so that no one takes them seriously, yet the power elite and their media shills tease the public with stories about mysterious lights in the sky and the occasional leaked video or document. Even with the recent Department of Defense acknowledgment of unidentified aerial phenomena, they won't come out and admit that they know—not yet, anyway. It's all part of the game to keep people partly in the truth and partly in the dark to confuse, manipulate, and obfuscate. Classic cover-up and propaganda techniques."

"You mentioned fakes. Who creates them, and what's their purpose exactly?"

"Artificial Intelligence robots built by the government to spook people and make them think the aliens are here to harm us. And why? Well, that's the worst part. We had the Cold War, then the Global War on Terror, and what's next?"

"Alien invasion," I grinned.

"That's right, Ben. Fake an alien invasion to expand military-industrial control."

"When do you expect that to happen?"

"By next year. That's why we're rushing to build our new facility and network." Daniel kept his eyes on Nadine.

I scribbled a note. "I saw your website, but tell me more about you about your mission."

Daniel leaned forward, holding up three fingers. "We have three primary goals. The first is research. We want to learn everything we can about the EBEs and what the government has been doing with their technology. Think of us as a central hub for scientists, sociologists, psychologists, and others who want to study alien technology and culture." One finger down. "The second is knowledge dissemination and training. We want to share what we learn and educate the public so they are no longer in the dark about all of this." Second finger down. "And three, we serve as cosmic ambassadors, so to speak."

"Ambassadors?"

"Yes, ambassadors." Nadine chimed in. "The more people who know the truth and how to communicate with our friends, the better."

"And people can receive training on this?" I asked.

"Yes. We have a training and certificate program, and we also have a publishing company," she added.

"So how many people are part of the Foundation now?"

"We're structured like other nonprofits," Nadine explained. "We have a Board of Directors and a leadership team, but we are also an organization made up of its members."

"We just hit 300,000 members worldwide this past week," Daniel said.

"Wow, impressive!" I said. "And you're building your new facility here. Can I get a tour of the compound?"

"We don't call it a compound. It's a ranch, so we call it that," Daniel corrected. "Our research and training center is in the pre-construction phase, so we're using a large tent for group assemblies. It's temporary."

"How many people are staying here?" I asked, thinking about the shipping containers.

"We have pods for two dozen visitors," he said, "and run it like a bed-and-breakfast. We're open to visitors who are here to participate in our visitation protocol and lectures, and to the general public."

Nadine smiled. "We have a five-star host rating online."

I smiled back. "Why did you decide to build here?"

"We considered other places too. Jackson Hole was one, but it felt better here. It's a good spot for the Center. Nadine and I felt like this is where we needed to be." He glanced at his wife, smiling and reaching across the white tablecloth for her hand. "Didn't we, honey?"

She took his hand. "The change of pace from Chicago is very nice, and we needed the space for the horses to run."

"I saw the corral. How many do you have?"

"Six—three thoroughbreds and three American quarter horses."

I thought about how expensive six horses were. "Did the Foundation buy the land and the new building."

"The land was donated by Robert Petulli Jr. You probably know who he is," Nadine said.

I nodded. "The son of Dr. Gordon Petulli, the Apollo astronaut. Robert's into UFOs, like his late father. Wrote a book, didn't he?"

"Yes, a very good one, too, about alien energy technologies," Daniel said. "He's been very supportive of our organization." He looked over his shoulder, pointing to a large house perched on one of the peaks to the east. "That's Petulli's place up there."

I squinted at what looked like a castle. "I'd love to talk with him. Do you have his contact information?"

"He's very private, doesn't like to talk to the press, but I can ask him about talking with you," Nadine said.

"That would be great," I said. "So, Mike, what exactly is your role with the Proxima Foundation?"

"I'm the Chief Operations Officer," Mike said through a mouthful of scrambled eggs. "I handle anything that needs getting done."

"Why the sidearm?" I asked.

He stared at me. "I provide security as well."

"He doubles as Security Chief," Daniel said before shoving a forkful of pancake into his mouth

"Why exactly do you need a security detail?" I asked.

"That should be obvious," Daniel said, giving me an appraising look. "We are dealing with a major government conspiracy here. Think about it. Everything will change if the public has access to alien energy technology. The government doesn't want us telling the truth to the public. They've threatened me before. I've got evidence."

"So protection from the government?"

"And their crony corporate henchmen," Mike said.

"So if this is all true, wouldn't they have already…"

"Assassinated me?" Daniel said. "If they do, a cache of information that blows the lid off the entire thing will automatically be released."

"We're lawyers, Ben. We think of these things," Nadine smiled.

"What kind of information cache are you talking about?"

Daniel crossed his arms and leaned his chair back. "Mountains of documents in our secure archives." "Like what? Are these documents anything I can see?" "We can share some, yes," he said, glancing at Nadine. "That would be great." I hesitated. "Don't take this the wrong way, but are you certain about this government conspiracy thing? There's a lot of government conspiracy stuff floating around on the Internet. Even with all the evidence you have, how do you know for sure?"

Daniel smiled. "My life's work has been about getting to the truth and knowing it for a fact by gathering and evaluating. Sure, we're trained as lawyers, not scientists, but we think like scientists do. We consider all hypotheses before ruling anything out, and we do so carefully. In the 1980s, I was fortunate to meet the famous Nobel Laureate physicist Richard Feynman at a quantum mechanics lecture. He said that the first principle of being a good scientist is that you must be careful to not fool yourself, and you are the easiest person to fool. To know, really know, you must be objective when looking at the evidence, acknowledge its limitations and remain aware of your own biases. These are standard Ranch principles."

"I get it. You don't want to just see what you want to see, but have reliable evidence to test hypotheses." I glanced at Daniel, then Nadine. "You need enough evidence to prove more than a reasonable doubt. That's how a lawyer would approach it in court, right?"

"In criminal law, yes," Nadine said. "Being satisfied with proof beyond reasonable doubt is the standard, but that doesn't mean there must be no doubt at all. It's about demonstrating evidence to show guilt or liability, not necessarily the truth. Our work here is also about demonstrating the evidence towards the truth while acknowledging the unknowns. Is that any different than how an investigative journalist would approach a story?"

"Journalistic truth is about gathering the facts and conveying them in a truthful manner while realizing that you may not know the whole truth yet."

"That's exactly it," Daniel said. "Our goal with the Proxima Foundation is to collect and make available information to help people judge on their own, but based on a preponderance of evidence. I'm not here to convince or make anyone believe anything."

"Makes sense to me," I said. "You ran a fundraiser this past year. It looks like you're raising a lot of money for the Foundation and the new Center. Congratulations. How much have you raised so far, and how much from donors and how much from membership?"

"It's all in our annual report," Nadine sighed, passing the pancakes to Daniel for seconds. "We'll get that to you, Ben." Her crow's feet crinkled as she smiled. "I can tell you really like what you do, investigating."

"Yes," I said. "I like getting to the truth, and I think that what you are doing here is very compelling. Another question; I read somewhere about a lawsuit between you and the editor of *Cynic* magazine, David Ellis. What was that all about?"

"That man is as crooked as a dog's hind leg," Nadine said. "He was spreading lies about us, so he got himself hit with a restraining order."

"The truth is, Ben," Daniel added, "he was on the CIA payroll, front publisher and part of a controlled opposition operation. You know about those, don't you?"

"The best way to control the opposition is to lead it yourself."

"Vladimir Lenin." Byrne smiled. "You know your history."

"I took a course on mass communications in graduate school."

"That's good, Ben. Then you know how governments use media to create deception. But don't print that about Ellis— we don't need to get his lawyers going again."

"Sure, I won't mention it," I assured him, doubting the CIA story, anyway.

"Good. You should come to my presentation at the 18th annual UFO Conference in McMinnville Oregon next weekend. It would give you an opportunity to learn more about the UFO topic, for your story. You'll meet all kinds of interesting people there too." He looked at Nadine. "Isn't that right, honey?"

"Always," she answered, tilting her head toward him.

I thought about it for a second. "I may be able to come down for a day. I'll have to clear it with my editor, but I think he'll be okay with it."

"Good. I'm giving the keynote on Saturday. It will include a major announcement," Daniel said, smiling enigmatically.

"What kind of announcement?" I asked.

Daniel looked at me. "You'll have to come and listen."

"Cool," I said stupidly. "Another question, this one regarding the death of Sally Jensen." Briefly, they riveted their eyes on me. Had they been worried that I'd bring it up?

"Obviously, you know about it."

"It was on the news," said Nadine, gathering up dishes, "terrible thing."

"Was she doing a story on you and the Proxima Foundation?" A shot in the dark, but—

Daniel shook his head. "Not that I'm aware of. Where did you hear that?"

I shrugged. "Her body was found not too far from the Valley of the Moon, so I thought maybe—"

Daniel and Nadine exchanged glances. "We don't know any more than you do," Nadine said. "I'm sure the police will figure it out."

"Did the police talk with you?" I asked, handing Nadine my plate.

"What do you mean?" Daniel asked, shooting Nadine another glance.

"No," Nadine said, looking at me. "I'm sure they would have if they had a reason to, but they didn't."

I tried to sound casual. "Yeah. I'm planning to stop by the Sheriff's office and see what else I can find out about her."

Nadine smiled at me. "Of course, you are, you're looking for a story."

"Never leave a good story," I said, smiling back.

When we finally finished brunch, I shook hands with Daniel and Nadine, reminding them about Petulli and the documents. Nadine promised to get them to me.

Outside, Mike shook my hand. "See you in McMinnville," he promised.

As soon as I got out to my car, I called Jennifer to tell her that I had one more interview and would take a later flight. Of course, she was all horns and rattles about my being late for Gabriella's baby shower, but I had to talk to law enforcement about the dead reporter. Getting a whatever hang-up from her wasn't good, but neither was a half-assed story.

I set my GPS and made my way to the Missoula County Sheriff's office in downtown Missoula. The deputy at the window, a tall, skinny guy with brown eyes and a tight mustache, said the Sheriff wasn't there. I asked if anyone else knew about the Sally Jensen case—and would they be willing to talk to me? He said no and took my name to give to the Sheriff.

As I left the building, the Sheriff arrived. He too was tall, in his late fifties with peppered gray hair and the usual police potbelly. I was betting that he was just coming back from lunch.

"Sheriff, I'm Ben Davenport, *Hot Reports*. I spoke with you on the phone last week. Can we talk about the Sally Jensen case?"

He talked as he walked me back into the building. "Kind of busy here. If this is a press inquiry, you can talk to Ms. Helens." He pointed to a woman sitting in an office down the hallway. "She'll let you know when we are having a press conference."

"I'm leaving town today. Just a few minutes of your time," I stressed.

"What's your name again?"

"Ben Davenport, *Hot Reports*."

He let out an annoyed sigh. "All right, only a few minutes, though."

He led me to his office and sat down at his desk. "What paper did you say you're from again?"

"*Hot Reports*," I said for the third time, taking a seat in front of his desk.

"One of those online papers?"

I nodded.

"Okay, what is it that you want to know?"

"What's going on regarding her murder? Any suspects?"

"It's still an active investigation. Because the body was found on the border of federal land, the FBI has taken over the case. My people are only assisting now."

I could tell from his tone that he wasn't too happy about the feds leaving him out. I also knew that this meant a bureaucratic no-go on getting any information. I would squeeze him, anyway.

"The news said a ranch worker found her in the Valley of the Moon. That's not all private land, is it?"

"Right. All that land there, except for the federal park land, is owned by Petulli. But the body was on the border between the two, like I said, which means it's out of my jurisdiction."

"How was she killed? The local news coverage didn't specify."

"Like I said, Mr. Davenport, this is an active investigation. You'll have to talk to the feds."

"Any idea on a motive? I'd think that would clue you into suspects."

"You're not trying to do my job, are you, Mr. Davenport?"

"Oh no, sir, I'm just trying to get what information I can."

"Does your being out here have anything to do with the UFO folks up there?" He was putting his own two plus two together.

"Yes. I'm doing a story on Daniel Byrne and the Proxima Foundation. Did you talk to them?"

"Why should we?" he asked. "Have you been talking with them?"

"Yes, last night and this morning. Why?"

"Just wondering." He looked at the clock on the wall. "When is your story coming out?"

"I don't know yet—soon. I'm still gathering information," I said.

"Do you mind if I get your contact information again?"

"No, not at all," I said. I gave him one of my cards. "Is it okay if I check in with you in a couple of days? See if you have any more information?"

"I don't see the harm in that. Anything else?" he said.

"I think I'm good for now," I said.

He escorted me out to the lobby. We shook hands, and I thanked him for speaking with me. After he strolled back into his office, his deputy from behind the glass partition, said irately, "Don't be printing no stories on our investigation. We don't need no big city hipster journalists getting in our way, talking to suspects."

I walked over to the partition. "Suspects? You just said you didn't want any journalists talking to any of your suspects, implying that you have some."

He began backpaddling. "Are you harassing an officer of the law?"

"That's enough!" the Sheriff shouted from his office.

When I got to my car, I called Ramblin' Joe's to see if Brenda was working. I hate to death-knock, but perhaps she'd be more willing to talk with me now that I'd talked to the Sheriff. She wasn't on shift yet. I headed to the airport for my flight to Seattle.

3

RABBIT HOLE

Jennifer was stretched out on our sofa in yoga pants and a sweatshirt, her blond tousles falling loosely around her shoulders. As usual, she was watching a celebrity dance show on TV.

"Nice of you to come back," she said, as I closed the door to our one-bedroom apartment. *Here it comes*, I thought, expecting her to rip into me for getting in so late and missing her friend's baby shower.

I kissed her on the forehead. "How was the shower?"

"Fine," she said, her eyes fixed on the screen.

I set down my overnight bag. "Did you eat dinner?"

"We went out afterward," she said. Her tone and lack of eye contact confirmed her irritation.

I went into the kitchen, hoping to find some leftovers but had to settle for a bowl of Cinnamon Toast Crunch. I grabbed a beer to go with it, set my laptop on the dining room table, and checked my email before visiting the Proxima Foundation YouTube Channel. There it was, the latest upload.

"Jennifer, come see this. They posted a video of what I saw at the sighting event."

She got up from the sofa after a few seconds' delay and

stood behind me. I clicked the play button.

On the monitor was the back of my head, barely visible in the darkness. "I was sitting there."

"What am I looking at besides the back of your head?" she asked, glancing back at her TV show.

"Just watch."

Amber lights appeared in the distance, fuzzy and blurry until the camera came into focus. We could hear Byrne in the background giving commands to Mike.

"Looks like some lights in the sky," she said. "It could be anything, airplanes probably."

"They weren't airplanes. Planes don't look like that."

She watched it with me until the lights disappeared. "Huh. What do you think they were?" she asked as she headed back to the living room.

"I'm not sure, but I want to find out. There's a UFO conference in McMinnville, Oregon next weekend. I'm thinking of going." I was hoping that she'd be more amenable if I made it sound like I hadn't yet made my decision.

"McMinnville? We've got dinner with James and Rebecca next weekend. Did you forget?"

I'd forgotten all about the dinner with her friends. "I have to go to this conference, I need more for the story," I said, speaking louder so she would hear me over the TV.

She sighed loudly. "I don't see why you need to attend a conference with a bunch of UFO nuts."

"I'm sure they aren't all nuts. Why do you need to be so judgmental?"

"Whatever," she said.

I started pulling up UFO videos on YouTube to see what was out there. If I could find some intriguing evidence, I'd show it to her. I came across one that showed footage taken from a Navy F/A-18 Hornet tracking an object off the coast of San Diego in 2004. I recalled having seen it on the news recently. Ping, another Navy F/A-18 video surfaced with footage of a fast-moving UFO taken off the East Coast in 2015. I'd caught that one, too, and remembered thinking that the footage was probably just an advertisement for a military contractor's new weapons tracking system. But the videos had been acknowledged by the Department of Defense.

"You know there's some pretty cogent evidence out there of UFOs—credible witnesses, reputable people."

Jennifer didn't respond. I looked at some more videos. I heard her get up to get something to drink. She stood in the doorway between the kitchen and the dining area, looking at me.

"I thought you were going to give up the freelance journalism. Why not write press for Amazon or some other company—one that pays benefits and stuff?" she asked.

I looked up. "We've talked about this before, Jennifer. I like what I'm doing, and I think this story is going to turn into something big. Maybe I'll write a book on UFOs or something." I wasn't serious about a book, but I said it anyway just to push her buttons.

"Tell me you're not serious," she said. "UFOs? Really? Why would you want to waste your time on a conspiracy theory?"

I went back to the 2004 UFO footage from the Navy F/A-18. "Look at this."

"What?"

"Just come here, I want to show you this."

She came and stood behind me, her hands on her hips.

"This is official government footage. The Department of Defense released this," I said.

"I'm looking at something flying in the sky. It's probably a drone or something."

"I don't know, maybe, but why would U.S. Navy pilots come out and insist that what they saw was a UFO? I'm mean, these people are highly trained, and their reputations are on the line."

"I don't know," she said. "Just because they see something in the sky doesn't mean it's aliens or whatever."

Whatever was her favorite word.

"I know that, but what if there is alien life out there?

Wouldn't you want to know?"

She went back into the living room and flopped down on the sofa. "Why do you need to know? We have enough problems on our own planet to deal with. I still don't know why you're doing a story on something that's in the National Enquirer. Maybe you should write for them."

I got up and stood in the doorway so I could speak directly to her. "I'm doing this because I'm creating a good story, not watching TV. And what if they are real? What if alien life is visiting us? It's kind of egocentric to think that we're the only life in the universe, don't you think?"

Her eyes were glued to the TV. "I thought you were going to do a story on a UFO hoax. Now you're a believer?"

It was true: I was no longer sure. "I want to find out what this is about, that's what an investigative journalist does. If you have to ask me why then you don't understand me or what it means to be an investigative journalist. If this thing with the Proxima Foundation is all a dupe, then I'll expose it. I want to get to the bottom of it, like all the other things I've investigated. Can't you see that?"

"I guess," she said.

Now I was pissed. I was tempted to go down to Jonesy's, the dive bar at the corner. Out the window, I could see the air dancer tube man in front, flapping and waving at me to come in for a drink. I switched the temptation and decided to watch UFO sighting videos and eyewitness interviews while I finished off my soggy cereal and beer.

Jennifer went off to bed after her show and I followed shortly after, setting my phone on the nightstand. I took a quick shower and once in bed, knew that I should make peace with her. I snuggled up to her. Needless to say, she was facing away from me. I put my arm over her affectionately.

"I'm sorry about missing the baby shower. I wish I could have been there," I said softly.

"Yep," she said, pulling the covers up to her chin.

"I just need to go to this conference next weekend. I should be able to write this story after that. Then I'll be done,

I promise."

"You promise?"

"Yes, I promise," I said, spooning her. "I missed you." I buried my nose in her hair and began rubbing her shoulders. Eventually, she turned towards me. We kissed again, and again. I wasn't expecting sex that night, but her willingness was a good sign. A minute later I was on top of her, going at it. About two minutes into it, my phone lit up, nearly vibrating itself off the nightstand. I leaned over and glanced at it, doing my best to keep the rhythm of my thrusts. It was a text from a Missoula, Montana number. I squinted but had no luck in reading the message. Was it Brenda? Nadine or Daniel?

"Are you looking at your phone?" Jennifer asked suspiciously.

I glanced down at her and realized her eyes were open.

"No," I lied.

"You are! Get off of me," she said, pushing me off and shoving me over to the other side of the bed so that I nearly rolled off.

"I wasn't looking at it," I said.

She sat up. "Yes, you were, I saw you. Who is it?"

"Jesus, Jenn, I don't know, it's a text. What's the big deal?" I knew I was in big shit now and likely wasn't going to get out of it anytime soon.

"You can sleep on the couch tonight," she said, turning away from me and pulling the covers back up.

"Fine." I put on my boxers, grabbed my phone, and went into the living room, closing the bedroom door on my way out. I sat on the sofa in the dark and read the text message. It was from Brenda.

Got some information today about my Aunt. You may be interested. Call me.

I checked the time. It was 10:35—late, but not too late to call. I paused for a moment to make sure Jennifer wasn't going to storm out and yell at me some more, then call Brenda.

31

I spoke softly. "Hi, Brenda? It's Ben Davenport. What's going on?"

She sounded incensed. "My aunt's funeral was today, a closed casket. They wouldn't let the family see her. My uncle told me that someone who knows one of the Sheriff's deputies said that she'd been burned and mutilated, her organs taken out, some sick shit."

"What?"

"Yeah, and the police won't talk to the family. The FBI wouldn't tell my uncle anything. I don't understand why."

"Who do you think did it?"

"I think it was the culties, maybe their leader—what's his name?"

"Daniel Byrne," I said. "What makes you think that?"

"I don't know. Maybe she was onto them or something, and he found out."

"Was your aunt into UFOs? I mean, was she doing a story on it?"

"My uncle said she became interested in UFOs lately, but I don't know if it was for an official story or not." Her voice cracked with emotion. "I just don't know why she was out there by herself at night."

I felt for her. "I'll tell you what—I'll call the TV station again tomorrow and see if she was assigned to cover the Proxima people or not. I'll let you know what I find out."

There was a long pause.

"I hope I didn't interrupt anything," she finally said.

"No, not at all, call anytime."

In the morning I went into the *Hot Reports* office in downtown Seattle. I checked my email and the fax machine, hoping for the financial documents from Nadine. Nothing.

I called Channel 4 in Missoula to see what I could find out about Sally Jensen's last story and what she might have been doing at the Valley of the Moon. I finally got through to Robert Shaw, the station manager.

"She was off duty," Shaw said. "We have no idea what Sally was doing over there that night."

I asked him for some more background on her, how long she'd been at the station, etc. Sally had been employed there for almost five years, having come from a local newspaper. Shaw said she'd done a small piece on UFOs, but that was it. I asked if Channel 4 was going to cover any information about the manner of her death.

"We've been told it's an active investigation and that the FBI will let us know when they have something."

"Do you have anyone on the story, following up on local leads?"

"We're monitoring the situation and will report it when we have all of the facts."

I thanked him for his time and hung up, discouraged. The FBI was being secretive, and law enforcement hadn't held a press conference. Why all the hush hush? There was nothing ordinary about this murder case.

I checked in with Marcus, my forty-something editor with salt-and-pepper hair and square-rimmed hipster glasses. He had a nice corner office with big windows overlooking Pioneer Square. I told him about my adventure in Missoula.

"Have you decided on your angle? If you're going with fraud, then you better have substantiating documentation," he said.

"I've got a request in on their financials. I definitely think the Proxima Foundation is bull-hooky."

"You have any idea how they may be gaming this stuff?"

"Not yet," I said. My plan was to drive down to McMinnville on Friday night for Byrne's talk and perhaps interview some of the attendees.

Marcus was skeptical. "Another trip? You're not going down a rabbit hole on this. Are you?"

"You want me to go down the rabbit hole, don't you?" I countered.

He looked at me for a moment. "What about the murdered TV journalist? Anything on that?"

"Yeah. Law enforcement isn't talking, but I've got a family member source." I told him what Brenda had said on the

33

phone the night before.

Marcus arched his back, lacing his fingers behind his neck. "Okay, keep working on it, but don't lose sight of the deadline. I need the story in two weeks."

I headed for the door.

"And stay somewhere inexpensive and keep your receipts," he said to my back. Marcus was cheap, but he gave me lots of leeway, a perk I'd never get at a corporate job.

On the way home that evening, I grabbed a bouquet of flowers, a quart of cherry-vanilla gelato, and some of Jennifer's favorite breakfast scones from the bakery down the street. I was feeling contrite about forgetting her social events and wanted to smooth things over. It took a little work, but we made up, cuddled on the sofa, and binged on ice cream and lord knows how many episodes of her favorite celebrity cooking show.

4

EXTRAORDINARY CLAIMS

McMinnville is surrounded by rolling green hills, vineyards, and fields that smell of fresh manure. On the 11th of May, 1950, local farmers Evelyn Trent and her husband Paul snapped several photos of what appeared to be a saucer-shaped craft flying slow from the direction of Mount Rainier. The Trent Farm UFO photographs are among the most iconic UFO photos ever taken. Independent photometric studies conducted at the time suggested the photos were of a distant object and not fakes. Some years later, someone noticed that the object in the Trent photos closely resembled the chrome side view mirror of an old Ford pick-up truck. There's a saying *that if it smells like bullshit, it probably is.* Curious, though, is the striking similarity between the object in the Trent photos and the 2014 Navy Thimble UFO I saw on YouTube.

McMinnville's 35,000 residents now had to put up with the buzzing of the UFO conference. The historic Hotel Oregon was full, so I settled for a hotel just outside of town. I registered for the conference and picked up my complementary bag of alien swag. Daniel Byrne was smiling back at me on page two of the schedule of events. He was indeed the keynote speaker and would be presenting after dinner.

With time to kill, I went to hear about "Deception and Disinformation: What the Government Doesn't Want You to Know about UFOs." About eighty people were in attendance in the Community Center auditorium. I sat at the back next to a middle-aged man sporting a dark brown Stetson-style western hat, sports jacket, and tan trousers. Maybe a retiree and self-proclaimed UFOlogist. We made eye contact.

"Jack Clark."

"Ben Davenport, with the magazine *Hot Reports*. I'm from Seattle."

We exchanged business cards. His read *Jack Clark. Washington State Mutual UFO Network (MUFON) Director.*

"Oh. Reporter. Have you been to this conference before?"

"No, never been to a UFO conference." I smiled.

"Get ready for a room full of mirrors."

"What do you mean?" I asked.

"You're going to hear all kinds of claims. Some true, some maybe not, but all interesting."

The first speaker was Dr. Max Steiner, a former nuclear physicist and government contractor, a short, round fellow, with a mustache and bald head. He wore a black suit and large-rimmed glasses that went out of style twenty-five years ago.

"I'm going to reveal to you the links between UFO technology, the monetary system, and what the government doesn't want you to know," Dr. Steiner promised. In a quick clip he covered official government investigations into UFOs (Project Blue Book, Majestic-12, the Condon Report, and the Advanced Aerospace Threat Identification Program sponsored by Senator Harry Reid, etc.), finishing with how they were all public disinformation fronts aimed at denying the presence of alien visitors and quelling public interest in the matter. His proof was slide after slide of leaked government reports with more black redactions than content.

"Don't you think it's suspicious that government inquiries into UFOs only report cases that are easily debunked, or that there are trite explanations for credible mass sightings? Mainstream media are just a wing of the government existing to mislead the public. The motivation for the secrecy and misdirection is obvious: keep the public in the dark about free-energy technology. This is all about military-industrial complex control over oil and thus our monetary system." I was sure that there were other machinations, but I kept listening.

He showed a few clips of government whistleblowers, mostly enlisted military personnel and contract technicians like Phil Schneider who had gone on record about having seen reverse-engineered alien technology, from antigravity generators to flying saucers, more than 35 years ago. There was an interview with NASA astronaut Gordon Cooper who claimed to have seen footage of a disk-shaped UFO that landed in the desert near Edwards Air Force Base in California in the late 1950s. The government had buried the original footage.

"When we have credible witnesses like these, we need to be paying attention," Steiner stressed.

When he took questions from the audience, I couldn't resist throwing one in. "Do you think it's possible that the documents you've shown were not about alien craft at all but sightings of classified aircraft, perhaps our own or from other countries?"

Steiner shrugged. "But then what do we do with all of the eyewitness testimony that corroborates the documents?" He flipped back to the slides loaded with the black redactions. "There's no doubt that alien spacecraft are here, and the government doesn't want the people to know about it."

I sat down, unsatisfied. I saw no link between so-called eyewitness testimony and redacted documents.

The next speaker was Dr. Richard Mazzotti, a former NASA astronaut with a full head of white hair. He'd witnessed a UFO on Space Shuttle STS-9 in 1983 and showed an image of a faint red object he'd taken through the window.

"What was it?" he asked the crowd. "Neither we, nor anyone else on Earth, have anything like what I saw up there."

He showed photos and videos taken from the International Space Station (ISS) and other shuttle missions, all fuzzy, floating, and darting about, looking like they could be satellites or out of focus ice particles. Dr. Mazzotti, however, believed: "Space junk doesn't change its trajectories like this. These are alien craft under intentional, conscious control."

The 2004 Navy video of the Tic-Tac UFO took a different trajectory, however.

"The *USS Nimitz* Carrier Strike Group had been tracking these tic-tac looking objects for a week," Mazzotti explained. "On radar, they appeared to be dropping from 60,000 feet to the surface of the ocean. This is some of the best proof we have to date that alien probes are here on Earth. The U.S. Navy has finally released this evidence to the public. As Carl Sagan said, extraordinary claims need extraordinary evidence. Well, if you were in doubt, here it is."

Why had the government released the videos to begin with? I wondered. There was speculation that the video was illegally leaked, but it seemed contradictory to what Steiner had said about the government and media misdirecting the public—or was it?

During the lunch hour, I grabbed a quick bite to eat and perused the books for sale at the registration booths. Byrne's new book was prominent, surrounded by other works like *Alien Species: What We Know* and *Roswell Revisited*.

After lunch, I couldn't pass up a UFO abductee "lived experience" panel. The sign outside the door said, *Please refrain from wearing costumes or masks of unfriendly alien species. These may upset some of the conference attendees. Thank you.* On stage were three seated people, all claiming to have been snatched up by aliens. Anna Jo, a portly young woman with curly blond hair, said she'd been repeatedly abducted by aliens for the purpose of researching her reproductive organs. With tears in her eyes, she said she'd been unable to have a baby ever since.

Mark was beer-bellied and middle-aged, an IT technician from Ohio who said that he'd been having sex with tall, blue-eyed, blond aliens for decades, having lost his virginity to one when he was thirteen. He stated that he might have seen one of his alien hybrid children on his last mothership rendezvous. I wondered what the blue-eyed beauties saw in Mark to begin with.

The third was Chester, thinner and younger, with black bags under his eyes. He claimed to have been abducted on a dark desert road outside Bakersfield, California three years before. "A week later I started seeing numbers, formulas," he said in a soft voice. "I'm convinced that they took me up because they wanted me to help build zero-energy technologies." Either he'd been through some serious trauma in his life or had been out drinking all night.

The audience was transfixed, whereas my bullshit meter was off the charts.

During the Q & A, I asked, "Do any of you have any hard evidence that you were taken up into an alien spaceship? By hard evidence, I mean a photo or another eyewitness account? Anything to corroborate what you are telling us?"

Mark glared at me. "I don't need evidence. I know what happened to me."

Anna Jo nodded, while Chester gazed blankly out at the audience.

All I could think was, *if all it takes is believing, then the world is in serious trouble.*

But Chester wasn't done. He pulled his shirt out of his trousers and showed his bare stomach and chest. "I have this," he said. Just above his sternum, a small, red mark in the shape of a hexagon was seared into his skin. "They marked me," he said.

Someone in audience behind me called out, "They do that, you know. It means you've been chosen."

At last, I headed to the main hotel ballroom for the keynote. The room was packed. Patricia Neumann, one of the conference organizers and author of a series of books about alien species, introduced Byrne.

"I've always thought, if an alien visitor came to me and said, *Take me to your leader*, I'd take them to Mr. Byrne. He's been called the guru of alien contact, the ambassador of intergalactic goodwill, and the keeper of cosmic truth. With no further ado, Mr. Daniel Byrne."

Applause erupted while Daniel mounted the stage with a tiny wireless microphone by his chin and a huge smile on his face. He wore khaki trousers and a white button-down shirt (no tie) displaying the Proxima Foundation symbol.

"Thank you, Patricia, and thank you, everyone." His face went serious. "We are living in the most important time in modern history, the turning point when we will be free from the shackles of fossil fuels. No more energy costs, no more pollution, no more global warming. Zero-point energy, brought to us by our extraterrestrial friends, is here. It will change everything. Are you ready for it?" He paused, looking out at the audience.

Several dozen people in crowd began shouting. "Yes!" and "We're ready!"

"But wait," said Byrne, his voice booming through the PA system. "The shadow governments of the world will not allow it. They will stop at nothing to keep the truth about this technology and our alien friends a secret." Walking back and forth, making quick eye contact with people in the audience, he continued. "You may have heard Dr. Max Steiner this morning. I hope you did. The government has been covering up the presence of aliens for 70 years. Up to this point, they haven't wanted you to know, but what I'm about to tell you should scare the living hell out of you."

The crowd went dead silent.

Daniel waited, then quietly said, "They're going to fake an alien attack. They're going to make you believe that the aliens are here to cause harm and they will use draconian scare tactics—that's right, another Pearl Harbor, Gulf of Tonkin, and 9/11 all rolled into one, except bigger, much bigger.

Once this happens, they will take what remains of your freedoms away from you and levy economic and social control like you've never seen."

I noticed how already he was becoming exhausted. He stood still for a moment, resting his arm on the podium, and exhaled, his face wet with sweat. He wiped his face and looked at the audience. "People ask me all the time, why do I do this? Why put myself and my wife and colleagues at such risk to bring the truth out? I'll tell you why."

He removed a piece of paper from his shirt pocket and unfolded it. "I just received this letter the other day from six-year-old Amy." He cleared his throat and read. 'Dear Mr. Byrne, I'm very worried about the world. I don't want the bad rich people on Earth to scare us. The people from space should be our friends. I want to play with them. Please, Mr. Byrne, tell everyone that we should all just get along and be friends.'

His voice cracked.

"Excuse me," he said, wiping his wet eyes.

Was this Harvard lawyer about to cry on stage? Were his emotions legit, or was this the TV evangelist? I was betting on the latter.

Daniel held up the letter for the audience to see. With crayons, Amy had drawn a large-headed alien holding hands with a stick figure girl. Three planets hovered over them in the paper sky. He folded the letter and stuffed it back into his pocket.

The woman in front of me was sniffling and wiping her eyes.

"Dear little Amy is right," Daniel continued. "We've got to stop the government from destroying our planet and our relationships with each other and with our extraterrestrial visitors. Our cosmic friends want to share their knowledge, but they are cautious. They've been watching us for thousands of years and know the destructiveness of our leaders. Humanity has let them down, and when they have tried to communicate with us, we've misconstrued the intent and demonized them. Those experiencers that do come forward to speak the truth about the objectives of the visitors are ridiculed. Cosmic racism, frankly. Just because the EBEs look different and we don't know them. They may have different DNA, but they are intelligent, sentient beings, made of the same stardust as you and I."

"That's the truth," an audience member shouted.

Daniel continued. "Our consciousness has been moving backwards. It's like we are stuck, stuck by primal needs of egocentric self-preservation and greed, and we keep doing the same things over and over again, hoping for a different result. You know what that equates to?" He paused, looking out at the crowd.

"Insanity," a few people called out.

"That's right, insanity," Daniel said. "It's nuts. But we can reverse this crazy path we are on, if we work together."

The audience erupted in applause.

He waited, then cleared his throat again. "I have to admit, there are times when I feel alone—like I'm Atlas, you know, holding the weight of all of this on my shoulders."

Someone in the audience yelled, "You're not alone, Daniel!"

"Thank you for that," Byrne said. He stood up straight and walked to the front edge of the stage.

"We need to step up contact with our visitors. It's more important now than ever before that we come together and honor their arrival. We need to let them know that we welcome them. And remember, there's no need to panic when we start seeing them. Panic and fear are just what the government wants you to experience."

A woman shouted, "I'm not welcoming them. I don't want to see them again. They are molesting me! You welcome them, but you shouldn't!"

I scanned the audience. It was Anna Jo. Her face was red, and she was breathing heavily.

Daniel looked toward the voice. "I'm not here to discredit anyone's experience. Whatever has happened to you is obviously unpleasant. It sounds like you are a victim of a secret government program to fake abductions. The military does that, you know. It's called MILAB. They can stage abductions to instill fear in good people like you. I invite you to come out to our facility in Montana. The Foundation would like to hear about your experience and learn from it to warn others of such abductions. What do you say? Will you come and visit us?"

Anna Jo nodded. "Yes," she promised, her eyes wet but her mouth smiling, the woman next to her patting her shoulder. The crowd applauded.

"Folks, we need to work together," Daniel said. For a brief second, our eyes met. "We must seek the truth. Now, let's watch some videos from our viewing events this past year. If you haven't been with us or seen these before, they will give you a sense of how wonderful it is to make contact with our EBE friends."

Here comes the sales pitch, I thought.

After several dozen photos and short videos of previous viewing events, he showed the video I'd been part of two nights before. The audience seemed to be astounded. The guy next to me leaned toward me and said, "It's the real deal, I'm signing up."

I nodded, saying nothing. Did Byrne have plants in the audience to persuade others to sign up?

Afterwards, Daniel introduced his new iM4ET or Intra-dimensional Meditation Assistant for Extraterrestrial Togetherness app. "It's a great way to learn our protocol and practice it on your own or with groups in our ambassador's program. It's free at all of the app stores. I hope that you will all download it," Daniel said.

I was intrigued by the app but suspected it was a marketing tool. Nonetheless, I planned to download it later.

He thanked the audience, bowed with his palms pressed together as the audience applauded, then descended the stage for the meet-and-greets and book-signing. The smile on his face told me that he was in love with the attention.

As I waited in line to speak to him, I pondered his real motivations. Perhaps the lawyer life got to him 20 years ago. Selling the aliens-are-here-to-save-us schtick is a great way to make some cash, given that there was no shortage of willing takers. Then there's the celebrity attention. But maybe he really did believe that aliens are here and had good intentions.

I shook his hand. "Nice talk," I said.

"Thanks, Ben. It needs to be said, but I've been saying the same things for two years now. I hope I'm getting through to people."

"From the looks of this crowd, I'd say you are."

"Well, the Foundation and our new facility is the best bet we have to move us forward." He put his hand on my shoulder. "Patricia has put together a dinner for the main speakers tonight. Why don't you join us as my personal guest? It will be good for you to meet them. They have a great buffet here in the hotel, it's out of this world."

We shared a smile over his *out of this world* allusion.

I agreed and asked him if Nadine would be joining us. I was hoping to ask her more about the Proxima finances. He said she was at the spa with some girlfriends in town. Maybe she'd been to enough UFO conferences. I found myself wondering about their marriage again.

5

RESONANCE

Dinner was at the restaurant in the hotel. In attendance were Daniel and Mike, Patricia Neumann, Dr. Mazzotti, Dr. Steiner, and Chester from the lived experience panel. I became a bit nervous and embarrassed when I saw them at the table. I hoped that the latter two weren't upset by my questions at their talks. Still, talking with these characters would make for excellent background.

Daniel introduced me and told them that I was doing a story on the Proxima Foundation. He also told them that I had an interest in UFOs, and that I'd been witness to the Phoenix Lights.

"Ah, so you saw them first hand," Mazzotti said, smiling. "Where did you see them and at what time was it?"

"We were camping up near Prescott. We had run out of wood for our campfire. My friend Jonathan and I went looking for more wood around our campsite. We had wondered off, I'd say, a few hundred feet, and then I think we both saw the lights at the same time. They were in formation and flew over. It had to have been around 8pm. Not sure."

"That would have been when the craft was heading south towards Phoenix," said Mazzotti.

"You think it was one craft?" I asked. "I've always assumed that there were several B-2 Stealth Bombers in formation or maybe several planes refueling in-flight. No one really knows, do they?"

"It definitely wasn't Air Force," said Mazzotti. "It was a giant V-shaped UFO, nearly a half mile across. Most people get confused by the Phoenix Lights because there were really two events that happened; One was the flares from A-10s that were in a military training exercise over at the Barry Goldwater Range on the other side of the Estrella Mountains. That was seen from Phoenix. The other was the V-shaped mothership fly-by that you witnessed."

"Governor Fife Symington came out that he saw it, too," said Patricia, "as did Kurt Russell."

"That's right, he did," said Daniel.

A waiter took our orders while I continued my questions. "So, if it was an alien craft, what do you think the EBEs were doing? Why fly so low over a major city area?"

"They could have been on a reconnaissance mission, maybe picking up probes. That's what I suspect," Mazzotti said.

"I think it was more likely Air Force," said Steiner.

I waited for Daniel's response. I was expecting him to tell some story about how he was meditating that night and caused the lights to appear.

"There's no doubt that there were two events that night. One was the A-10s maneuver, the other was most likely a TR-3B test flight." Daniel looked at me. "The TR-3B is a giant V-shaped spy craft built by reverse-engineering alien craft. They look almost identical to alien craft. They would have been flying south from Nevada, and the timing makes sense."

"I saw one of the V-shaped motherships the night I was abducted," said Chester, speaking slowly with his usual blank stare. "I saw it fly over the road. At first, I thought it was a big jet. Next thing I knew, I was twenty miles away and it was three days later."

I bet he was naked too, I thought unkindly. "What did the EBEs look like?" I asked.

"They were the greys and they told me that they were from the planet that orbits the red dwarf Proxima Centauri."

"That would be Proxima b," said Daniel.

"Are you absolutely certain about that?" asked Patricia. "Maybe they were from Zeta 2 Reticuli, unless we are talking about a completely different species here."

"I have to agree with Patricia on this," said Richard. "There are massive solar winds on Proxima b, as far as we can tell. It would make it awfully tough to build a civilization there."

"Oh, I'm certain about Proxima b," Daniel said. "Remember, it's just over four light-years. That's nothing in interstellar travel terms, and it's quite habitable for a technologically advanced civilization."

Patricia smiled. "Daniel knew about Proxima b before it was discovered in 2016. Can't argue with that."

Daniel nodded self-assuredly.

"That's incredible. How many species of extraterrestrials are there, anyway?" I asked.

"Sixty-four known species have been documented," said Patricia. "Only about five have been visiting us regularly, though."

Mazzotti interrupted. "The greys, the reptilians, the blond Nordics, the short blues...."

"And don't forget the cat people," added Patricia, "they come from Lyra..."

"But we are mostly visited by the Proxima greys," said Byrne. "The ones with the small eyes. That's who we've been in contact with, and they are friendly, regardless of reports of some abductees."

I looked at Patricia and then Daniel. "Why is it that all of these alien species are humanoid? In theory, couldn't they be in other shapes and forms? They could be like dolphins or something, couldn't they?"

Daniel smiled. "Have you ever heard of Morphic

Resonance Theory?"

"No." I was curious but expecting nothing more that some New Age pseudoscience explanation.

"Morphic resonance theory was developed by the evolutionary biologist Rupert Sheldrake. His theory states that each individual life form inherits a collective memory from past members of its species, or other species. This process also feed backs into the collective memory, which will affect other members of the species in the future."

I saw where he was going. "So, the human form, the upright biped with a head, two eyes, etcetera, is found elsewhere in the universe because of this resonance theory?"

"Yes. And it's more than just physical attributes, of course. How our minds work is influenced by the resonance as well. Our memory, our awareness, our consciousness, is not hard-stored information but influenced by the collective. Think of it like this: our minds are not video cameras, watching the world and recording what we directly experience. They're more like television receivers picking up information, whether we are conscious of it or not. This is also how collective mediation can influence the world; the more people resonating with a particular thought, the more powerful the influence will be."

Patricia smiled widely. "It's marvelous, isn't it Ben?"

I nodded. "Yes." I looked at Chester. "Chester, I'm wondering about these visions you said you have. Anything come of that?"

Daniel answered for him. "I should have mentioned earlier. Chester is one of our consultants on a very special project we are working on."

"What kind of project?" I asked, intrigued.

Byrne grinned. "I wish I could tell you, but we are keeping it secret until we finish running proof of concept tests. Mr. Petulli is helping us out with it, and we have the project funded through the end of the year, but it's going to need more."

Of course, it will, I thought, more funding is always needed.

"It's a zero-point anti-gravity device, isn't it?" asked Mazzotti.

"We'll make an announcement soon. But for now, let's just say that the device will disrupt every industry. It's a game-changer."

I saw images of Daniel and his assistants in a basement laboratory, trying to make bowling balls levitate.

"I've been experiencing high strangeness, too," blurted Chester, "a lot recently."

Everyone went silent, all eyes on him.

"I've seen things. Little orbs in the sky, in my room at night. Ghosts, too."

"Ghosts of people?" I asked.

"Yeah, people, what else?" he shot back sarcastically. "I don't know who they are, but I see them at night sometimes, walking around my house. They are apparitions, definitely humanoid. They seem friendly enough."

"It's not uncommon for UFO experiencers to have what is called high strangeness," Patricia explained for my benefit. "Aliens have a connection with other dimensions of reality. Given that there are portals into other dimensions, you know, it seems experiencers are more sensitive to comings and goings through portals. I describe this in my new book."

"We've been studying the phenomenon at the Foundation," said Daniel. "There's so much yet to learn about intra-dimensional travel. In my estimation, Chester is being visited by EBEs through remote viewing. It's much like what we do to see them. We'd be naïve to think that EBEs don't meditate like us."

Patricia had her eyes on me. "You look surprised by all of this, Ben."

"Maybe a little. These are all extraordinary experiences."

"It's okay to have doubt," Daniel said, "history is replete with extraordinary claims. If someone tells you about something they experienced and know to be true, do you outright believe it as if it were your own experience? Of course not. The credibility of the claimant, their motivation

for telling the story, as well as the details of the
circumstances, are all relevant." He smiled at everyone. "But
once you experience it for yourself, your perspective changes,
doesn't it?"

"That's it," Patricia said.

We talked for another hour or so after dinner. Everyone
wished each other well when we were done. I made sure to
get each person's contact information in case I wanted to
check facts later for my story.

Daniel walked me to the hotel exit. "I hope you found this
useful for your story."

"Definitely. Thank you, Daniel."

He put a hand on my shoulder. "Ben, you've entered a
whole new world here. I'd like to show you more of it. Why
don't you come to another viewing event? We are having one
again next weekend. Same place. You should get there early
and participate in the learning lecture on Saturday. We'll
waive the fee, of course."

His hand on my shoulder and the "I'll be your teacher"
thing was creeping me out, but I knew that I wanted to
experience a sighting again, whether it was the real deal or a
hoax. If the whole thing was bunk, I would need evidence of
it, as well. Daniel seemed to trust me, which would give me
the opportunity to learn more about him and the Foundation
and its's financial paper trail. I could hear Marcus and
Jennifer giving me hell about another trip already, but I'd
already made my decision. "I'll be there."

Daniel smiled. "Excellent."

"I want to make sure I get those financial documents
about the Foundation. Can you remind Nadine?"

"Of course," said Daniel. "I'll remind her right away."

In my motel room, I sat on the bed exhausted, and
downloaded the iM4ET mobile app. I filled out the required
registration and toggled through the app's features. I found
the 3D map feature to be of most interest. Apparently, the
app could track the location of all of its users on a virtual 3D
animation of the Earth, as well as where EBE craft were

supposedly spotted. Curiously, the disclaimer stated that the Proxima Foundation made no guarantees of sightings, nor was it liable if injury, psychological or physical, occurred during a sighting. *Typical lawyer cover-your-ass jargon*, I thought. I was about to doze off when my cell phone rang. The caller ID read Private. I answered the call. An unfamiliar male voice spoke slowly and softly. "If you want to know the truth about Daniel Byrne, then listen to me. He's got people launching drones from the north side of the Valley of the Moon. If you want to catch his ruse, you can do it there."

"Who are you? How do you know this?" I asked.

"Trust me, I know. Good luck Mr. Davenport."

The caller hung up. I paused to think about what I'd just heard and who the caller might be. Someone from the inside of the Proxima Foundation? An enemy of Daniel Byrne? Whoever it was, they knew that I was doing the story and what I was looking for. I hit redial. A recorded voice said the number was blocked. *A mysterious anonymous tip.* I was ecstatic. Sometimes they are an investigative journalist's dream come true.

6

SEEING IS BELIEVING

I ran into Brett Spearman at Jonesy's on Thursday night—a U.S. Army veteran, Special Ops, with a couple of tours in Afghanistan and Iraq in the mid-2000s. He wore a camo Carhartt cap over his curly, dirty-blond hair hanging over his ears. He had fully tattooed arm sleeves, and judging by the size of his biceps and beer gut, I suspected he was surviving on a diet of creatine powder and lager. Jennifer absolutely hated the guy, but he had become one of my best drinking buddies over the past year, and he was into hunting and wildlife photography, which meant he owned cameras and night vision goggles.

"Any interest in helping me with a UFO debunking surveillance mission this weekend?" I asked.

He swiveled toward me. "Sounds like fun, tell me more," he said, shoveling beer nuts into his mouth.

I told him about my story and the suspected hoax. I made it clear that all I needed was some help with filming, but I also thought he'd be good to have around for other reasons. I wasn't sure whom I might run into out there in the darkness in the Valley of the Moon.

Brett belched loudly. "Count me in."

Our plan went like this: Friday night, we'd take my car to

Missoula and tag team driving duties. I'd get us a motel room and pay for all expenses, including beer. I'd drop him off Saturdey morning to scout the north side of the valley while I attended Byrne's lecture at the Proxima Foundation ranch property. Brett would hang out and call me mid-afternoon. I'd pretend the call was from Jennifer, calling me home because of a family emergency, and skip out of the viewing event, then rendezvous with Brett back at the motel room. We'd wait for dark and then go to the north side of the Valley. I wasn't going to let him gather the evidence for my story without me as a witness. I was also thinking that if we were successful at filming the hoax, then I would need to disclose my findings to Daniel before I ran the story—basic journalism courtesy, plus his reaction would make great copy.

We arrived in Missoula late Friday. I got us a room at the Motel 6 where I'd stayed before. We went over to Ramblin' Joe's for some dinner and beers. It was busy. Brenda was our server.

"Hey," she said, handing us our menus, sadness was still in her eyes.

I introduced her to Brett and told her about our plan for the evening.

"Be careful over there," she said.

I nodded. We ordered beers and food. Brett leaned sideways and rubber-necked Brenda's ass while she walked away. "Damn, dude, she's hot." He looked at me and smiled. "You were blushing. You like her, you dog."

I was probably blushing again. "No, I wasn't, and don't be a dick. She just buried her aunt this week. She was murdered, pretty close to where we're going tonight. She was hacked up pretty bad, mutilated, organs removed, burn marks on her, too. I've been trying to get information on the case."

"No shit? So they haven't caught the fucker who did it?"

"No, not yet. She was a TV reporter doing a story on UFOs, I think."

"Really? Kind of sounds like one of those cattle mutilation experiments."

"What are you saying? You think it's possible that aliens killed her?"

"Dude, if a flying saucer flew out of your ass right now, I still wouldn't believe in aliens. I'm talking about secret military experiments. They used to test chemical warfare stuff on farm animals, spray them with chemicals, pick them up in helicopters, dissect them, and dump them out afterwards. You said she was investigating UFOs, and she was found gutted with burn marks, right? I'm just saying…"

"You're not serious, right?"

"Trust me, man. The military does all kinds of experiments, and they're not picky about who they use."

When Brenda returned with our food, she asked me if I'd learned anything from the TV news station. I told her I had no further information. She looked at me with lovely but discouraged eyes. "Thanks for trying, I appreciate it."

She walked away and Brett looked at me. "Dude, I think she likes you."

"I doubt it," I said, squirting ketchup onto my burger. "I really do feel bad for her."

Brett was shaking salt onto his rib eye. "How's things with…what's her name?"

"Jennifer? Okay. Mostly," I lied. I wasn't looking for any relationship advice from Brett, divorced twice before age 30. "Everything's fine."

He nodded as he stuffed a forkful of meat into his mouth.

I had Brenda transfer the tab to the bar. Brett and I looked at a map of the area and determined our route while we pounded a couple beers. The road we planned to take wound into the valley and up a ridge. Brett suggested we hide the Jetta off to the side about a mile in and hike the rest of the way. It made sense, even in my beer-buzzed state.

A while later Brenda came over and sat on the stool next to me. She looked tired.

"Do me a favor," she said, "let me know if you catch them."

I turned to her. "Yeah, I will, and I'm really sorry about

your aunt." It sounded awkward the way it came out.

She shook her head. "It's just not making any sense. They should have suspects by now."

"I'll see what else I can find out," I said. "I'll try talking to law enforcement again. My journalist badge gets me some privileges."

"Thanks," she said, getting up to run the tabs of the people lined up at the register. Brett bottom-upped his beer and bro-punched me on the shoulder. "Come on, chief, no time for chasing skirts. We've got a mission tomorrow."

***

In the morning, we ate a quick breakfast of protein bars and got ready. Brett put on camouflage fatigues and checked and racked his Glock that he kept in a concealed holster under his beltline. I was a little worried that he was becoming overly zealous about the mission. I didn't really know him all that well, and I sure didn't need him shooting anyone or jumping from the bushes to snap necks.

We headed down North Valley Road. At the intersection with Mountain Road, Brett told me to slow down. He had his back pack in his hands and his wrap-around Oakley's on.

I glanced over at him. "You want me to stop here?"

"Don't stop, keep rolling."

"Don't stop?"

He cracked the door open. "No, keep rolling."

I slowed down to about 10 miles per hour. Brett had the door all the way open now and was half hanging out. I slowed some more, and before I knew it he was gone. I looked in the rear view and all I saw a cloud of dust from the road. Crazy bastard.

I sped over to the Proxima Foundation Ranch. I was running late. I parked in a large dirt parking lot and followed the signs to a large white tent where I signed the attendee roster at the entryway and picked up a protocol instruction manual. There were about 40 people inside the tent, sitting in a circle, some in lawn chairs and others on mats. Daniel was in the center, sitting in the lotus position. I sat in a chair outside the circle.

"Breathe in. Now exhale," Daniel intoned, his eyes closed. "Focus is important. We start by honing in our breath, then focus on our intention."

After a few minutes, he spotted me. "Ben, come and join us. Have a seat over here." He pointed to a large mat, half of it occupied by a large woman in sweatpants with curly hair and glasses.

The meditation exercise was painfully uncomfortable for me.

Daniel then explained how the EBEs respond to meditation. "We share the cosmos through what is called unity consciousness. Remember, the most profound level of communication is not communication but communion. When we do the protocol, we are connecting at a much deeper level with our visitors."

During a break, I spoke with a man sitting across from me named Robbie Spence. His forehead was covered in sweat, and I noticed the pit stains in his button-down safari shirt.

"Is this your first time at a viewing event?"

"This is my third. Once in Sedona, once at Mount Shasta, and now here. My wife and I make a trip out of it several times a year."

"So you've seen objects in the sky before at these events?"

His eyes lit up. "Oh yes, almost every time. It's incredible."

I nodded. "So you think these objects are from another planet?"

"Absolutely. Seeing is believing." He smiled at me. "I can't wait until it gets dark."

"I can't wait either," I said, though I was thinking about Brett's recon mission, hoping he'd find us a hiding place and remain unseen.

Next, Daniel explained the characteristics of the EBEs, where they are from, and how they travel inter-dimensionally. He lectured about the protocol, covering the rules and plans for the evening. At lunch, Mike handed out sandwiches and cans of soft drinks that they had catered in. I hesitated, hoping that I wasn't getting myself into a Jonestown situation and then wondering about my level of paranoia. No one else had keeled over yet, so I figured the eats were safe.

"What are you thinking about the conditions tonight for viewing?" I asked Daniel who was sitting across from me.

He looked through one of the tent's plastic windows, still chewing on his sandwich. "I'm not entirely sure. Weather looks like it will hold out. Moon will be starting to come out tonight, but that shouldn't matter."

My phone rang. "Hello?"

It was Brett, doing his best high-pitched effeminate voice. "Hello, sweetie, I need you to come home right now and tend to me."

I got up and stepped away, still close enough to Byrne so that he could hear me.

"I understand. Is he okay? I'll be home tonight." I threw in a, "love you, honey," just to throw Brett off.

Byrne was looking at me. "Everything okay?"

"That was my girlfriend. She's got a family situation, and I'm going to have to go home. I'm sorry. I'm going to miss tonight's viewing event."

He looked disappointed. "I'm sorry to hear that, Ben. I hope everyone is okay."

I thanked him and told him I'd be following up with him soon. I got out of there fast and headed back to pick up Brett at our rendezvous point. I rolled along, expecting him to emerge from the sage. He did. I kept rolling, thinking that's what he wanted me too. He ran along beside me, trying to open the door. It wasn't opening.

"Stop!" he yelled.

I slammed on the brakes. He jumped in.

"Shit, dude, when someone yells stop, stop!"

I hit the gas. "Sorry, man."

We went back to the motel and hung out until sunset. Brett made me put on my navy-blue sweatshirt and a camo baseball cap. He also insisted on driving. I gave him the keys.

He stopped the Jetta just before we turned onto the road leading to our destination on the ridge. A sliver of a moon was rising to the west. He wiped on black face paint and donned his night vision goggles, then proceeded forward, now with vehicle lights off.

"I hope you know what you're doing," I said, still a little worried.

He glanced over at me with the googles. "Do I look like I know what I'm doing?"

I kept reminding myself that the military had trusted him, so I should too.

We went more than four miles in. Towards the end, the ride got bumpy, the bottom of my Jetta scrapping on rocks and threatening to bottom out. Brett reassured me he'd adequately scoped the terrain out and that he already knew where he'd hide my car. He made a three-point turn and got the car facing the other way. "In case we need to get out of here fast," he explained. "I'm going to need you to put your watch and cell phone in the glove compartment."

"What for?" I said.

"They make sounds and give off light," he said.

I threw them into the glove box, and we started down the road, the moon lighting our way.

It wasn't long before we saw a 4x4 Ford Explorer parked on the side of the road up ahead. With no one else out there, it had to be Daniel's people. Brett threw his arm out to stop me. I froze. He scanned our surroundings with his night vision goggles. I couldn't see shit, but I heard a rustling sound up ahead in the bushes.

"Did you hear that?" I whispered. Brett listened attentively.

Then strange sounds were coming from above. My heart was racing. We looked up and saw a dark V-shaped formation flying south, then we heard the honks of geese.

We shared a look, and Brett gestured silently to proceed. A few dozen yards further and we came to a jack knife in the road overlooking a ridge.

"This is the spot," Brett whispered.

We ducked into the sage and kneeled down.

"Can I try the goggles?" I whispered.

He handed them to me. After a minute, I spotted three figures, that looked like green ghosts through the night vision, about sixty feet ahead. My heart felt like it was going to jump out of my chest. They were each carrying something— drones? Brett already had two cameras on them. One of them released a drone, a large quad with its four propellers whizzing in a high pitch. As it lifted, I saw a flare hanging below it, similar to what you find in an emergency roadside kit. It was making sense: electrical igniters to light the flares upon cue.

"You tracking that?" Brett said softly.

"Yeah," I said. "you filming it?"

"Affirmative."

The first drone ascended, then the second, then the third. As they went up, I instinctually stood up. Brett grabbed the sleeve of my sweatshirt and pulled me back down. The first flare lit up, then the second, then the third. The drones hung in the sky and spread out in the shape of a triangle several hundred feet above us.

"Son of a bitch," I said. "I knew it! We've got 'em."

"You call that a UFO?" Brett said.

"Only a distance," I confirmed. The flares would look like what I saw from a few miles away. They were similar in color and shape, this time only three lights, not five. Maybe they were short a drone or two that night.

We filmed until the flares started to burn out, then double-timed it back down the road and jumped into the Jetta, lights off. My adrenaline was pumping as we barreled down the dirt roads and back onto the highway.

When we got back to the motel, we reviewed the video. Perfect. Afterwards, I sat back on my bed and began to worry that maybe we should have stayed somewhere else. My Jetta was parked outside, and I'd told Daniel where I was staying the last time I was here. If anyone had seen us tonight, they could have alerted Daniel. A few seconds later, there was a loud rap on the door. In an instant, Brett was on his feet and turned off the one lamp that was on. I went to the door and looked through the peep hole. It was Daniel and Mike.

"Ben? We want to talk to you," Byrne said, his voice loud but muffled by the door.

I looked at Brett. He nodded, affirming that I should go ahead and respond.

"About what?" I said.

"We just want talk to you," Mike said.

I flashed on a fist fight turned gun fight in the parking lot, that would make the local Channel 4 news for sure. *Journalist confronts UFO Hoaxer in Parking lot, Shootout Ensues.*

I glanced at Brett, confirming that he had my back. I puffed up my chest, opened the door and stepped outside, ready for a cockfight if it came to it. "Let's talk out here," I said confidently as stepped out behind me.

"Who's this guy?" Daniel asked.

Brett and Mike were sizing each other up and staring each other down.

"A friend of mine," I said.

"What was going on on the other side of the mountain tonight?" Daniel asked.

"I don't know, you tell me," I said.

"We got a tip that there were government agents over there trying to hoax a sighting to discredit us. I sent Mike over to check it out, and he said he saw them and your Volkswagen. Isn't that right, Mike?"

"I was out there," said Mike, "I saw them, and I saw you."

I had my hands on my hips. "Oh, really? That's not what we saw. What about the drones and flares?"

"Listen, Ben," Daniel said, "this is all part of a government denial plot to bury the fact of extraterrestrial visitors. Can't you see? They wanted you to find them."

You've got to be kidding me, I thought, *he's a charlatan and trying to confuse and conflate with yet another conspiracy.*

Daniel shook his head in disgust. "This is right out Phillip Klass's playbook."

"Phillip Glass, the composer?" I said.

"Klass," scoffed Mike, "the government agent UFO debunker."

"Did you receive an anonymous phone call, Ben?" Daniel asked.

I wasn't buying it. "I'll review my sources when it is appropriate to do so. If what you say is true, why would they wait until now to do this?"

"Because this is about you, Ben, and about the Proxima Foundation. They want to confuse you, get you to report that what we are doing is all fake, but it's not. The real story here is what *they* are trying to do with tactics that cover up the real contact and progress we're making."

I raised my hands and dropped them in mock exasperation. "Well, Daniel, all I know is what I saw, and seeing is believing, is it not? As a journalist, I have an ethical obligation to report facts and support them with evidence. I think I have enough to show that what you are doing here is all a ruse."

"Come on, Ben, please don't do this. You need to listen to me." He stepped toward me, so I stepped back.

"Don't touch me," I said. Mike and Brett looked like that were about to go at it.

Daniel dropped his hands. "Look, everyone, let's all calm down. I urge you, Ben, to not run with that. You'll set everything we've done back twenty years."

"I don't know what else to say, Daniel. We've got video of a hoax here and no other evidence to support what you're saying. I'm just not buying it. We'll let the public judge the evidence."

"Ben, if you run a story like this, I can sue you for defamation."

"Go ahead and try. I know what I saw, and we've got it on video."

"This won't work out for you, Ben, this I know," Daniel

concluded. "Come on, Mike, let's go."

Mike slammed his palm into the top of my Jetta's hood as they walked by it.

Assholes, I thought. Fuck Byrne. I had found the truth, and I was going to let it be known.

7

UFO HOAXES, TOO

Do you ever wonder what makes some people more gullible than others? How some people choose to ignore facts contrary to what they believe?

One of my favorite electives in journalism school was a psychology class that covered why people believe what they believe. It's not because some people are just more stupid than others; there's far more to it than that. It has to do with how our brains are wired, and how conscious and subconscious cognitive processes, emotional states, and biases influence our decisions. Some of these processes are adaptive, meaning they're helpful, but it is also why well-meaning people are susceptible to manipulation through misinformation and propaganda.

Knowing all of this doesn't make me accept or justify others' actions, but it does help me to frame how people will interpret the information I write about, and what they may or may not react to.

I had this in mind while drafting my 2000-word exposé on the Proxima Foundation, "Seeing is Believing: UFO Hoaxes, Too." It was done in two days, and I presented it to Marcus on Wednesday morning.

Marcus clicked on the YouTube link showing the viewing

event I attended, then the night vision video Brett and I filmed. He watched with interest while I waited confidently for his reaction. The reflection of the video flicked in his hipster glasses.

"I like what you did describing the meditation thing, and the videos are great. What about the financial documents form the Proxima Foundation?"

"I never received them from Nadine Byrne, and I'm not expecting them at this point," I said. "The videos tell it all."

"Financial documents would make this even better, but the video is good," Marcus said.

I smiled. "Seeing is believing."

He nodded. "What about the murdered TV journalist. Anything on that?"

"Nothing. I called the police and the news stations again this morning, and the case remains unsolved." Brenda had crossed my mind just that morning. I hadn't called her after Brett and I caught Daniel in the hoax, but I was wondering how she was doing. I decided I would call after my article came out.

Marcus nodded. "Very well. I'm good with this. Get it over to the web department ASAP and run it."

By the end of the first day, the story had more than ten thousand hits. By the end of the first week, it had half a million. Reuters picked it up, and I was getting interview requests from TV stations and other press outlets across the nation and a few from overseas. The story wasn't going to get me another Pulitzer nod, but it was a success as far as an online investigative magazine article goes.

I was also getting hundreds of comments from anonymous readers on the *Hot Reports* website. AliensAreReal67 wrote: "Another hoaxer bites the dust. Doesn't mean aliens aren't real."

SiriusBoy88 wrote: "This story is obviously bogus. Got to be another government disinformation campaign."

Rollergirl87 said: "Fuck you, Ben Davenport, you corporate hack piece of shit."

This kind of vitriol didn't bother me all that much. The same type of thing had happened when my Hanford waste story came out. It just comes with the territory.

Marcus called me into his office two days later. "Nice work on the UFO story. I've got another assignment for you. Looks like the Yakima Indian tribes are resisting the installation of a new cellular tower network on their land. They just filed a Federal lawsuit. Congressman Mathew Young from the 4th District has agreed to talk to us about the situation over there. He's siding with the tribes and giving us an exclusive. Wants to meet with you on Saturday. I need you on this right away."

"An exclusive? Why?" I hadn't met the Congressman in person, but the Hanford Nuclear Reservation was in his Congressional district and I wondered if my fraud waste and abuse investigation had anything to do with why he gave me an exclusive.

Marcus shrugged. "Apparently, he likes your work. He asked for you specifically. Can you get out to Yakima by Friday? He wants to meet with you on Saturday."

"Sure," I said, "I'll get right on it."

"Oh, one more thing," he said. "You're coming up on your three-year anniversary with us. I'm giving you a raise. Congratulations."

We shook hands.

"Thanks, Marcus, I really appreciate it." I was riding a wave of euphoria now.

Marcus glanced at his computer screen for a moment. "I've never seen so many comments like this after a story. You really hit a nerve."

"Byrne has quite a following. Some of those people mortgaged their homes to give him money and participate in his sighting retreats. They're in denial."

"UFO nuts," he said.

I smiled. "Yeah, for sure."

Just before I headed out of the office, a package arrived for me. I studied it, contemplating whether or not I should call the bomb squad. I decided to open it. It was the Proxima Foundation annual report and copies of tax returns for the last three years with a hand written note:

"Dear Ben, I regret that I couldn't get these documents to you sooner. I read your story, 'Seeing is Believing: UFO Hoaxes, Too'. I'd hoped that you would have put more effort into understanding what is really going on. Sometimes things are not as they appear. Apparently, this type of drivel is what the millennial generation has come to accept as adequate journalism. I wish you all the best on your journey. Nadine Byrne."

I set the note aside, annoyed. I didn't need to be lectured by a con-artist. I looked through the documents: no red flags in the tax docs, nor was there anything of substance requiring me to make corrections or amend my story. If Nadine had given me the documents when I asked for them, would it have changed what I wrote? It all looked pretty clean, but that didn't matter; a hoax is a hoax, and I'd exposed it. I buried the documents and Nadine's note in the bottom drawer of my desk.

Nadine's comments about my "drivel" hadn't fazed me, either. In fact, thanks to the raise and praise, I was feeling more optimism about my writing career and outlook on life than ever before, and it made me think about Jennifer and the rough spots I blamed myself for. Should I pop the question? I was thirty-one and feeling ready for the commitment.

On Friday night, I took her out to dinner. I'd gone to a jewelry store in the mall earlier in the day and purchased a three-quarter karat engagement ring, four months of my new salary. I hoped to hell she'd be satisfied with it. I reserved a table for two at an expensive restaurant in the Elliot Bay Marina. The Space Needle and city skyline were lit up and reflecting across the Sound. I insisted she sit in the seat with the best view. When the waiter came around, I ordered a hundred-dollar bottle of champagne.

Jennifer smiled at me. "I told you it was a hoax."

I smiled back. "Yeah, you were right. It doesn't explain

everything, but it shows how easy it is to fool people."

"No more UFOs and aliens, right?" she said.

I was still smiling. "No more UFOs and aliens."

The waiter brought the Champagne and poured.

"Before we toast…" My throat was suddenly dry and my heart starting to race.

Jennifer looked at me.

I stood and went down on one knee in front of her, took her hand, and said, "I know a writer can be difficult at times, but I hope you forgive me. I want to be with no one else in the world but you." I pulled the ring out of my pocket. "Will you marry me, Jennifer Martin?"

She froze, staring at the ring. Then inspecting it for a moment longer. Blood was pulsing in my face. She looked at me. I was about to panic, but then she smiled.

"Yes."

Thank God, I thought. I slid the ring over her finger. We stood up, embraced and kissed. Some of the people at adjacent tables applauded. I heard a few whistles.

After dinner, we went out for drinks at one of her favorite bars in Ballard. She called a few of her girlfriends and spent half the time texting and on social media while I got wasted.

That night I fought off the whiskey dick, and we had the best sex we'd had in months.

In the morning, we went out for brunch. Jennifer wanted to discuss a date for the wedding and what she wanted for our special day. My stomach churned with anxiety: it was going to cost a fortune. I reminded myself that the bride's family pays for the wedding. Her parents had the money; they lived in Bellevue. Jennifer's mother was a lawyer, and her father a psychiatrist. Mine were in Spokane, my mother a librarian and my stepfather a plumber. My biological father, a captain in the U.S. Navy and a physician, had died when I was eleven. Why a Navy officer was stationed in Arizona was never clear to me. As far as I knew, he had worked with a Department of Defense contractor on aerospace medicine systems.

We had just ordered our omelets when my cell phone rang. I glanced at the caller ID. It was Brenda.

"Excuse me a second," I said, standing up.

"Who is it?" Jennifer asked, eying me suspiciously.

"It's work related, won't be a minute." I headed toward the restrooms in the back. I stood against a wall answered the call, my finger in my other ear to muffle the din of the packed restaurant.

Brenda was irate. "Did you forget about me? I saw your article. So you are done with it all? What about my aunt?"

"No, I didn't forget about you. I've been thinking about you actually. Are you doing okay?"

"I guess so. What the news is reporting out here is bullshit, all bullshit. The FBI were at my uncle's a of couple days ago. They said they were investigating links to the bastard who killed her, which doesn't make any sense to me. What would my aunt have to do with an escaped convict?"

"Did she do a story on him or something?"

"Not that I'm aware of. They took my aunt's laptop and her notebooks, and they grilled my uncle, too, which didn't seem right. He sent me a voicemail that my aunt Sally left him the night before she was killed. Apparently, she was out investigating lights in the sky."

"Can you send it to me? I'd like to hear it."

"Maybe. The file is pretty big, I'll have to email it."

"But what she was working on?"

"Give me a minute, I need to get onto my computer."

I waited a minute. I glanced out into the restaurant and saw that Jennifer was glued to her phone, probably shopping for wedding dresses or on social media.

Brenda returned. "I'm sending it right now."

Jennifer was zeroing in on me now.

"I got to go, Brenda, can I call you later?"

"Yeah, sure."

I hung up and got back to the table. Our omelets had arrived.

Jennifer set down her phone. "Everything okay?"

"Everything's fine. It's just some details about the story I'm working on. No big deal. I'm going to be interviewing U.S. Congressman Young in Yakima this weekend. It's an exclusive interview. I'll get national coverage for sure."

She seemed to be impressed with who I was going to be interviewing. We finished up our breakfast and when we got home I listened to the audio file Brenda sent.

"I'm on Deer Creek Road, just south of the tower. It's 9:20pm. There are lights in the sky, two—no, three. They look like they are heading this way." I could hear her walking through the sage. "I'm still seeing three lights. They are definitely getting closer." Her breathing increased. "It's going to fly over me. *Our Father who art in heaven*...It's a triangle of lights, a perfect triangle. Is it an airplane? No, definitely not an airplane. I can't see the stars in between the lights. It's got to be a solid craft, silent, no sound. Holy Jesus." There was a long pause, perhaps 15 seconds. "It's gone. It flew over, accelerated, and was gone." She giggled. "It was a UFO. Hot damn! I'm going to have to come back out here tomorrow night. Sally out."

The recording ended. *What the heck did she see?* A Proxima Foundation's hoax? Maybe, but what she described on the recording sounded a lot like what I remembered from 1997. A formation of lights flying silently overhead.

That evening, I started the shower and tried calling Brenda from the bathroom. She didn't answer. I shot her a text. No response. I planned to call her in the morning while on the road to Yakima.

8

DARK DESERT HIGHWAY

U.S. Representative Matthew Young greeted me at the door of his residence. He was fifty with dark hair and chiseled face. His thick-rimmed glasses gave him the appearance of a college professor. He was dressed in a navy blazer and tieless white dress shirt. We shook hands.

"Welcome, Ben, thanks for coming out and agreeing to do the story."

"Thank you for meeting me, sir."

"I hope you're hungry," he said. "Esmeralda, our help, has prepared a nice lunch."

The place wasn't as opulent as I was expecting for a second-term U.S. Congressman, but it still had hardwood floors, classic wainscoting, and tall ceilings. On the wall was a large painting of a barred owl, its wings spread, its big eyes beholding its prey. We sat at the dining table.

"My wife is out of town this week visiting family. She would like to have met you, we've both enjoyed your articles." Was he buttering me up?

Within seconds Esmeralda, a middle-aged woman with a warm smile, served us a delightful dinner of roast chicken, new potatoes, roasted artichokes, and a nice Washington Sauvignon Blanc.

The U.S. Representative poured my wine. "What made you want to give us an exclusive story?" I asked innocently.

"Well, I'd read your article on the Hanford Nuclear Reservation thing, seemed fair and objective, the way journalism used to be, and you obviously care about this region and the people living here, which matters to me." He sipped his wine.

In between mouthfuls, I began with background questions. He was born in Washington, and his family owned one of the largest apple orchards in the Northwest.

"I grew up a farmer and still am at heart. I love the land and the people out here, including the tribes. When this cellular tower thing happened, I had to get involved."

I savored the wine. "So what is the issue?"

"The FCC approved one of the nation's largest cellular carriers' bids to build a major network installation in the Yakima and Tri-Cities area—part of the nationwide 5G upgrade extending wireless broadband coverage over the entire reservation area. The tribes aren't too happy with having new towers on their land. They want to protect the natural beauty and health of the area. I agree with them. I'd like to see the company move the towers to the east. It's a logical concession, if you ask me."

"What's the resistance?"

"This new shorter range 5G technology requires a lot more transmitters and it's just easier to run them along the highway. The company has demos of how they can camouflage the towers to look like trees, but the tribes don't care." He took a bite of his chicken. "It just went to court this past week. I'm hoping this gets resolved and doesn't get into a larger lawsuit. These cases can take years."

"Can you convince the company to move the towers with your influence?"

He stared at me. "You know I can't interfere with the courts like that. I can publicly express my opinion and show my solidarity with the tribes, but that's all. That's what I've always done, and that's what I plan to do with this situation.

I'm hoping your story on this might help build public pressure. The local newspapers covered it, but with no effect. Of course, you'll look at both sides. Fair and honest reporting." He glanced at me.

"Of course," I responded, knowing now there wouldn't be any grand controversy to unveil. He was just looking for some publicity for his future re-election campaign. Nonetheless, an exclusive interview with a Congressman made it worthwhile and guaranteed me a slam-dunk article.

We went over a few more details about the tribes and transmitters through lunch and Esmeralda's apple pie. Stirring cream into his coffee, the Congressman switched gears, "I read your story on the Proxima Foundation. So I assume you don't believe we're being visited by alien beings. Is that so?"

I smiled. "I still can't say with any certainty whether or not we've been visited, but I'm certainly a lot more skeptical after catching the Daniel Byrne UFO hoax."

He got a little more serious. "You know, I saw one once myself, at an airshow in Spokane a couple of years ago. I tracked a white object moving fast across the sky, and it wasn't a jet." He smiled. "Nor was it a sparrow, swamp gas, or the planet Venus."

"Do you think that whatever you saw was from another planet?"

"It was definitely something not of this world as I know it. There's a video of the sighting on YouTube, maybe under Spokane UFO."

"I'll look for it. People see all kinds of things in the sky, but it doesn't mean it's aliens, right?" I didn't want to come off as being disrespectful. "I don't mean to discredit what you saw, of course."

"To tell you the truth, Ben, I've had a personal interest in this topic for a number of years. To think we are alone in the universe is ridiculous. But don't get me wrong: I'm a religious man and believe in Jesus Christ our savior, but God's universe is a mysterious place. We don't know for sure what may be out there. Wouldn't you agree?"

"Yes," I said, biting into my second piece apple pie, the flaky crust melting in my mouth.

"Can't rule it out." He kept looking at me thoughtfully, watching me eat the pie. "Washington apples. Esmeralda does a great job."

I looked up and nodded, my mouth stuffed. Having savored and swallowed, I responded, "You must have inside access to data on UFOs. Does the government know something?"

"It would really change everything, wouldn't it?" He smiled meaningfully at me. I was beginning to see that this visit wasn't really about the 5G towers or his career, nor was he having fun with me.

I decided to be more direct. "Can you confirm that the US government knows for certain there's alien life out there?"

"Even if I knew, Ben, I couldn't tell you." He continued looking at me.

I went a little further. "What about any new government black programs, like the Advanced Aerospace Threat Identification Program? I read that the former program manager, Luis Elizondo, said he believed there was very compelling evidence we may not be alone."

The Congressman was dismissive. "That's just one man's opinion. He no longer works for the government. People say all kinds of crazy things when they retire from security positions."

"He's part of the To The Stars Foundation, isn't he? They have some kind of contract with the government related to anti-gravity, don't they?"

The Congressman rubbed his chin. "I admit I'm not in on this stuff, but I'll look into this for you and let you know what I find out. How does that sound?"

I was surprised. What did he want in return? "That would be great, sir," I said, scraping the plate to the last dregs of Esmeralda's pie.

At the door, he shook my hand again and said, "Good luck with the story, Ben. Don't hesitate to call my office if you need any more information. I look forward to seeing your article."

Walking down the driveway to my car, I was thinking it was no coincidence that the Congressman was interested in UFOs, and yet he said he didn't seem to have much information on black government programs investigating them—SAPs, the government calls them—Special Access Programs. Wouldn't he have known more? Or did he actually know and pretend he didn't know? With all of that staring and smiling, I suspected he did.

In the car I shot Jennifer a quick text to let her know I was on my way. The map on my smartphone told me there was an accident at Snoqualmie Pass. I'd have to take Interstate 12 south of Mount Rainier to get home before midnight.

About an hour into the drive, Steve Miller Band's "Fly Like an Eagle" came up on my phone play list. The sun had set and the sky was dark, no moon, just like it was during the first sighting event. My phone lit up. I glanced over: the Proxima Foundation's iM4ET app had launched. How, and why, did the app start by itself? I force closed it.

In less than a minute, a large white light was in my rearview mirror to my right, above and behind my car. It had to be an Army helicopter spotlight, maybe on maneuvers from the Army National Guard base near Yakima or Joint Base Lewis-McChord near Tacoma. If it was, it must be on whisper mode. It seemed to be trailing me, then the light was gone. Had it changed course or gone behind a ridge?

A moment later, a blinding green-white light enveloped my car. I slammed on the brakes, my mind scrambling for an explanation. Then my engine cut out. The Jetta had completely died. I felt a vibration, a high-frequency buzzing as if it was coming from inside my body and resonating in my skull, then a tingling sensation. All the hair on my body rose up, responding to the static electricity. Leaves and dust swirled around my car in a vortex of wind and pale green light.

Out of instinct, I grabbed my phone and fumbled to turn

on the video app. A ringing tone began in my ears and grew louder until it felt like my ears were popping from low air pressure. I remember the panic, then I lost consciousness. I came to in a room unknown to me. Except for a bright pin-point of light emanating from the ceiling, it was dark. The air was thick, very thick, and smelled sour and stale, like a refrigerator after no power for a week. I was having difficulty breathing and realized I couldn't move my arms and legs. In fact, I couldn't see or feel them. *Was I in an ambulance? the hospital? was I dead?*

Peripherally, I caught movement to my left. Two humanoid beings were on the other side of what appeared to be a glass wall. They had large hairless heads and two small completely black eyes. Like the Congressman, they were staring at me. I stared back, terrified. Their arms and torsos were thin and spindly in grey body suits of some kind. What were they planning to do to me? I tried to get up and get away. It was useless. I must be strapped down. Their stares seemed to be connected to slowing my thoughts, perhaps due to my state of panic. My jaw felt weighed down from the inside, but I managed to shout, "What are you doing? What do you want?"

I scanned the room for other possible threats. When I looked back, the two figures were standing over me, their pale skin as textured as fine cloth with long ridges from their foreheads down to two small nostrils and no nose. I could smell them—spicy and cinnamon-like.

The beings backed away and exited. That's when I noticed a narrow, metallic robotic arm above me with something rectangular at the end of it, transiting my face. Something was positioned over my eyes, covering them completely. Suddenly, I felt a horrendous pain in my groin. Something, some kind of instrument had been shoved up the urethra of my penis, but how? Feeling as though I was going to pass out, I began seeing images, symbols, some sort of star map. Then I heard a garbled voice say in English, "You are special to us. We will be coming for you again, Ben." Then a bright flash, a loud noise, and a booming coming from within my head.

I was sitting on the edge of a road, facing a large drop-off, hundreds of feet above a valley. It was still dark. A white light was approaching just above the ground, shining into my face.

"What are you doing there?" asked a masculine voice.

The man was wearing a hat, a light blue uniform, and I saw a badge. *Washington State Patrol Trooper. What the hell happened? Where am I? Was everything that I'd just experienced a bad dream?* I realized then that I was naked and shivering from the cold. A few cars and a tractor-trailer truck crept by us, rubbernecking the scene.

"What are you doing up here?" the trooper repeated, towering over me, holding a blanket.

"Up here?" I looked around. I was in the mountains, a hundred feet above a valley. Was it still Snoqualmie Pass?

He handed me the blanket. "Have you been drinking? Taking drugs?"

I draped the blanket over my body. I couldn't get any words to come out of my mouth. I shook my head, indicating no to his drug use question.

"What's your name?' he said.

I struggled to get the word out. "Ben," I said.

"Okay, Ben, let's get you up and somewhere safe, what do you say?"

I was shivering uncontrollably and my head was pounding with the worst headache I've ever experienced. I stood up and almost instantly the trooper spun me around and had handcuffs on me. He secured the blanket over me and then made a call on his radio. "10-73 in custody." He then told me that the restraints on my wrists were for my and his safety.

He walked me back to a patrol car and had me sit in the back, then he shut the door. I watched him do a quick walk up and down the side of the road, presumably scanning for anything that would serve as a clue to who I was and what was going on. He picked up what appeared to be my smartwatch.

"This yours?" He held it up when he got back to the car and I grunted a yes, still in migraine pain.

"I'll keep it for now," he said.

He took me to the State Police station in Morton where I was booked, fingerprinted, given an orange jump suit, and placed in a holding cell. Three days had passed since I had left Yakima. They gave me a medical exam and told me that there were no obvious signs of a head injury. There was nothing wrong with my man parts, either. They located my car, 10 miles away from where they had found me.

Later, a young woman who introduced herself as a mental health counselor questioned me.

"Any idea what you were doing up there on the Pass, Ben?"

"I don't know. I remember seeing lights, I don't know what happened." I thought I'd be better off not mentioning the details of what I'd experienced for fear of them thinking I was a psych case.

"Lights? You mean headlights?"

I remained silent.

"Have you been having thoughts about suicide?"

"Suicide? No. Like I said, I was driving home and I saw some lights. I don't remember. Did you find my car? I must have been in an accident."

"Your car shows no signs of an accident."

"I just want to go home," I said, exhausted.

"Is there anyone that you want us to call?"

"Yes, my fiancée, Jennifer."

They made me take a shower. I stripped down and noticed a red spot in the center of my chest—six raised holes in a circle, as if I'd been pricked or embossed. I leaned against the wall of the shower stall, letting the water cascade over my body, images of the black-eyed beings flooding my mind, their eyes looking through me, their strange cinnamon scent, and that voice in my head, *You are special to us. We will be coming for you again, Ben.*

I began to cry, my mind racing. What was happening to

me? Am I crazy? What is this mark on my chest? Was I now a UFO abductee? Why did they pick me? What did they want from me?

Jennifer arrived in the morning. I changed into the clothes she brought, and the booking officer gave me back my smartwatch I'd completely forgotten about. I sat in the waiting area, watching Jennifer on the other side of the glass, talking with an officer. Once I was buzzed through, Jennifer looked me over but didn't say a word. She was saving it for the ride back to Seattle.

At last in her car, she sat and looked at me. "What the fuck, Ben? Where in the hell were you? What happened? Were you drinking?"

"No, I wasn't drinking! Can we go, please?"

"Then what in the hell were you doing on the side of road with your clothes off? Were you going to jump or something?"

I put my hands on my head. The bright sunlight was triggering another migraine. I felt like someone was sticking a knife in my right eye and out through my left.

She looked at me. "Are you okay?"

"No. I'm not, let's just go home."

She started the car. "You'd better call your parents, they're worried."

I knew I should, but I didn't want to talk to anyone.

Once on the road, Jennifer started her interrogation again. "Are you on meth or something?"

"No!" I was staring out the window, suddenly very tired of her endless suspicions, wanting her to just leave me alone.

"What then? Are you into some kinky shit or something I should know about?"

"Goddammit, Jennifer, no!"

"Then what's going on?"

I was growing angrier by the second. "I don't know. Something happened to me! I just need to get home and sleep."

"What happened?" She glanced over at me, newly

concerned.

"I think I was abducted, okay?"

A look of terror and disgust went across her face.

"Abducted? You mean like aliens?"

"Yeah, like aliens."

She rolled her eyes and sighed. "Here we go again with the aliens. What are you talking about, Ben?"

I remained silent. I felt like kicking out the windshield. After a minute, she put on the radio, and I turned it off, making it clear that I wanted quiet.

"Why won't you talk to me?" she said.

I kicked the dash. "Just drive! Please, Jennifer! Just get me home!"

"Okay, okay, take it easy!"

I leaned against the glass of the passenger door and within minutes, I was asleep.

9

HIGH STRANGENESS

The ringing in my ears sounded like cicadas on crack. The sound ebbed and flowed over long cycles, with its most intense peaks coinciding with pounding migraines. My sleep was terrible. I was having dreams of being on a highway at night only to lose control of the car after being blasted by bright lights from above. My restlessness in bed was driving Jennifer crazy.

I got a new cell phone and called my insurance company. A local tow company had retrieved my car, and its transport to Seattle was covered by my insurance. Luckily, I didn't need it right away. Marcus agreed to let me work from home as long as I got the cell tower story done. He gave me two weeks. I went to work on it, but couldn't focus worth a damn. I was spending hours on the Internet, searching and reading everything that I could about alien abductions and what people experience afterwards. I downloaded a bunch of books, including John Mack's *Abduction: Human Encounters with Aliens* and Budd Hopkin's *Intruders*. I watched documentaries on Betty and Barney Hill and Travis Walton. I needed answers, and what I found were similar themes among what ufologists call experiencers. The bright lights from above and being examined by large-headed beings while strapped to a table were common themes. Some of the details were the same too. In the book *Communion*, Whitley Strieber mentioned the odors of burning cardboard and sometimes cinnamon when his abductors were present. He mentioned the small triangular mark on his son's body; for me, it was a hexagon on my chest.

One night, I had a particularly terrifying dream. Two dark figures entered our bedroom and stood over me, watching me. I tried to jump out of bed only to find my body paralyzed. I yelled for Jennifer to wake up, but my mouth wouldn't move. At last, the specters disappeared. I awakened from whatever state I was in to find Jennifer out of bed and staring at me from the far side of the bedroom. She was terrified, her face lit up dimly by the night light in the bathroom.

"What's going on, Ben? You kicked me really hard."

"I don't know, I just saw..." Before I could finish my sentence, I spotted several translucent balls of light about the size of grapefruits floating in the air.

"Right there!" I pointed to the balls of light. "Do you see that?"

"See what?"

"Balls of light!"

Jennifer looked around the room.

"There's nothing there, Ben."

As soon as I pointed to them, they faded away.

"I don't know, I thought I saw lights floating in the air, right over there." I pointed.

"You were having a nightmare again, Ben. You are hallucinating. I think you should see someone about this."

I sat up on the side of the bed to think, feeling another migraine coming on. "I need some water. I don't want to talk about this now."

Jennifer was still staring at me.

"Maybe you should sleep on the couch."

"Fine," I said, not wanting to argue. I went out into the kitchen for the water, popped a couple of Excedrin, and spent the rest of the night in the living room.

A day later I began to notice something going on with the thoughts in my head. Sometimes a thought would come into my mind, and I would find myself putting it into my own· words and then acting on it, whether it was to get up and pace the room or get a drink of water. They were benign behaviors, but the thing is I'm sure the original thought was not my own. It would just appear, and I would believe it was true or that I needed to carry it out. Only afterward would I question it.

People with schizophrenia have conversations with phantom voices that sometimes tell them what to do, or tell them they are a worthless piece of shit. What I was experiencing was different. I wasn't hearing voices; I was having thoughts telling me what I needed to do or believe. But where were they coming from? Why was this happening to me?

In the morning, while I was putting on my smartwatch, an idea came to me. Did the watch capture my heart rate and GPS from the night up on that ridge? Would the data prove my abduction experience? Why hadn't I thought of checking before?

I synched my watch to my laptop and looked at the data. My heart rate was a normal 74 beats per minute up to about eight-thirty, and then it shot up to 110, which must have been when I spotted the lights in the sky trailing behind me. Then my heartbeat rocketed to 120 for about two minutes before plummeting down to 56 for about a minute, and then— missing data. I checked the GPS map feature. It showed me on the highway, then stopping on the ridge, then missing data until about 7 am, a mile down the road.

I sat back to take it all in. If I had been taken up into a ship, then the data would look just like it did. I had to show Jennifer. I took my laptop into the bedroom. She was still in bed.

"Look," I said, sitting on the bed next to her with my laptop in hand. "My smartwatch recorded the whole thing. It shows my heart rate increasing, and then the GPS does something crazy. This proves something happened to me up on the ridge. I was taken up into a ship."

She pulled the covers over her head. "I'm not hearing this," she said, her voice muffled.

"Why won't you look?" I said. "This proves something did happen to me up on the ridge. It was an abduction, Jennifer, I'm certain of it."

She didn't respond, but her crying told me enough. It must be too much for her—too outside her worldview. She wasn't ready for this.

I left her and went out to the kitchen to make some coffee and conduct more research online.

The next evening Jennifer requested a sit-down talk.

"I'm really worried about you, Ben, you're not sleeping, and I'm still not sure what is going on with you. I think it would be helpful if you saw someone. My mom gave me the name of a psychiatrist who's close by."

She dropped a piece of paper with a name, number, and address on the coffee table.

"Make an appointment. I think it would be a good thing."

I picked up the paper, glanced at it, and then tossed it back onto the table. If I saw anyone, it was going to be a neurologist, not a headshrinker. Whitley Strieber went to see a neurologist and got tested for epilepsy. Did I have a tumor pinching up against the occipital lobe? Was this the cause of the orbs of light that I was seeing at night? Could something like this be affecting the thoughts in my head, too?

Perhaps it would be better that I talk to someone who was an expert on alien abduction. When conventional medical explanations failed, Strieber had sought solace by talking to the UFO abduction expert Budd Hopkins. John Mack would be an ideal option, too if only these prolific men weren't deceased. I wasn't sure who I should call. I just knew that it needed to be someone I could trust.

I leaned back on the sofa and stared at the floor.

"I think I need to talk to someone about aliens

abductions."

She gave me an annoyed look. "Here we go with aliens again. You weren't abducted, Ben. Just make the appointment. You're not in a good state of mind. You need to get some help."

The ringing in my ears started up again. I leaned forward and cupped put my hands around my face. "It's not going to help. I need to know what has happened to me. I just need some time to figure it out."

She shook her head. "Well, you can't just sit around here all day reading and looking at UFO videos. You need to do something."

I'd been pushed enough. "I don't need this. I'm going out!" I headed for the door, grabbed my keys and jacket, and glanced back at her. She was red in the face, and her eyes were twitching with frustration.

"That's great!" she yelled. "Go drink your problems away! That's really going to go well!"

I opened the door. "I'm just going to get out for a bit. It's no big deal. Don't be such a shrew," I said.

"Don't be such an asshole!" she replied.

I flung her favorite word at her. "Whatever. I'm going." I walked out, letting the door slam shut behind me.

I could hear her yelling from behind the door. "If you do that, you can sleep somewhere else tonight!"

"Fine! I will!"

I got down to Jonesy's. I was fuming mad and needed a drink.

Brett was sitting at the bar. I sat beside him and ordered a shot of whiskey. I told him about my experience on my way back from Yakima and all of the strange symptoms that I'd been experiencing. I wasn't worried about risking ridicule with him. He was a little crazy anyway, and I trusted him. I figured that just maybe he'd have some ideas for me.

"Occam's Razor, man," he said. "Maybe someone gave you some LSD in your food that night?"

"I had dinner with U.S. Congressman Young. He's not

going to put a roofie in my wine."

Brett looked at his drink. "Never trust a politician." He took a sip. "Ever see the movie *Jacob's Ladder*? Trippy psychedelic shit. They really did BZ experiments in Vietnam, you know."

I'd seen the movie and wasn't buying the government conspiracy-inspired LSD trip.

"Something has definitely happened to me. I didn't hit my head either. The insurance company told me that my car wasn't that damaged when they found it, so that can't be it."

He sipped his beer, pondering what happened to me. "You smoke some bad weed?"

"No, not at all. I'm not taking any drugs."

He took another sip. "There's another explanation."

"Yeah, what's that?"

"A staged abduction. Like I was telling you, how do you really know that you aren't part of some government experiment?"

At least I was interested. "How would I know?"

"Got to look at the evidence. Maybe you should talk to someone, maybe one of your UFO friends."

I wasn't buying the government experiment theory, but talking to a UFO expert was a possibility. Just then, I remembered the guy I had met in the hallway at the UFO convention in McMinnville—Jack Clark, the State of Washington MUFON Director. I still had his card in my wallet. He was local and would be interested in what I'd had to say.

Brett bought us a round of whiskey shots. We took them and slammed our empty glasses down on the bar. "How's what's her name taking all this?"

"Jennifer? She thinks I'm two cans short of a six pack. She doesn't believe me at all."

He leaned closer. "Just pretend you're 100 percent sane. Show no signs of the weird stuff you are experiencing. That's what I do."

Wise advice from the relationship master. The thing was, I

knew he was right.

"Yeah, but she's pretty pissed off at me right now. I don't think she is going to let me in tonight."

"Sweet talk her, man. Say you are sorry. Get her a gift or something."

He was right about that, too. I sent Jennifer a text on my new phone, telling her that I was sorry and that I wanted to come back home. She texted me back and said that she was in bed and that if I came back, I'd have to sleep on the couch. I told her that would be fine, and that I'd be there soon.

Just then, I noticed the icon for the iM4ET app on my home screen. *I don't remember downloading that*, I thought. Once again, it downloaded automatically from the Cloud. I was too drunk to think any more about it and stumbled out onto the street. Brett followed me. That wind sock was flapping about outside of Jonesy's, its skinny arms, long, tubular neck, and black eyes staring me down. I was paralyzed at the sight of it. A thought popped into my mind, and I found myself saying, "They are coming back for me." Panic consumed me, but I couldn't get myself to run. I dropped onto the concrete and crawled into a ball. My mind was flooded with the same thought. *They are coming for me! They are coming for me!* A few minutes later, hands were on me, pulling me up off of the concrete. It was Brett.

"Come on, man, I'll get you home."

10

SHRINKED

Dr. Chu was at her desk. Plants and Asian lamps reflected from the lenses of her thick rimmed designer glasses.

"So what brings you in to see me, Ben?" Her voice was soft, and her face friendly.

I'd debated whether or not I should tell her about my abduction experience. I figured that she'd think that I was out to lunch and marbleless. My insurance was paying for the visit, and I didn't see the need for that information to go on my medical record. I decided to keep it conventional.

"I've been having sleep problems—trouble falling asleep and nightmares. I've also had a very loud ringing in my ears for the past couple of weeks."

She reviewed the health-screening questionnaire I'd completed in the waiting room. "Do you feel depressed?"

"No. I mean, I'm not feeling good, but I don't have clinical depression or anything like that."

"What about thoughts of harming yourself?"

"No, I'm not suicidal, if that is what you are asking."

"You mention ringing in your ears. Have you been checked out for tinnitus?"

"It's not that. The ringing is not normal, and I never had it before."

She continued down the list, ruling out head injuries based on my history, and in 15 minutes had prescribed 50 milligrams of Zoloft plus a referral for outpatient counseling. She said to see her office assistant on the way out to book another appointment in three weeks, and that was it. I hadn't expected more.

I made the follow-up appointment and stopped at a pharmacy down the street, then headed to Sumner, fighting mid-afternoon traffic all the way.

Jack Clark was sitting in the back of Starbucks. He smiled when he saw me and shook my hand. He was still wearing that hat. I sat down, and he opened up his laptop.

"Is this private? Do I have to give my name?" I asked.

"Well, we respect your privacy, Ben. We won't give out any of your personal information. I just need to fill out this report. It shouldn't take more than 45 minutes or so."

"Okay. I just don't want anything going in that will identify me, okay?"

"Sure, let's proceed. What was the date of the event?"

"November 12th, Thursday."

"Tell me where you were and what you were doing."

"I was driving back from Yakima. It was evening. I'd just done an interview with U.S. Congressman Young about the cell phone tower controversy in Yakima County."

"Congressman Young, uh huh." He scribbled his name down.

"Is that important?" I asked with interest.

"Maybe. Keep going."

"My smartphone started to buzz. It was Byrne's Proxima Foundation app. It lit up on my phone like it had started up itself."

His eyebrows rose. "I'm curious about this app. Can I see it?"

"Sure," I said, pulling my new phone out of my pocket and showing him the iM4ET app.

He looked it over. "Interesting," he said, then handed it back to me. "Tell me what happened next."

"I saw a light trailing me, then it disappeared, and then I was surrounded by light. Then it…"

"Hold on. Tell me more about the lights. What color? Size? Shape? In a formation?"

"Triangular, definitely triangular. It seemed pretty big."

"How big would you say?"

"I don't know. Forty of fifty feet across, maybe more."

"Did it have color on its surface?"

"I'm not sure, it was dark. I couldn't see the stars, so it had to have been solid." I struggled to form the memory of what I had seen. "I'm not certain, but I'm pretty sure it was one big object."

"And it was flying in what direction?"

"Northeast."

"Towards Mount Rainier, right? Not the only sighting over there."

"What do you mean?" I said.

He smiled. "That's near where Kenneth Arnold had his sighting back in 1947. Those were flying disks, according to Arnold, not a triangle UFO. Anyway, what did you think the object was when you first noticed it?"

"A helicopter, I guess." I felt less certain now. "It happened so fast."

"Can you describe your feelings during and after sighting the object?"

"I was freaked out, half paralyzed. Who wouldn't be?"

"That's common," he said. "Anything happening to your vehicle at this point?"

"Yeah, it shut off. Everything went dead. Kind of like in the movie Close Encounters."

"Any magnetism effects? Hair standing on end, that kind of thing?"

"Yes, definitely. And there was this buzzing sound that got louder. Then I must have blacked out. When I woke up, I was strapped down on a table. I couldn't feel my arms or legs, then I noticed I was being watched by two figures."

He kept reading off of the checklist on his screen. "Tell

me more about these figures. Were they human-like? Ape-like? Reptile-like? Insect-like? Robotic? See-through apparition?"

"Definitely greys, but with smaller eyes and a ridge going from the forehead down to their nose. They were the ones that the Proxima Foundation people say they've been in contact with, but the ridge made them look meaner."

Anxiety and fear began to creep over me. Jack must have noticed.

"You doing okay, Ben?"

"Yeah, I'm okay."

"Other than the two beings you mentioned, were there any others? Anything or anyone else there with you?"

"No, I don't think so."

"Okay, I need to ask you a few difficult questions. It's routine."

"Yeah, sure," I said, ready for anything.

Jack looked at his screen again. "Did you experience any penetration during the experience. By penetration, I mean by a needle or other instrument, into the skin, mouth, nose, or any other orifice."

A middle-aged woman at the table behind us overheard and looked at me. I glared back, and she returned to her café-mocha-slurping husband.

I spoke more softly. "I think something was inserted into my man part. What do you think they did that for?"

"That's not uncommon," Jack said. "Experimentation with human genetics and reproductive processes. What about marks on your body?"

I pulled up my shirt and let him inspect the six dots on my chest. "Have you seen this before?"

He leaned, squinting at it. "Well, what do we have here? It's not uncommon to have some kind of mark after an abduction. Do you mind if I take a photo?"

"I guess," I said, "just don't get my face in it."

"No problem." He took a photo on his smartphone, then I put my shirt down. Jack made a few more entries on his laptop, then returned his attention to me.

"Just a couple more questions, Ben, and then we'll be done. Are you on any antipsychotic medications?"

"No, not yet, anyway."

"Has anyone ever told you that they thought that you were fantasy-prone?"

"Fantasy-prone? No."

"Ben, I'd say that you have a very credible story here, at least as far as self-reported alien abductions go. I've been monitoring the national database. We've had a lot of similar cases over the past two years. We've also had more than 300 reported sightings in Washington this year alone, more than in any previous year. Once it was cigar-shaped and classic disc shapes, but now we are seeing more triangular ones like you described. Of course, I still think 90% of all the reports we get are either natural phenomena or bogus, but this increase in sightings is the highest we've ever seen in any one year. Something seems to be going on."

"Can I see this data?"

"Well, anyone can look up the MUFON national data base. You can access it on our website."

"What about radar? Do you have any way to tell if any tracked objects are a spaceship or helicopter?"

"Yes, I have a friend with the FAA. They've tightened up quite a bit, but I can probably still get it. I'll look into it and let you know what I find out. It could take a couple weeks."

I exhaled out of frustration. I was hoping for immediate answers. "Do you think I was abducted by aliens or could it have been faked?"

"I can't say for sure, Ben, just be patient. We'll look at the data objectively."

I nodded. "So what about Congressman Young? You seemed to suggest that my meeting with him was important."

"He serves on the House Strategic Forces Committee, and is one of the supporters for the new Space Force. It is kind of odd that you meet with him and then have an abduction experience."

"Do you think that the Congressman has something to do with it? Like a secret program or something?"

"If there are secret programs, I'd suspect he'd know. But then again, it's all so compartmentalized in government, who the hell knows? Best thing for you now is to document everything that's happened to you."

I still wasn't satisfied. "Who would know more about this?"

"Well, there's Daniel Byrne. I'd suggest him, but I'm sure you're one of the last people on Earth he wants to talk to."

"He probably wants to kill me."

"I could see why, but it may be worth a try. You never said who was your source for the tip on the Byrne hoax. Any idea?"

"I have no idea. I suspected it was someone who worked for him, maybe in the past."

"Drone with flares, yeah, I could see how that could be used to fake a sighting. But you yourself said that two flares is not what you saw on the sighting event you went on. Are you absolutely, one hundred percent sure that Byrne was behind the hoax?"

"What are you saying? Byrne's events aren't a hoax?"

"I don't know, Ben. I've seen just about every possible hoax there is in this job. I get crackheads calling me up all the time. People see airplanes with the navigation lights on, and it's an alien invasion. Drones are so common these days, and with people flying them at night, it's easy to fool people."

"What about you, Jack? Do you think we're being visited by aliens?"

"I've never even seen a UFO." He smiled. "Not even once. I hope to see one before I die."

"What should I do next?"

"Write it all down. Make a record of all of what you went through before you start forgetting things and people you talk to change how you remember it. You're a journalist; this will be easy for you. Then I'd talk to some experts. You know, there is a support group for alien abductees in the Seattle area. I know it sounds wonky, but a friend of mine runs the group. He's a psychologist named Jeff Swanson. The group meets once a week."

I was skeptical. "Are the people who go to it...normal?"

Jack smiled. "They have all had experiences similar to yours. You can always try it. If you don't like it, leave."

"Okay, maybe I will."

"It won't hurt." He wrote down the group's website information on one of his cards. "I'll be in touch soon, hopefully with some information from my FAA contact."

I thanked him, and we parted ways.

I felt better after talking with him. Jack seemed like someone I could trust with my personal information, and he was a skeptic but still knowledgeable and accepting of abductee experiences. That made me trust him even more.

On my way home, I picked up a carton of Jennifer's favorite gelato and scones from the bakery down the street. I found her sitting on the sofa. Her eyes were red from crying.

"How did it go?" she asked. I could tell by her tone that she was trying to hide her emotions.

"She gave me candy," I said.

Jennifer watched me as I set the drugs on the kitchen counter.

"Was it helpful?"

"All she did was give me drugs and a referral to a counselor, if you call that helpful."

"Did you tell her everything, I mean, about the UFO thing?"

"I told her about my symptoms. No, I didn't tell her the back story. But I did learn about a group, and I may go to it."

"A group? What kind of group?"

"A support group for people who have had experiences like mine."

She looked at me deadpan. "You mean for people who think they've been abducted by aliens? Sounds like a bunch of crazies," she mumbled.

"It's a therapy group led by a psychologist. He's supposed

to be pretty good. Why can't you support me on this?"

"I do support you, Ben. I just think…"

I was getting irritated. "What?"

"Nothing. Go to the group. I hope it works for you."

I finished setting up my laptop while she continued. "Don't forget, we've got the Fourth of July party this week. Let's not screw this up, okay?"

"Yeah, why would I screw it up?"

"Just take your medications," Tears were streaming down her face, "I want to get back to normal."

"Okay," I said, en route to the kitchen to get us spoons for the gelato. I knew she'd be calling her mother later that evening.

11

THE GROUP

The abductee group meeting was held in a corporate building in downtown Seattle. I sat in a circle of about a dozen people. Dr. Jeff Swanson, a thin, tall, middle-aged man in jeans and untucked button down introduced me.

"Everyone, this is Ben Davenport. Please welcome Ben."

"Hello," I muttered flatly, making eye contact with an overweight woman with oversized black-rimmed glasses and blood-red lipstick.

"Ben, what we do here," Swanson continued, "is share our experiences, talk about how they have affected us, how they have changed us. We explore them together in the safety of our group. We have just three rules: share what we believe is truthful, show respect for each other, and keep what we discuss in group private."

"What's said in group, stays in group," proclaimed the woman with the giant glasses.

"That's right," clamored several other members of the group.

I nodded. "Okay." I sat back to listen, thinking, *Jesus, what am I doing here? Am I like these people?* The entire set-up reminded me of the support group scene in the *Communion* movie where Christopher Walken, playing an apprehensive

Whitley Strieber, arouses paranoia in the group because he's a writer.

Swanson looked about the group. "Who wants to start?" His eyes came to rest on an overweight man in his thirties with a dark beard, polo-shirt and jeans. "Mark, why don't you lead us off?"

"Well, I have something new to report. I was in Belltown this last Tuesday at like two in the morning. I noticed a light in the sky, green, trailing behind me. I walked faster but the light kept up. When I got to my apartment building, I saw a grey in the alleyway just standing there, peering out from behind a dumpster, like it was waiting for me. I attempted to speak to it, it raised its three-fingered hand as if greeting me back, then was gone. I looked back up into the sky and saw the light again, darting off fast. That was it."

"They didn't speak to you telepathically?" asked a woman in the group.

"No. I think it was just saying hello. You know, like, I'm here, still keeping an eye on you."

I raised my hand and Swanson called on me. "What did it look like?"

"He was a grey, you know, the ones from Proxima Centauri b, just like the ones Daniel Byrne communicates with."

"Can we not use gendered language?" said the woman in glasses. "We don't know them to have a sex."

"The ones I've seen were definitely male. Definitely," said the man next to me.

"There are the male and female Nordic Whites too, let's not forget," said another group member.

Swanson reminded the group to keep gender pronouns neutral. To stay out of trouble, It was okay, but EBE or visitor were better. "Please continue," he said to Mark.

"So yeah, that was it. I don't know if I'll see them again tonight or not."

"Were there any witnesses?" I asked. "I mean, did anyone else see the light in the sky? Film it?"

"Maybe someone did. I don't know. But I can tell you that it was there."

"How can you be sure?" I asked.

Mark was irritated by my question. "I know what I saw was real because I experienced it."

"Me, too, I know what I saw," said the woman across from me.

"And me, too," another attendee insisted.

The woman in the lipstick took a turn. "I learned this at the Proxima Foundation ranch last year. Daniel Byrne says they are intra-dimensional and can slip in and out of this plane of existence. If you are tuned in, then you can see them."

I recalled hearing Daniel say that, but I wasn't satisfied. "So you are saying you see them in your mind? They're not here in the physical world?"

"No, that's not quite right," the lipstick woman said in irritated tone. "I don't know how else to explain it to you. Can someone else explain it to him?"

"Let's not rush things, we'll get to that," Swanson interrupted. "What about you, Ben? Do you want to share your experience?"

Reluctantly, I told my story, starting from the lights in the sky to waking up on the side of road naked.

"How are you coping?" said the older woman next to me.

"Fine. It's just the ringing in my ears and the sleep problems that are bothering me."

"Ringing in your ears? Tell us more," Swanson said.

"It's a buzzing sound, sounds like cicadas. I don't know what it is."

"Ever heard of The Worldwide Hum?" asked Mark.

"You mean the Schumann's resonance, the Earth's natural vibration?" I said.

"No, this is different. A small percentage of people from around the world hear a persistent oscillating low-frequency hum from an unknown source. It's louder at night and while indoors. Some think it's caused by vibration in the inner ear, others think the source is environmental, far-off radar or microwave stations, industrial equipment or something."

"What does the Worldwide Hum sound like?" I asked him.

"Low frequency rumbling sound, like a street sweeper or engine idling in the distance."

"I think the hum is caused by HAARP," added a middle-aged man sitting across from me, "you know, the High-frequency Active Auroral Research Program. It's an array of high frequency radio transmitters and antennas in Alaska. It's not to study the ionosphere—it's for mind control experiments. I saw it on an episode of Conspiracy Theory With Jesse Ventura."

"Here we go again with the mind control conspiracies," said the lipstick woman in glasses. "Can we stay on topic, please?"

Neither of these explanations made any sense to me, nor was it tinnitus from what I could tell. My sound increased in frequency and intensity with time and began after my abduction experience—it had to be related to whatever happened to me.

"You seeing things? Orbs?" asked the woman in glasses.

"Yes, I have. At night."

"That's common."

"What do you think causes them?"

The middle-aged man said, "I think they're intra-dimensional. Just like the EBEs."

Another man said, "I think they are projections, caused by signals from satellites, black satellites."

"Black satellites?" I asked.

"Secret government program," he replied.

Swanson turned to me. "It's a good idea to rule out natural causes. Physiological explanations."

"You might want to see a neurologist and an audiologist, just as a rule out," said another one of the attendees."

It seemed like a good idea. My insurance would cover it. I had an annual physical coming up and could see about getting a referral.

Swanson smiled. "We can all agree that we've experienced something not ordinary."

Everyone nodded.

More group members provided their updates in turn, but my mind wandered to my own experience. I wanted answers, but found myself more disillusioned than ever. Then, Swanson made an assertion that grabbed my attention.

"Last time, we talked about the link between experiences in adulthood and during childhood. It's helpful to trace back your experiences into your childhood, isn't it?"

"Yes," more than half the attendees murmured.

I hadn't thought of that. Perhaps the Phoenix Lights, but hundreds of people saw them, and the experience was far from the horrors of abduction.

"What about Ben? Any abduction experiences as a child?" asked the lipstick woman.

"I don't see what my childhood has to do with what I experienced. It wasn't like anything I've ever been through."

"Are you so sure?" she asked.

"I'm not even sure now if what I experienced was real. All I know is what happened to me was physical, but now it all feels like a dream."

"It wasn't a dream," one of the men said quietly, looking at me.

"Anyone can say they saw anything, can't they? Who knows what is true?" I said, crossing my arms.

Swanson, sensing the tension in the group, attempted to calm everyone as the meeting time was winding down. "There are levels of truth, Ben." Sometimes truth has to be viewed from a cultural perspective—through the eyes of our ancestors if you will, not just how we think it to be now in front of us. Does that make sense?"

"You mean truth is relative?"

"In a way. It depends on one's perspective and on one's experiences."

I scoffed. "So, what if someone is crazy or high on LSD?

Their perception of reality isn't the truth, regardless of what their culture is."

"What we are saying, Ben, is that you can't view reality without the lens of your experiences."

I sat back, my arms still crossed. What he was saying wasn't making a whole lot of sense to me, but I kept on listening until the group's time was up. Swanson approached at the door. We shook hands as others were leaving in pairs and alone.

"Ben, thanks for coming. Did you find this helpful?"

"I don't know. I'm just looking for some answers about what's happened to me."

"I know you are, just like the rest of us. You might want to take the advice of some of our members and consider reaching out to the Proxima Foundation. They have some good workshops."

"I'll consider it," I said, thinking how ridiculous it would be for me to contact the Byrnes.

"I hope you can work this through. Come back when you are ready."

"Thanks," I said and turned toward the door.

12

JONATHAN MAHUE

I kept thinking about my experience and its possible relationship with my childhood. Jonathan Mahue—what was he doing now? Maybe he'd had weird things happen to him, too, since we were ten. It was worth a try.

Several Jonathan Mahue's popped up in the online public records search websites. There was one with the right age, and to my surprise, he was in Portland, Oregon and married to Elizabeth Mahue. I found him on LinkedIn, too: a software engineer and developer with a Masters from Stanford in Computer Science. He still looked like the adolescent I remembered, shaggy blond hair and all.

I emailed him, saying nothing other than I was hoping to catch up with him. He replied the following day with his phone number. I called that evening.

"Jonathan, this is Ben Davenport, how are you?"

His voice was soft and distant. "I'm fine. Surprised to hear from you. It's been what, eighteen years?"

We spent a few minutes catching up. He'd seen my Proxima Foundation UFO hoax article and it had made him think about our time in the Cub Scouts and the Phoenix Lights. I suggested we should get together sometime that week, saying nothing about my abduction experience for fear that it might freak him out. I'd wait until we were in person.

"We're going out of town to visit Elizabeth's parents this weekend."

"I could come down before then." Could he hear how desperate I felt?

There was a long pause. I could hear the baby crying in the background. Jonathan said something to his wife, his voice muffled by his hand over the phone, then was back.

"Want to come down tomorrow? We can go out for dinner or something."

"Yes, I can be there tomorrow. That would be great."

I took the Amtrak down to Portland in the morning. Jonathan picked me up outside the station. We bro-hugged, then he introduced me to his wife, Elizabeth, and daughter. Elizabeth jumped in back and insisted I ride up front. We went to a restaurant called Theo's On the River, ordered dinner, and started to catch-up.

"So you're a big-time journalist," Jonathan said, teasing me.

"So you are a big-time software developer?" I countered.

"Software engineer. I've been in a couple start-ups, developing mobile apps, cloud-based applications and stuff. I lived in San Jose for a while after school." He smiled at his wife. "That's where Elizabeth and I met."

Elizabeth looked up from wiping the baby's face and smiled.

"You in a relationship?" said Jonathan.

"Yes. I'm recently engaged."

Elizabeth smiled "Congratulations."

"Yeah man, congratulations. So why did you decide to contact me now?" he asked.

"I thought I'd reach out to you because I had something happen recently and, well…I'd like you to tell me what you remember about when we saw the Phoenix Lights."

His wife looked up, then at Jonathan. The mood definitely shifted. *Something happened*, I thought.

Jonathan haltingly started. "Okay. Well, I remember we

were sent off to get some kindling for the campfire. I think…"

'Yes," I said, "that's my memory."

"…and we were looking around. It was getting dark, making it difficult to see. We didn't have flashlights with us, and we were worried about snakes and scorpions. Do you remember that?"

"Yes, I do, but we were determined to have a fire for s'mores."

"Exactly." He glanced at Elizabeth. "And the stars were out. We could see the Milky Way, I remember that. Then, I don't know, it must have been around 8pm or so, we saw lights in a V-shape formation. Seven lights, I think, flying from north to south. Silent. When it flew overhead, I remember ducking down, like I was afraid it might see us or do something to us."

"Yes," I said, "I was freaked out, too. We dropped the wood we'd found and ran back to the camp site."

"We were both freaked out," Jonathan repeated slowly.

"Did the others see it, too?" asked Elizabeth, now lightly rocking the baby in her arms.

"No, it was just us. For some reason, it was just us," Jonathan said equally slowly.

I looked at Elizabeth. "Others saw the lights, too, just not in the group we were with. They must not have been looking up or something. A lot of people saw the lights. Thousands, that night…"

Jonathan took a deep breath. "It's still a mystery. We'll likely never know what it was. Why are you bringing all of this up now? Are you doing another story or something?"

"I saw something like them again, Jonathan. And I had something else happen to me that I'm trying to understand." My heart was beginning to race.

They both had their eyes on me, waiting on what I had to say next.

"I was abducted. I think I was abducted by aliens."

I watched for their reaction. Both stared at me in silence.

"You're messing with us, right?" Jonathan said.

"No, I'm dead serious. I wouldn't make this up. I mean, you read my article; I'm a skeptic. I was driving home from an interview I had with Congressman Young. I was coming over the pass, south of Mt. Rainier on Route 12, and I saw these lights behind me. Next thing I know, I'm in a vortex and strapped to a table somewhere, I guess on a ship."

"And you saw aliens?" Elizabeth asked.

"Yes, two of them, and they...well, they did stuff to me."

"You're shitting us, right?" Jonathan was smiling, more out of uncomfortable shock than anything else.

"No, Scout's honor. I wanted to catch up with you to see if you've had anything strange happen. I know this all sounds crazy. I'm just trying to get to the bottom of it."

Just then, the waiter brought us our food.

"Have you told anyone else about this?" Jonathan asked.

"Yes, a few people. My fiancée knows. I'm not crazy. I've been evaluated by a psychiatrist."

They both poked at their food, not saying a word.

"You think I'm crazy, don't you?"

"No, not at all," said Elizabeth. "Are you going to write a story on your experiences, or something?"

"I don't know yet. I'm not sure what I'm going to do. I'm just trying to talk to people who I trust. Like I said before, I want to figure this out."

We dug into our meals, discussing alien abductions for a bit. I eventually brought up the iM4ET mobile app.

"I'd like to see that," said Jonathan.

"It's no longer on my phone, I had to get a new phone."

Then I glanced at my phone screen and saw that the app's icon was there.

"That's strange. The app is on this phone."

"You must have had it on automatic backup and it reloaded," said Jonathan. "Can I see it?"

"Sure."

I handed him my phone. He opened the iM4ET app and went through its features.

"This is an interesting design. Looks like its mostly cloud-based, and it has access to lots of your phone's features, like Bluetooth and GPS."

"Does it? That's probably for the geolocator functions. It can tell you where other people are meditating and when ETs are in the area."

He handed the phone back to me. Just then, my ears began to ring with great intensity, and I felt a migraine coming on. Both Jonathan and Elizabeth noticed something was wrong.

"Are you okay?" Jonathan asked.

"I keep getting these headaches, and I hear this ringing in my head. It started after I had my experience."

"Did you see someone for that?"

"Yeah, the psychiatrist. She just gave me some medication, but nothing helps."

Elizabeth looked up again. "Maybe you need to see a neurologist."

"Yeah, maybe," I said.

The baby began to cry. Elizabeth slid out of the booth. "We'd better get going," she said to Jonathan.

Outside the restaurant, Jonathan pulled me aside. "Elizabeth hates the UFO stuff. I usually keep it to myself, but I'm actually into this. Ever since we saw those lights, I've been fascinated with it. There just so much stigma associated with it. People think you are nuts when you talk about it."

"I know how that goes," I said.

He gave me another bro-hug. "Hey man, let's stay in touch, okay?"

"Sure," I said.

On the way back on the train I got a call from Jack Clark. "I've got some news for you, Ben," he said excitedly. "I talked to my friend over at FAA. He sent me the logs and some screen shots from the radar data from the day and night of your abduction in June. There were definitely some anomalies that evening, in and around where you said the abduction experience took place. This is very interesting."

"Really? What exactly?"

"Well, there was an interesting hit of a large object that flew in from the northeast. It was big, maybe the size of a 747, only it was moving too slow to be fixed wing. I asked my contact for the data before and after the event. This is where it gets strange. He said the data leading up to and after the date you had your experience was missing."

"Missing? Like someone deleted it?" My mind went straight to a cover-up.

"I've seen patterns like this before, where FAA radar data gets censored. Usually, it's because of military exercises in the area. That could explain some of this."

"Well, what do you think? Was it an alien craft or the military?"

"I think this data is inconclusive. I'll see what else I can find out. I'll call you when I learn something."

Inconclusive. *Interesting*, I thought.

I got home late. Jennifer has just started her bath when I told her about what I had learned from Jack Clark.

"So what?" she said, as she headed into the bathroom and turned on the water. "I don't know why this is important."

I stood in the doorway, annoyed by her lack of understanding about the importance to me. "It's hard evidence that there was something big in the sky that night. It proves it wasn't in my head."

"It doesn't prove anything, Ben." She threw off her robe and got into the tub. "You said there was missing radar data or whatever."

"Yeah, but not the night it happened. Whatever was in the sky wasn't normal."

"Could have been a blimp or a flock of geese, couldn't it?"

"It wasn't a blimp or geese. Jesus, Jennifer."

She turned the water off. "Don't forget we are going to my parents for the 4th. I'm expecting you to be normal. Will you be normal?"

"Yeah, I'll be normal." I said. I knew the engagement party get together was important for her and us. Our parents had met the previous summer when mine came out to visit on their summer vacation. We'd gone out to eat at a restaurant on the waterfront. The entire day was an embarrassing and nerve-racking experience for me.

"I picked out some dishes. Let's finish up the registry tomorrow, okay?" she said from behind her *Vanity Fair* magazine. "And close the door, will you? There's a draft."

"Sure," I said, leaving her alone. The wedding planning pressure was driving me almost as insane as the ringing in my ears and the phantom orbs at night. I just wanted it all to be over.

13

BREAKDOWN

My mom and stepdad flew in from Spokane for the Fourth of July weekend. Jennifer and I picked them up at the airport and took them to a hotel in downtown Seattle. My mother was concerned about the dark bags under my eyes and asked me about my sleep. I reassured her that I was okay, just overworked. I still hadn't told my parents about my abduction experience, and I wasn't planning to.

In the morning, Jennifer drove the four of us to her parents' place in Bellevue, whispering to me before we got out of the car, "You look like shit. And why didn't you shave today?"

"Don't worry about it," I said. The truth was the ringing in my ears had increased in pitch and amplitude that morning, and I was hearing it now over ambient sound.

"Let's be normal, okay?" she said.

"Whatever," I said. Was she worried I was going to play with my potato salad like in the scene in *Close Encounters of the Third Kind* when Richard Dreyfuss's character was playing with his mashed potatoes? Was she afraid that I was going to embarrass her in front of her family? Probably.

Jennifer's mom met us at the door, and after hellos and hugs, we headed to the backyard where everyone gathered by the pool. A large tent was set up over a couple tables. A Mariners and Padres baseball game was on a large TV screen set into an outside gas fireplace. My step-dad and I made drinks and we sat to watch the game while Jennifer's dad tended the grill. Jennifer's brother Bradley was there too. He was into finance, a jock type. I didn't like him that much and got the sense that he didn't like me either. When we shook hands, he squeezed mine tightly so I wouldn't forget who the alpha was.

I sat in one of the lawn chairs and had half the whiskey and Coke gone before the end of the first commercial break. The game was in San Diego, and the announcers went on and on about the lineup. The camera went to a shot from high above the stadium.

"We've got the blimp flying overhead, Jim," said one of the announcers. "Some people out there might think we've got a UFO over San Diego." The announcers chuckled. "Hopefully our little green friends won't abduct the pitcher."

The other announcer chuckled back. "Maybe they're coming for the Gatorade, Jim."

Bradley laughed and looked over at me. "Maybe they're coming to get you," he said, smirking.

I looked away. Apparently, word had gotten to Jennifer's entire family about my abduction experience.

I got myself another drink and after a few minutes my mother came over to check on me.

"Are you okay, Ben?"

"I'm just fine," I said.

"Leave him alone," my step-dad said, "let the man relax."

I could hear my mom and my future mother in-law talking about me from across the lawn. Jennifer came over a minute later and saw that I had a fresh drink in my hand.

"Can I talk with you for a minute?" she said softly.

I knew what was coming. I got up without saying a word, and she led me behind the cabana where we were out of sight.

She whispered loudly, gritting her teeth. "What are you

doing? Are you getting drunk? We're supposed to be celebrating our engagement and enjoying being with our families. Get yourself together!"

She reached for my glass, and I pulled it away from her. "Chill, Jennifer. What's the big deal? I'm just having a drink with family."

"You're not supposed to be drinking with your medication. Did you take your medication today?"

"Yeah, I took it."

"Jesus, Ben, just try to be normal, okay?"

"Everything is fine." I said, wanting her to leave me alone.

Ten minutes later, Jennifer's dad served up the burgers and hotdogs. Everyone took their seat at the tables set up by poolside. I sat next to Jennifer. Bowls of salad and sides arrived from the kitchen, and we began to spread the plates around, talking as we ate. When the main course was finished, it was champaign and desert time. In front of me was an apple cobbler, the scent of cinnamon wafting up from it. Anxiety rushed through me. I felt like I wanted to crawl out of my skin. I kept staring at the plate while Jennifer's father gave a toast.

"To our future family," he said.

Jennifer had a huge smile across her face. She glanced at me, and kicked my shin under the table to get my attention. Everyone raised Jennifer's mom's fine crystal and drank, but I couldn't stop staring at the cobbler. The ringing in my ears had increased in frequency and with more intensity. I could feel the eyes of everyone on me. My mother's voice kept saying, "Ben? Ben? What's wrong? Ben?"

I had my elbows up on the table now, my hands over my ears.

Then I heard another voice: *We will be back for you.*—the same metallic voice I'd heard during the abduction coming from inside my skull. My heart began raced and panic swept over me. Was it the greys? Were they about to take me again? I just wanted to get out of there. I should hide somewhere they wouldn't find me, but where?

I heard my mother's voice again. "Who, Ben? Who will be back?"

"The greys! They are fucking coming to get me! I've got to get out of here!" I was speaking aloud, but I could not control my speech, nor could I control my bodily functions all that well, either. I vomited over my plate of food and onto Jennifer's thigh. I could feel my bowels suddenly give out, causing me to shit myself. I could hear Jennifer's mother scream.

I stood up, knowing that I needed to get out of there.

Jennifer stood up, too. She had the look of terror in her face. I pushed her out of my way, causing her to fall backwards onto the floor.

"Hey!" yelled Bradley, as he got up from his seat. "Don't touch my sister!"

I ran through the house to the front door, struggled to get it open, ran out into the yard, and ran to Jennifer's car. It was locked. Bradley caught up and shoved me from behind, nearly causing me to fall face forward onto the driveway.

"Hey asshole! What do you think you are doing?"

I turned and faced him. "Fuck off!" I said.

He shoved me again, the palms of his hands landing on my chest and throwing me backwards onto the grass. I could hear the others screaming and yelling. I curled up on the ground in the fetal position. Bradley stood over me.

Jennifer's mother was yelling. "Bradley, no!"

"Fucking UFO freak!"

I must have blacked out because I don't remember anything until two Bellevue police officers were standing over me. An ambulance showed up a few minutes later. My mother's voice was trying to calm me down. I cried, lying on my fiancée's parents' front lawn, on the Fourth of July, my pants soiled from my own shit.

14

NERVOUS BREAKTHROUGH

Jennifer didn't want to press charges, but the State of Washington has mandatory arrest laws for domestic violence. My mother had pleaded with the police to let me go to the hospital instead. The police did take me to ER, in handcuffs. Jennifer had to go to another ER for a broken wrist. I was then checked out of the hospital and taken to jail, where I had to sit in a cell for three days. My parents stayed in town through the holiday weekend, but had to return home on account of their jobs. My mother told me that I just needed a break, it was just a hiccup, she said, I'd be okay. I wasn't so sure.

I was given the option to either stay and face the charges or seek voluntary inpatient psychiatric treatment at Harbor View Medical Center in Seattle. I chose the latter. My first day, I went to a compulsory group therapy session where I was forced to listen to people talk about their coping skills. Otherwise, I slept. They gave me a neurological work-up and told me that it checked out normal. I was diagnosed with psychotic episode, unspecified, likely triggered by stress. A nervous breakdown. I was discharged from the hospital three days later with another prescription for psychiatric meds.

I called Jennifer and told her that I was coming home. She

told me that she would be there. When I got back to the apartment, my belongings were out of my dresser and closet and stuffed in several black garbage bags and my suitcase, my books in three cardboard boxes, along with my laptop. Jennifer was sitting on the couch, her wrist wrapped.

I stared at my stuff, then looked at her. "What's going on, Jennifer?"

"It's over, Ben, I can't do this anymore."

I sat down on one end of the sofa and faced her. "Do what?"

"Jesus, Ben, you broke my wrist. I don't want to get married."

I noticed then that she wasn't wearing the engagement ring. She pulled it from a drawer and set it on the coffee table.

She started to cry. "I can't do this…crazy stuff…this alien stuff."

She had never understood. "God damn it, I can't control what's happened to me. They did this to me!"

She continued crying.

I grabbed the ring, thinking that I'd end up hawking it somewhere for cash. "Fuck you, Jennifer."

"Just go, okay?"

"Fine. I'll go!"

I then threw my stuff out into the hallway outside the apartment, then loaded up my Jetta and called Brett to ask him if I could crash at his place for a couple of days until I figured out what to do next. He agreed.

Brett and I talked that night.

"She wasn't the one for you, man. Have a drink, it'll make you feel better."

We finished off a bottle of whiskey.

I pulled myself together and went into the *Hot Reports* offices in the morning. Marcus called me into his office first thing and had me sit down.

"Ben, this is one of the worst things that I have to so as an editor in chief. I've got to let you go."

"What? Why?"

He slid a printed page across his desk. It was an article from Channel 5 News Missoula website that read: "Local Teenagers Admit to UFO Hoax." I read it quickly. Apparently, two 16-year-old boys had come forward to claim responsibility for several UFO sightings in the Missoula area, including the one I wrote about in my article.

"Looks like you missed something important," Marcus said. "Not what we want to happen."

As I processed the new information, I knew I was in journalistic trouble. "This is bullshit. I saw two men in an Explorer. We've got video. You saw the video!"

"I've looked at the video several times. Could be anyone. Could be those boys, they are old enough to drive."

"I know what I saw."

He exhaled. "Do you know how this makes our magazine look? We could be sued for journalistic malpractice and defamation. Jesus, Ben, we can't afford this. *Hot Reports* is hanging by a thread. This could ruin us."

I was speechless.

"Regardless," Marcus said, "you've left me with no choice but to give the cell phone tower story to someone else."

"Why? It's my story? I'm still working on it. I'll do a retraction story on the Proxima Foundation, but please don't take this story from me," I pleaded.

"A retraction is out of the question. I gave you three weeks on the cell tower story and it's been six. I've got to let you go. I need you out of here today."

I stood up. "Whatever." I exited his office, humiliated and furious. I went over to my desk to pack my things and found a box on the floor with my name on it: Marcus already had someone clean out my desk. I grabbed it and went out to my car, set the box on the trunk while I fumbled for my keys. The box slid off the trunk, all my belongings scattered with the note from Nadine Byrne on the very top. I picked everything up and threw it all into the backseat, then I went to Jonesy's and threw back three or four drinks. My life was over.

Brett showed up a few minutes after five. "Another day, another dollar," he said eagerly as he sat on the bar stool next to me.

"Not for me. Marcus fired me today." I told him about the article.

"Marcus sounds like a real cunt. First round is on me," Brett said.

We did a round of tequila shots.

I told him about my conversations with Jack Clark.

Brett set his glass down. "Maybe there's a link between what happened to you and the aunt of that hottie waitress. What's her name?"

"Brenda. Why do you say that?"

"Seems like too much to be all coincidences, don't you think? You should call her. You're single now, anyway." He reached for my cell phone. "Here, give me the phone, I'll call her."

I moved it away from him. "No way. I'll call her later."

He leaned closer to me. "Just be careful. The government's not going to like it if you know too much. Bad shit happens to people."

"Like the bad shit that's happening to me lately?" I said it flippantly, but began to wonder. Ever since I'd written the UFO hoax story…

He took another slug of his beer. "So what are you going to do, man?"

"I need answers. I can't go on like this forever. Maybe I should go talk with Daniel Byrne. He might be able to help me. What do you think?"

"Maybe. Just be careful."

"Careful about what exactly?"

"Dude, did you hear about that guy in Texas who was kidnapping people, wearing an alien mask, and butt-raping them?"

"Yeah, so?"

"You better watch out, just saying. It could get worse."

I chuckled and we threw back one more round. Brett may have been joking around with me, but I knew he was serious about his concerns with the government. Considering Jack's strange FAA data, someone in the government, the military or NASA most likely, had to know something about what happened on the ridge in Yakima. Who knows? Maybe Daniel would have some answers or at least know how I could get them.

Later that evening at Brett's, I sent an email to Daniel apologizing for the article and that I was hoping he'd be willing to talk to me about some events I'd been experiencing.

Right on cue, my headache returned. I took some pills and finally managed to doze off.

In the morning, Nadine Byrne called. Her voice was warm and calm.

"We received your message, Ben. Why don't you come out to the ranch and visit us?"

"I could be out there on Saturday. Are you sure that it's all right? Is Daniel okay with it?"

"Yes, he's looking forward to talking with you. We'll see you on Saturday."

Late the next morning, I loaded all of my worldly possessions into the back of my Jetta, and headed east on 90.

15

NONDISCLOSURE

Nadine opened the door. "Hello Ben. It's nice to see you again. Please come in." She was wearing a flannel shirt and jeans, and her long, cornsilk hair was tied back in a ponytail. "Daniel's out back working on his new book. He's waiting for you."

"Thank you, Nadine" I said, stepping through the doorway and walking through the house to the back porch. Daniel was in a wooden Adirondack chair, reading Dolan and Zabel's *A.D. After Disclosure: The People's Guide to Life After Contact.* A notebook and a mug of hot tea were on the table next to him.

He tilted his reading glasses to look at me and in a tranquil voice said, "Hello again, have a seat. Join me."

I sat in the chair next to him, not sure what to expect.

"Nadine mentioned that you think that you may have been abducted. I'm glad that you contacted me, Ben. If you were abducted, it would be good for us to talk."

"I didn't know where else to turn. No one can give me any answers."

He put his reading glasses on the table and looked at me. "Who else have you told about this?"

"Just my fiancée—ex fiancée. Her family knows about it

too. My parents know about it. My friend Brett knows. I also told Jack Clark from MUFON. I went to him after I told Jennifer."

"I know about Jack. I get reports from the National UFO Reporting Database. Why don't you tell me about everything? I'm all ears."

I told him about my interview with Congressman Young and up to the point of when I saw the greys.

"Hold on, Ben. You said that they were greys with small eyes, and a ridge down to the nose. Are you sure?"

"Yes. I can't get the image of their faces out of my mind. They had small, dark eyes. No whites. They were like the typical greys."

"Can you draw what they looked like for me?"

"I guess so," I said, assuming that he wanted to be sure of the species that had abducted me. Byrne handed me his notebook and a pen and I took a minute to draw what I could remember. I handed the notebook back to him.

He held it in his lap to look at it for a moment. "Yep, that looks like one of the government fakes all right. See here?" He pointed to the nose ridgeline. "This is characteristic of government imposter EBEs. They have a distinctive raised arch above the eyes."

I looked up from the drawing. "So you think this was a fake abduction? How can you be sure?"

"I'm certain of it. But why don't you tell me what happened next? Tell me everything."

I told him about being strapped to a table and seeing the star map.

"Keep going," he said, looking at me attentively. "Did they probe you?"

"Yes. I think so. I remember feeling a pain in my man part. It hurt like hell."

"A urethra probe. I bet it did. Tell me more."

"Then I heard a voice."

"A voice? What did it say?"

"It said that I was of use to them and that they would be

back for me."

"They want to scare you, the government. Tell me what happened next."

I told him about how I had ended up naked on the side of the road, three days later.

"Your experience is a lot like Travis Walton's. I'm sure you've seen the movie *Fire in the Sky*, although what was depicted in the movie is very different from what Travis says actually happened. His experience wasn't as sinister as what they showed in the film. You could say artistic license, but really it was government license. They wanted to scare the shit out of people, and that they did."

"How did they do it? Were the lights that I saw helicopters, then? The black helicopters? Where did they take me?"

"You are going to want to read my book. I cover all of this. They likely picked you up in a TR-3B, took you on board, did their thing, and then dumped you out two days later. Sometimes, they use short people dressed in body suits to look like EBEs, no different than Hollywood costumes, or it could also have been robotic simulations. They spray a psychoactive agent and memory-wiper chemical to confuse the victim and create amnesia. What about high strangeness? Experiencing anything weird?"

I told him about the orbs floating around in my room, the strange humming in my ears. I also told him about my bowel blowout on the Fourth of July. "If it was a fake abduction, then why would I have these hallucinations? It just doesn't make sense."

"Actually, it does make sense, Ben. It sounds like you are experiencing psychotic symptoms induced by specialized chemical agents. You most definitely received an implant that controls release of the agent. This approach has been used by the CIA since the 1960s. Ever heard of MKUltra?"

"Yes, a top-secret program, conducted by the CIA to test the effects of LSD and other mind control agents while programming spies who wouldn't remember anything. But how did they implant me?"

"Injected through the skin or swallowed."

I was staring off, thinking about what Daniel was saying. It made sense. "You think I may still have something implanted in me?"

"Have you been experiencing any of the high strangeness since the Fourth of July?"

I thought about it. "No, not at all. I assumed it was the drugs they were giving me at the hospital."

"I think you either threw up the implants or crapped them out. They can also control when they are to leave your body too. It's impossible to trace the implant once that happens."

"So what about that guy at the conference in McMinnville, the abductee? You still think that his abduction was real and not a government fake like mine?"

"You mean Trevor? Yeah, his was real. His experience was nothing like yours."

"How can you be so sure?"

"Do you have a mark on your chest, Ben?"

"Yes, a hexagon, just like Trevor's."

"Let's have a look," Byrne said, scooting himself forward in his chair and turning towards me.

I pulled up my shirt. The hexagon had almost completely disappeared.

Byrne looked at my bare skin. "Do you mind if I touch it?" he asked.

"Why?"

"I want to see if it's raised."

The request sounded a little off to me, but I wanted an answer. "Go ahead."

He put the tips of the fingers of his right hand onto my sternum and rubbed lightly over the area where the hexagon was. He pulled his hand back and I put my shirt down.

"Yep, it was a fake. The government just can't seem to recreate the real thing. If you stick around, you'll have a chance to ask Trevor about his mark. You'll see what I mean."

I reflected on why the military or CIA would want to abduct me. "Do you think I was abducted because I did the article on you?"

Daniel put his fingers up to his lips and thought for a moment. "I suspect there is another reason connected to your experience with the Phoenix Lights. Your father Michael Davenport was there with you, wasn't he?"

"Yes. He was our Cub Scout Master. How do you know about him?"

"It's in our archives. Now tell me, did he witness the lights with you?"

"I'm not sure if he saw the lights, but I presume so. After Jonathan and I saw them fly over, we ran back to the campsite to tell him. He listened to us and then told us to keep quiet about it. He said people would think we were nuts. We never talked about it after that, at least from what I recall."

Daniel nodded. "Your father was a Navy 0-6 Captain and physiologist. He died by suicide. That wasn't a coincidence."

His reference to my father's suicide shook me to the core. "What do you mean, it wasn't a coincidence?"

"What I'm about to say may be difficult for you: Your father was assigned to work with Northrop, one of the contractors for the Aurora Project. He was the lead on a secret synthetic biology program, a compartmentalized sub-program under the Aurora Project. They were engineering EBEs out of a facility in northern Arizona, they were testing the synthetic aliens during the late 1990s by running abduction experiments with TR-3Bs." He sighed. "Your father could have protected you, but instead you were used in their experiments. He gave you up, Ben. He allowed you to be abducted and molested by this secret government program. There's no doubt about it."

Fury erupted in me.

"That's crazy! Just because my father worked with Northrop doesn't mean there's any connection to what happened to me. I can't believe that what you are saying is true."

"I'm sorry, Ben, it's true. Here, let me show you something from our archives." He pulled up some files and handed the laptop to me. One file was a scan of a phone directory showing my father's assignment at the facility. Another was a patent for synthetic exo-tissue; my father was listed on it. A third file was a heavily redacted document showing that my father was one of several project managers in a program code-named *Operation Green Snatch*. All of the documents appeared to be legit.

"I had been tracking his work for years. I even confronted him and other officers at various events in the late 1990s through the early 2000s." Daniel pulled up a photo of my father on stage and Daniel yelling into a microphone. "This was taken at a conference in Nevada in 1996. They weren't expecting me to be in the audience, but I let them have it. They denied everything, of course."

I couldn't believe it. Daniel had an encounter with my father! I was sick to my stomach. I didn't even want to think about what my father "giving me up" meant. "So you think he killed himself because he felt guilty about these experiments?"

Daniel closed his laptop. "He may have had second thoughts, sure, or the government forced him to kill himself. Either way, we'll never fully know the story, I'm sorry to say."

"Why didn't you mention this to me before I wrote my story on you? When did you discover this?"

"Nadine and I dug into your background *after* you wrote the story. We are, after all, lawyers, Ben. Nadine and I had seriously considered suing you for defamation, but once we discovered that you were a victim like so many others, we decided to just let it go. This is the truth, and now you know."

I sat back to take it all in. Was my deceased father responsible for my abduction experience? Did my mother know about this, and if she did, what did that mean? My entire worldview was, once again, turning upside down.

"But why abduct me now?"

"Think about it, Ben. Not only are you being tracked by
the government because of whatever was done to you in the
past, but you are a journalist possibly programmed to make it
public that aliens aren't real. Your interest in me was part of
it, with even a little bit of good old-fashioned revenge for
tangling with Congressman Young thrown in for good
measure."

My hands were trembling. "What are the odds that they'll
come back and abduct me again?"

"There's always the risk that once you are targeted, you'll
continue to be used in some way. But would they be so
brazen now? It's a good thing that you came to me."

"Why not expose all of this now and put an end to it?"

"They would deny it like they always do and we would be
the 'nuts'."

"But wouldn't they think I'd figure all this out? I'm here
with you talking about it, aren't I? Wouldn't they think that
I'd write about it? I could blow the whistle on the whole
thing as my father's son. Could I see more of the files in your
archives, especially the ones about my father?"

Byrne smiled. "Slow down a bit, Ben, there's a lot of
information to digest and you need to pace yourself. First, we
should make sure we have a detailed account of what you
experienced. As far as writing a story about this government
scam, I'm almost done with my book. Maybe I could add a
description of your experience, or maybe you could copy edit
my draft for me? How would you like to be my assistant on
this?"

I wasn't really interested in being his copy editor. If I was
going to do anything with this, I would write it.

"Let me think about it," I said, wondering what else
Daniel had in his document vaults. "But what about the files?
I'd really like to learn more about what you have, especially
about my father."

"In due time. You're still in trauma. It's best that we focus
on your recovery for now." He sat back in his chair. "You've

entered a whole new world of both lies and truths. Unfortunately, so much of this whole UFO thing is cloaked in disinformation. Most stories about UFOs and EBEs are fake and strategically designed to discredit the real experiencers and witnesses and scare people at a deep psychological level—like Hollywood, with a few exceptions. The mainstream press is just another wing of the shadow government, and they know what they are doing. If you tell a lie big enough and keep repeating it, people will eventually come to believe it. You know who said that?"

"Goebbels, wasn't it?"

"Correct. These techniques are long-standing and designed to control the minds of the masses. This is why we put so much emphasis on writing all of our own press releases. We want to put out the truth."

I exhaled. I wanted to know everything about my father's involvement with my abduction and *Operation Green Snatch.*

Daniel, seeing my frustration, opened his laptop again to the photo of my father. "Take a photo of this with your phone. I'd email it to you, but it would be tracked by the government. Let them speculate about how much you know—no need to make it obvious."

I took the photo as Nadine came to the door of the porch. "Why don't you two take a break and come join me for dinner?"

"We would be delighted," said Daniel.

I had so many more questions, but my stomach was growling.

Green curry tofu and a bottle of Riesling, again. Daniel poured.

"A toast?" Nadine said, holding up her glass.

"Before we toast, I just have to say I'm sorry about the article," I said. "I didn't believe that the government was behind this."

Daniel smiled. "We've had people attacking us for years and have thick skin."

Nadine smiled, too. "We forgive you, Ben. You are young

and need to slow down and listen to those who have life experience that can teach you."

We toasted and dug into Nadine's dinner. A feeling of resolve and comfort washed over me. She was right. I needed to slow down and assume less. I needed to listen more. Learn.

Nadine turned to me. "How are things at home, Ben? Your girlfriend?"

"Well, that's over. We broke up and she kicked me out. Just as well, really. She didn't want anything to do with the UFO stuff."

Byrne looked at Nadine and then back to me. "Well, we can understand that. It takes a special partner, someone on the same wavelength, to make things work."

Nadine looked at me. "We have an opening for a Social Media Manager at the Foundation. Maybe you'd be interested in helping us—writing some copy and assisting with marketing our work? We can't pay you much—we are a not-for-profit, after all."

"I'll need to think about it," I said. "Thanks for the offer."

Daniel smiled. "We've already been talking about Ben copy editing my book."

"Good idea," Nadine said. "So you said you were staying at the Motel 6. I can't imagine that you are enjoying it."

"It's the least expensive place near here, and temporary until I figure out what to do next."

"If you need a place to stay, we could offer you one. One of our minihouses on the property just opened up. You are welcome to stay there."

"Wow, thanks Nadine, let me think about it."

"Also, I was thinking, you might be interested in meeting Dr. Petulli. I could make that happen for you now."

"That would be great. When?"

"I'll give him a call this week. I'll let you know."

After dinner, Daniel suggested we return to the back porch and talk a while longer. We discussed methods of fake abductions. Nadine brought a tray of hot tea and a couple slices of apple pie. She handed a blue legal-sized folder to

Daniel.

Daniel smiled. "Thank you, my dear." He placed the folder on his lap.

We talked for a bit longer, finishing off our tea. The sun had already set, and I could feel the anxiety coming on. Daniel must have sensed it.

"Don't worry, Ben. Everything is going to be okay. Understandably, you have the symptoms of Post-Traumatic Stress Disorder. You are with good people here, and I assure you, at a cosmic level, that the only thing to be afraid of is the government." He grabbed the blue folder and opened it. "Before you leave us tonight, we've got an NDA for you to sign, Ben." He handed me the folder with several pages of small print documents and an arrow sticker that said "Sign Here."

I looked through the pages. "A non-disclosure agreement? For the documents?"

"It's routine. I've got to do this before we brief you in on more of what we are working on at the foundation, including the files about your father."

Eight pages of small print. I glanced over it, signed, and handed the folder back to him.

We walked through the house. Nadine was in the living room and called out, "Dr. Petulli said that he'd be delighted to meet you, Ben, when he gets back to town in a few weeks."

"Great. I look forward to it," I said, though I was unsure where I'd be then.

Daniel shook my hand. "I'm glad that came back to visit with us."

I looked him in the eyes. "Thank you, and again, I'm really sorry about the article."

He smiled. "Aristotle said the search for truth is in one way difficult and in another way easy, because no one can master it fully or miss it completely. But each adds a little to our knowledge of nature, and with all the facts put together there arises a certain grandeur. I look forward to more discussion with you, Ben."

"I'll walk Ben to his car," Nadine said, taking me by the arm.

We walked out to my Jetta. It was dark now, and the sky was filled with stars in radiant splendor.

She glanced up at them. "Will you look at that, Ben. It's so beautiful, isn't it? To know that we are not alone and a part of a much larger universe. Sometimes when I look up, tears come to my eyes and my knees shake."

I nervously looked up, scanning for anything flying.

She took my hand in hers. "I really hope you will consider coming to work with us. I think it would be good for you to be with us here. You'd be a part of something that will forever change the world."

"I need to think about it, Nadine. I'm planning to visit my mother in Spokane for a few days."

"Of course, Ben, you need to do what you need to do. Just know that you are welcome here if you choose to return."

We hugged, and I returned to the Motel 6. In the morning I'd head to Spokane. I had questions for my mother.

16

CONFRONTING MOM

I arrived at my mother's, mid-afternoon. Mom threw her arms around me, and Harry welcomed me with a handshake. I sensed their trepidation. Other than a few video calls, I hadn't seen them since the 4th of July incident. They didn't know about my post-abduction experiences or that I'd visited the Byrnes. What they did know was Jennifer and I were over, and I was unemployed and sleeping on my best friend's sofa.

Mom heated up a plate of leftover tuna casserole and sat with me in the dining room of her late Seventies remodeled ranch. Harry returned to the living room to watch a football game.

"What have you been up to?" my mother asked.

"I've been doing research," I said, shoveling a forkful of noodles into my mouth.

"Research? Are you writing again? Did you find a job?"

"No, but I've been researching a lot of things, and right now, I'm researching what happened in my childhood."

"Your childhood? What about your childhood?"

"I want to know more about my father and what he was doing for work before he died."

"You know that, honey: he was a doctor and worked for

the government."

"Doing what exactly?"

"Research. You know he couldn't tell us the details."

"He never told you anything?"

"He had a security clearance, remember? What's got you so interested in this now?"

"Do you know who he was working for before he died?"

"In the Navy, he ran a clinic and delivered babies. When he got out, he went to work for a contractor and was doing something with medicine for astronauts or something. You know that." She smiled awkwardly.

"Are you sure about that, Mom?"

Her voice rose. "Yes, of course I'm sure! Why are you asking me about this?"

"Game is coming on at seven. Going to be a good match-up between the Seahawks and the Rams," Harry announced from his recliner. He was obviously listening to our conversation and wanting to break the building tension, I paid no attention to him. Football was the last thing on my mind. I needed to know what my mother knew.

"He was working for Northrop Corporation, Mom. Do you know what he was working on?"

"No. He was a doctor. I'm sure it was a routine work; whatever it was he was doing."

"He was working on building human-like robots for a secret space program."

"Robots? Secret space program? What are you talking about? This isn't about the UFO thing again, is it, Ben?"

"Do you remember March 1997 when Dad took us on the camping trip near Prescott?"

"Yes. So?"

"The Phoenix Lights. You remember that, don't you, Mom?"

"I don't know." She looked at my plate. "Why don't you eat your dinner? Your food is getting cold."

"Don't tell me you don't remember the Phoenix Lights. It's the most famous mass sighting of alleged UFOs in modern history, Mom. It was on the news, remember?"

"Yes, the Phoenix Lights." She called out to Harry. "You said the game was on?"

"Why don't you come join me, Ben?" Harry said on cue.

Again, I ignored him. "Did Dad ever mention anything about the lights?"

Mom got up from the table abruptly and went to the kitchen. "No, I don't think so. I don't remember. Why are you asking me these questions?"

"Because I have seen evidence that he was involved in a secret project involving fake UFO abductions. I want to know what you know about it."

"Here we go again with the alien abductions. I don't think this is helping you any, Ben."

I could hear the clanking of dishes going into the dishwasher.

"Was anything different after we came back from the camping trip?" I asked, raising my voice so she could hear me.

My mother glared at me through the kitchen pass-through. "What do you mean, different?"

"Did I seem different to you?"

"I don't know, Ben, it was a long time ago."

"Mom, was I different after the camping trip?"

"It was a difficult time for you then. It was a difficult time for all of us. Let's change the subject, okay?"

She was covering up for my dad and I knew it.

"I've got something I need to show you. Come here." I took my phone out and showed her the photo of my father and Daniel Byrne. She studied it for a moment.

"That looks like your father. I've never seen that before. Who is that other person?"

"That's Daniel Byrne from the Proxima Foundation. This photo was taken at a conference in Nevada in 1996. Daniel confronted Dad about the secret government program involving faked abductions called MILABs. They were kidnapping children in secret aircraft."

"Kidnapping children? Oh, come on, that's ludicrous!"
She stormed back to the kitchen.

"What do you know about this?" I said in raised voice.

"That's just crazy," she replied.

"I'm going to get to the bottom of this," I said. "I want to
see whatever you have about Dad—photos, records of his
employment, everything."

"I don't have any of that stuff. It's all gone. Why don't you
join Harry and watch the game?"

I got up from the table and went over to the closet in the
front hallway. "Mom, where are the old photos?" I said,
rummaging through the shoeboxes and other junk on the top
shelf.

"They are gone. We lost them when Harry and I moved
here."

"Are you serious? You lost them? You lost the family
photos? How could you do that?"

"They are gone."

"Those were the only photos we had!"

"I don't know what to tell you," she said.

Not finding what I was looking for, I went to the garage to
hunt through the storage bins. Buried under Christmas
ornaments and a bin of mom's collection of knick-knacks, I
found a box containing my Cub and Boy Scouts Merit Badge
sash, brass skill award belt loops, and patches. Also, in the
box were old notebooks from elementary school and high
school. On one notebook's cover I'd scribbled: "1997". I
flipped through the musty pages. Several drawings showed
UFOs in V formation, obviously the Phoenix Lights. There
were also drawings of hexagons and large headed, dark-eyed
alien beings with the telltale ridge of a MILAB fake. I stared
into the graphite-blackened eyes.

I'd completely forgotten about these notebooks and the
drawings. Just as Daniel said, I would have repressed all the
memories, but they would still come out in dreams and in
drawings. *Daniel was right: I was a childhood victim of a MILAB!*

"Ben, come inside, it's getting late," Mom announced

from the doorway.

I was pissed. She'd kept my notebooks but had thrown out the photos of my dad. Why would she get rid of our family photos? She was trying to cover up our past.

"Mom, I'm determined to know what happened to me on that trip when I was ten."

My mother stepped into the garage and began replacing the bins on their shelves. My stepdad poked his head through the door. "What's going on out here?"

"None of your business," I snapped.

My mother wagged her finger at me. "That's no way to speak to your stepfather. You apologize right now."

I opened up my notebook from 1997 and held up the page with the figure strapped down to a table. "Do you know anything about this?"

She stared at me in horror.

"They were molesting kids, Mom, don't you see? Dad was not delivering babies or finding a cure for cancer. He was involved in this. You must have known about this!"

"I don't know what you are talking about, Ben." She stormed over to me, grabbed the notebook, flipped through a few pages, then tossed it into a plastic bin.

I was growing angrier by the second. "What do you mean you don't know? You had to know!"

"That's enough, Ben," my stepfather barked.

I glanced at him for a furious second. "Stay out of this! This has nothing to do with you!"

I turned back to my mom. "You knew about it, didn't you?"

"I don't know what you are talking about." Her voice cracked. "Tell him to stop," she pleaded to Harry.

Harry stepped into the garage and came towards me. "Ben, you're not doing well. Why don't you take a walk and cool down?"

"Listen to your stepfather, Ben."

I toppled Mom's Christmas ornaments off the shelf and onto the concrete floor. "Fuck you! You are not my father, and never were!"

"Benjamin!" my mother shouted. She came toward me. "You get out of this house! You're crazy, absolutely crazy!"

Harry leaped over the mess on the floor and grabbed her. "Let's all calm down now!"

My mother burst into tears in his arms. "I don't know what to do," she muttered.

"Go outside, Ben." Harry pleaded. "Take a walk and cool down."

"To hell with this!" I yelled, grabbing my notebook. I stormed past them into the house to get my jacket and overnight bag.

"Ben! Where are you going?" My mother yelled.

"I'm getting out of here, and I'm going to get answers!" I slammed the door of my Jetta and headed for 90 East. Daniel Byrne was right. My father was linked to a military black project involving fake alien abductions and his 10-year-old son. Daniel Byrne was going to help me get answers, and I was going to help him.

17

NADINE'S SUGGESTION

Mike ushered me up to Nadine's private office suite. A bouquet of flowers in a teal green vase was in bloom on her desk. Mahogany Barrister bookshelves lined the room. Above was a wood paneled ceiling, and a statue of Quan Yin, the goddess of compassion, was on display on one of the shelves. Through an ajar door on the side was a private bathroom.

"Have a seat," Nadine said, "I'm delighted that you've come back to us." She pulled a portfolio of paperwork out of a drawer and presented it to me. In it was a lease agreement for the pod, and an employment contract that said that I was there "at-will." There was also a list of rules I was to agree to. I glanced everything over and signed the documents without reservation. Then she slid an access card over to me.

"Here is the key to your pod. Mike will take you down there later. Daniel is meeting with the contractor and surveying the site right now. They are breaking ground on the new facility in the morning. Why don't you go and see him? I'm sure he's like to show you what is planned."

"I will. Thank you, Nadine."

She smiled. "So good having you with us, Ben, you will be at home here." She pulled a couple brown vials of essential oil from a desk drawer and handed them to me. "A gift. The scents will help you to relax."

I thanked her. I was feeling good.

Mike met me outside and we walked over to the construction grounds. Several dozen wooden stakes with bright orange streamers where in place, marking the site plan. A bulldozer and backhoe were parked and ready. Daniel saw us and came over to pick us up in his golf cart.

"So, you've decided to join us?" he asked.

I smiled and took out the access card to the pod. "Yes. I'm excited to get to work and learn more."

"Good. I'm excited to have you here." He pulled out a copy of the survey plan and blueprints. "Wait until you see what we have planned," he said as he unfurled blueprints on the hood of the golf cart.

The design was impressive and far more than what I expected. Daniel pointed to a spot in the field. "Over here is where the theater and planetarium will be. We'll have several video and theater rooms. The labs will be on the lower section, and a new secure archives vault."

"And a new fitness facility," Mike added.

Daniel smiled widely. "They are going to break ground tomorrow morning. Exciting times, Ben."

They drove me down to the apartment pods. Mike carried my duffle to the door, and they left me alone to settle in. There were twin beds inside, one on each side, two small built-in desks with desk lamps, an essential oil diffuser, and a kitchenette with a portable refrigerator, microwave, and hot plate.

I set my bags down on one of the bunks and began to unpack my things. The entire set-up reminded me of Boy Scout camp, which in a way revived my suspicions about the Byrnes.

I fell into the routines of life on the Proxima Foundation Ranch over the next few weeks. During the day, I stayed busy writing press releases, helping with correspondence, and updating social media sites. Over most lunch hours, I'd get a workout in with Daniel and Mike at the small gym attached to the main house. In the evenings, Daniel and I talked. We'd sit on the back porch and have lengthy conversations about UFOs, mediation, and metaphysical topics. The depth of Daniel's mind was impressive, and I could see why he was called the "Cosmic Guru". He knew all about major historical UFO sightings and abduction incidents, as well as names and backgrounds of the people involved in them. The man was a walking UFO encyclopedia.

One night, while staring at the foundation footings of the new facility, I asked him if he had ever doubted his certainty in the existence of the extraterrestrials. Was he one hundred percent sure that they were visiting Earth, or could there be some other explanation for the phenomena?

"I've never doubted it, not since that night on the lake back in 1978."

"How can you be sure, though?" I asked. "What makes you so certain?" I can't count the number of times I always come back to this one question.

"My life's work has been at getting at the truth and to know it for a fact by carefully evaluating the evidence and testing it. Remember, I may be a lawyer, but I think like a scientist—a real scientist who keeps an open mind—and I know how to be aware of my own fallacies."

"Just like Richard Feynman said, and journalistic truth," I blurted, thinking of the article I'd written that fell short of journalistic truth.

"Regarding your abduction, you know you were taken, albeit by the government, because the experience was real. You have physical evidence on you, and you know something about the motive of why the government would do this to you. We also have the experiences of others documented, supporting our hypothesis. The preponderance of the evidence tells the reality of the situation, even if people think it's crazy."

I nodded thoughtfully. "I just feel like I'm lost—like I don't know if I can trust myself to know the truth."

"Don't be so hard on yourself, Ben. The way to truth is

through questioning what you believe to be reality. You have to. You perceive things through lenses, and those lenses are based on your previous experiences, social influences, biases, whatever. Once you've considered your biases and all possible explanations, you have to trust that what you believe is true until something convinces you otherwise."

"Sounds a bit like faith," I said.

"Faith is the substance of the things to be hoped for, the evidence of the thing unseen: Hebrews 11:1. But there's also a truth you discover on your own or is revealed to you, in time. It's about trust. Trusting in yourself and the universe. And sometimes you just know what's true. I know we're not alone, that there's meaning in all of this. Our alien friends are trying to help us, but there are people on this planet who want to deceive and exploit them, and us. Let that scar on your chest remind you of that. Don't worry, Ben. There's a lot to learn, and your experience has awakened you to a whole new journey ahead. You are not alone and I'm going to help you. You can trust me."

I nodded, feeling less unsettled.

Daniel wasted no time planning the journey for the next several weeks. We were going to Yakima first to visit a friend of Daniel's and participate in a sweat lodge ceremony. Next, a visit with Dr. Petulli. They were going to resume testing on the device they were developing in his basement. Daniel was still keeping it secret, but I was to take part. I was excited to witness the device in action, whatever it was. Chester was taking the bus up from Fresno and would occupy the empty bunk in my pod. I was less happy about sharing my space, but I didn't have a choice in the matter.

Daniel also had a briefing planned at the National Press Club in Washington DC where he planned to make another push for full government disclosure of peaceful alien visitation. Next, back to Missoula for a speaking event at the Cosmic Woodstock festival, and then to top it all off, a trip to LA for an appearance on *60 Minutes*. I was to accompany and assist him, and while being in the public eye did not appeal to me, I felt honored to be invited.

The day before the Yakima trip, Nadine invited me to lunch. I sat at the table in the dining room while she served up some BLT sandwiches and iced tea.

"Ben, you've been doing a great job with the social media and public affairs work for the Foundation. Daniel and I really appreciate it."

"Glad to help," I said before gulping my tea.

She poured a refill. "Have you thought about writing an article about your abduction experience? Perhaps it would be good for you."

"Actually, it has crossed my mind, but I'm not sure..."

"What's stopping you?" She looked concerned.

"I don't know, I just..."

"Embarrassed to write about your personal experience because it involves extraterrestrials and government conspiracy?"

I smiled. "Maybe a little."

"But it would be cathartic for you—getting out whatever is on your mind, telling your story as you see it. Why don't you start with a short article for the Foundation web site?"

I took a bite of BLT and thought. I wasn't sure if I could write anything worth a damn. Writing form letters and making Facebook and Twitter updates are no brainers, but writing something substantial, and the lingering guilt over the hoax story that had blown up in my face all but erased my confidence as a journalist.

Nadine let me ruminate. "Well, if you feel like getting started on it, I'll let you off early today. Daniel will be supportive too. He admires you as a writer, you know."

"You sure he won't mind? I'm supposed to be helping with his book and if I start writing my own thing..."

"Daniel and I already talked about it. Daniel believes in you, Ben. In fact, it was his idea to send your article to his agent in New York, Howard Dulci. He's connected with the major publishers. May be your story could end up in the New Yorker or turn into a book contract."

"Really? Daniel would do that?"

"Yes," Nadine said. She cut a piece of pie for me. "Your exposé article hit Daniel especially hard. He's very trusting of others because his intentions are good. He cares. A couple of articles about your experience would be a great way to fix your previous journalistic error by telling the truth this time."

I sat back and chewed a large mouthful of pie. Writing an article sounded great, but I wasn't comfortable making promises.

"You're a writer, Ben. You'll know when you've got something good. Just tell your truth in the way you know how. I'll even copyedit it for you."

Daniel walked in. "What are you two talking about?"

"Writing," said Nadine.

Daniel grabbed a piece of pie crust and shoved it into his mouth. "Oh yeah?"

"Ben is going to write an article about his abduction experience." She smiled at me. "I think it's a great idea. Don't you, Daniel?"

Daniel nodded, still chewing. "Writing can be cathartic. I support."

"Well, there you have it, Ben. Daniel thinks it's a great idea."

I went to work on the articles, a short one for the Foundation website and extended one for Daniel's agent. Words flew out of me at lightning speed. I couldn't believe it. I wrote about what happened that night en route from Yakima to Seattle, what happened to me afterwards, the PTSD, the breakup with Jennifer, everything, all the while questioning the reality of my experience. Was it a fake abduction, or was it a real abduction? I focused on my interpretation of the experience, it's meaning to me. I drew parallels and comparisons to a few other notable documented abduction experiences, from Strieber to Walton, Betty and Barney Hill. Always the questioned loomed: were they real, or were they fake? I was hopeful for the answers.

18

SWEAT LODGE

We stopped at an outlet mall outside of Spokane for lunch and some shopping. Mike made a tank top acquisition at the NIKE outlet, and Daniel picked up a new pair or Ray Ban aviators. In the food court, we indulged in ice cream while discussing our plans for the next twenty-four hours.

"We'll check into the hotel in Yakima, and then head up Route 12," Daniel said, licking his salted caramel sugar cone. "We'll take a look around and see if we find anything left behind by your government abductors."

"What? We're going to my abduction site?" It was news to me, and it was almost one-thirty. I sure as hell didn't want to be up there on the ridge after dark.

"Yes," Daniel said, "returning to the scene will help you get over what they did to you, and we should do some investigative work."

"What are you expecting to find?" I asked, doubtful we'd find anything of substance to link my experience to a government abduction operation. What was he expecting to find—indentions in the dirt from the black helicopters or TR-3B landing gear?

"TR-3B residual energy fields. We have a special device for detecting them."

"Really? Energy traces after all this time?"

"Sure. The craft create so much electromagnetic energy that they charge rock, mostly basalt, given its rich iron ore. There's no guarantee we'll detect it, so we'll have to really scour the area. It will take some time."

"I don't want to be up there in the dark if we can avoid it," I said assertively, setting my bowl of macadamia nut ice cream down. "And won't us being there draw attention? Wouldn't the government have interest in us being there?"

Daniel wiped ice cream dribble from his chin. "Don't worry, we'll be back to the hotel before dark." His eyes were empathetic. "I know this is difficult, Ben, but everything will be fine. Trust me. I've helped many people with abduction trauma before. And no, I'm not too worried about the government. They won't even know we're there, especially if we keep our cell phones off." He looked at Mike. "Or we get pulled over for a speeding ticket—"

"I'll be careful," Mike replied.

"—like on our Peru trip last year," Daniel added, grinning.

"That wasn't my fault. I didn't know it was kilometers per hour," Mike said before taking a mammoth bite of his cookies and cream double scoop.

"You went to Peru last year?" I asked.

"A group of us went down for a sighting event and ayahuasca experience. It was incredible," Daniel said. "Have you ever experienced a DMT trip?"

Dimethyltryptamine. "No, but I've read about it. What was it like?"

"It takes a moment to cross the threshold, and then you are there in another dimensional realm. It's no hallucination—vivid, with geometric shapes and the entities are human-like but they glow as if from an inner sun. Their eyes glimmered like diamonds, and they smiled when they saw us, welcoming us to their realm. Others sang to us. It was beautiful."

"And the green stick figures," Mike blurted, "the ones with the large eyes."

"Like Gumbi?" I said, thinking about the stop-action cartoon character.

"Oh no, Ben," Daniel said, "these were intelligent intra-dimensional entities. Everyone with us saw the same entities at the same time. Others who have been on DMT have seen these same entities."

"Interesting. Is there a connection to the EBEs?"

"They are not the EBEs we have been in contact with, but other entities. Like the Proximians, they wanted to show me things and share their knowledge. It was a very special experience. I will have a chapter in my new book about the connection to the EBEs."

Daniel and Mike continued reminiscing while I went over my usual dilemma. How did Daniel know that what he experienced was real and not a hallucination? What about my own abduction experience? Sure, there was a mark on my chest, and I was sure I didn't put it there. Jennifer thought I did.

Daniel interrupted my thoughts. "Ben, you look perplexed. What's on your mind?"

"How can I be sure what I experienced was real? Maybe I was just hallucinating." I looked at him. "How can you be sure that each and all of the things you've experienced were real? How do you know for sure?"

He smiled. "First rule is you must be careful to not fool yourself and…"

"You are the easiest person to fool," I said, smiling back.

He licked his dwindling ice cream and nodded. "It's been well documented in the scientific literature that people have the same experiences with the same type of entities when experiencing DMT. How else can you explain that? It's no different from abduction experiences. It's a *cosmic connection*, and it's real, not a hallucination."

I finished off my macadamia nut, pondering the idea of shared metaphysical experiences and *cosmic connections*. Three months ago, I'd pass these off as crazy ideas—but now, I wasn't sure.

We continued our journey east. In Yakima, we checked into a hotel, and then headed up on Route 12 to the spot where I first noticed the lights trailing me, and the approximate location where my car lost power. Mike pulled into the next turnout and parked. We sat in the van for a moment while Mike readied his handheld electromagnetic field reader and Daniel surveyed the canyon and surrounding hills. "This was a perfect spot for them to take you," he said, pointing to the terrain, "the ridges provide cover, and they must have blocked the road behind and in front to make sure you were alone." He looked at me one last time before we got out. "Don't worry, Ben, you'll be fine. It's okay if you want to stay near the van."

I stepped out of the van.

The air was crisp, and the late afternoon sun gave the surrounding hills a yellow-orange glow. Daniel walked the road ahead of us while Mike walked the opposite side with his sensor in hand. I walked alone, scanning the skies and ridge tops for lights. After a minute, I found myself at the edge of the road in a daze, unable to keep out images of dark, lifeless eyes. A semi-truck blasted its horn, causing me to jump.

"You okay, Ben?" Mike shouted from across the road.

"I'm fine," I shouted back, but I wasn't. Fear and anxiety were tearing me apart.

Daniel called back to Mike. "Anything yet?"

Mike's meter was beeping and chirping. "Getting above background now."

Daniel disappeared into a ravine and emerged a minute later with something in his hand. "Look what I just found," he announced excitedly as he approached Mike and I.

It was the iPhone I lost the night of my abduction. I inspected it. The screen was cracked in one corner, and the battery was dead. We let it charge in the van for a few minutes, then Daniel made sure I set it on airplane mode to prevent cell tower pings. I scrolled through the last texts and calls from that fateful night. The last call was the one I made to Jennifer.

143

"Check the photos and the videos," Daniel said.

I opened the photo app and viewed the most recent images. Nothing out of the ordinary, just a handful of photos of Jennifer and me from our engagement weekend. Then I remembered that I had taken a video the night I was abducted. I checked the videos, and what I saw nearly made me drop the phone: the greenish white light and in the lower left corner, for an instant, an image of a small gray being with skinny arms outstretched toward me. The video ended abruptly.

"Holy shit! Look!" I yelled, playing the video for Daniel and Mike, pausing the frame when the first being appeared, and zooming in for its slit mouth and telltale ridge from the nose up to the giant forehead.

Daniel grabbed the phone and inspected it while Mike and I leaned over his shoulders. "Just what I thought, a robotic fake. He looked at me. "This video was planted by the government," Daniel said. "They wanted your phone to be discovered." He handed it back to me.

I played the video again, wondering if what he said was true. Then I remembered my smart watch data: hearty rate normal, then 120, then plummeted, then missing data. Was that government too? I mentioned it to Daniel.

"The government likely manipulated that data, too, just like your phone. They weren't counting on me finding it. I've got people who will help us with full in-house forensic analysis of the phone."

Did the government manipulate the data, or cause my heartrate to go squirrely while they took me up into a TR-3B?

I watched the video a third time. The government alien abduction hypothesis, Daniel's discovery of my phone, and the EBE shot—was it any less plausible than aliens from a distant star in the Goldilocks Zone taking me up into their ship? Something happened to me, and here was video evidence to back it up. I wondered about Congressman Young too. Was he linked to the government abduction program?

We headed back down into the valley and to the hotel. The next morning, we drove to Yakima Indian Reservation, southwest of Yakima. Yakima is the proper name of a people who've lived on the Columbia River Plateau for thousands of years.

We drove down a dirt road, past a cellular tower, and several apple orchards, and we pulled up next to an old tin roof trailer at the end. A dog barked and scurried around to the back as a middle-aged man in blue jeans and t-shirt with a greying ponytail stepped out to greet us.

Daniel and Mike shook the man's hand, Daniel and the man with the fervor of old buddies. Daniel waved for me to come over.

"Ben, this is Chief John Lightfoot."

We shook hands. We went inside the trailer and sat down in his living room. Daniel asked him to tell us what he knew about Congressman Young.

"He's a corporate man through and through," the Chief said, "don't trust him at all. He said he was going to help us with the cell towers, but he was really on the side of the cellular companies. He sold us out."

"And he's linked to government black ops program involving fake abductions," Daniel added.

"Yes, it's true," the Chief said. "My niece was taken a year and a half ago about ten miles from here, then was returned to us a week later."

"Is she okay now?" I asked, assuming she'd experienced the same post-abduction symptoms as I. "I'd like to meet her."

"She will be here anytime now. She wants to see Daniel and meet you."

Just as he said that, the door opened to a young woman in her early twenties with jet black hair and a one-year-old in a sling.

She and Daniel hugged. "So good to see you, Uncle Daniel."

"And who's this little one? Mia?" Daniel took the baby

145

and sat down, cooing and bouncing the baby on his knee.

The Chief introduced Maria to me and told her that I was working with Daniel.

"We know my abduction was a fake abduction," she glanced at Daniel and back at me, "done by the government."

"Why do you think they took you?"

Daniel interjected. "Tell Ben what happened to you."

Maria nodded to Daniel. "I was on my way home from visiting my sister when I noticed lights following me. Everything lit up around me, and then I was inside a craft with alien greys with small black eyes."

I pulled my old phone out and played the video for her.

"Oh my, that's exactly what I saw."

"Did they do anything to you?" I asked.

She became visibly uncomfortable. "Yes. I don't like to talk about it."

The baby started to cry.

"Oh, she's getting hungry, Uncle Daniel," Maria said, as she took her baby into her arms.

"Maria was in the wrong place and the wrong time," the chief said sadly.

"They fly TR-3Bs through this area," Daniel explained. "An air corridor runs south of Mount Rainier and north of Mount Saint Helens to the ocean. Isn't that right, Mike?"

Mike nodded. "They fly at night and low to avoid radar."

"But the Proximians are here as friends," the Chief said. "Our ancestors have been visited for hundreds of years."

Daniel looked at John and smiled. "We've done a lot of spiritual work together with the EBEs."

"Yes. Daniel and the Proxima Foundation are doing great things to bring our worlds together. Are you going to the sweat ceremony tonight?"

"Of course, we'll be there," Daniel said.

"Good. It will be an honor for us to have you join us tonight, giving gratitude to the great spirit together." The Chief turned to me. "Ever been to a sweat lodge ceremony, Ben?"

"No, never," I replied, wondering why this part of the itinerary hadn't been disclosed to me. "How long does it last?"

"It can be several hours in the hut. Cleansings can take longer. Daniel tells me you've been through a lot at the hands of the government—that you are hearing the voices of evil spirits, too. The ceremony will shake those spirits out of you. "Ben, you'll never by the same after connecting to the Great Spirit."

The three of us returned to the hotel to relax until nightfall. Daniel assured me that the sweat lodge experience would be well worth my time. *Therapeutically cathartic*, he promised. We skipped lunch and dinner. "Better to fast before a sweat lodge experience," he explained.

As the sun was setting, we returned to the reservation, but a different part where a large fire was already ablaze in front of a domed hut. Just under a dozen people were there, Indian and White. We stripped down to our underwear, and draped our clothes over a log laid in the grass. One by one, we entered the lodge in the center of which was a pit loaded with hot stones pulled from the fire outside. The flap over the door was lowered and we were immersed in darkness. An elder poured water from a ladle onto the stones and steam shot into the air. Soon, it was extremely hot. Prayers and chants began. I wasn't sure how long I could hold out. About five minutes in, I panicked and ran out into the cool evening air. Daniel came after me, sweat dripping from his face.

"You are experiencing repressed trauma, Ben. Everything is going to be okay. Just take deep breaths."

Mike fetched a blanket, and Daniel wrapped me in it. "Your reaction is a normal response for someone who had been abducted." Mike retrieved our clothes while Daniel stood with me as I caught my breath. I felt better. Daniel's voice and encouragement were invaluable. Soon, we were on the road back to the hotel.

"I'm embarrassed," I said, looking out the window into the darkness.

"You shouldn't be, Ben," Daniel said, looking back at me, "this experience tonight is part of your transformation. You're on the mend now and working with me at the Foundation is good for you. We have a lot of work to do together."

"Thank you, Daniel. I just need to get some rest."

"Of course," Daniel said, "knock on my door if you need me."

That night, curled up in bed, I cried like a baby.

19

THE DEVICE

Chester my "roommate" appeared at the doorway of my pod late Friday afternoon. He was wearing a sweatshirt and an old pair of jeans with a black backpack slung over his shoulder and a small olive drab satchel in one hand. I said hello as he stared at me suspiciously with his deep-set eyes with dark bags under them. He dropped his bags on the empty bunk.

"All of the other pods are full. Nadine said I was to stay here," he said glumly.

I was in my bunk and working on my article.

"Okay," I said, clearly feeling the territorial threat he was experiencing. "I understand that you've been making some progress on a special device. I'm excited to see this thing in action."

He unzipped his satchel and began removing his belongings. "We've got to keep what we have a secret or the government will be all over us and shut us down."

"Don't worry, Chester, I signed a non-disclosure agreement, and Daniel invited me to go to Dr. Petulli's with you this weekend."

His eyes were still on me. "Just don't touch anything."

"I won't. I'll just watch."

He nodded and went on unpacking while I finished my

article and sent it to Nadine for review. Nadine was right—
the writing exercise was cathartic. That evening, after dinner,
I supplemented my knowledge by reading more MILAB
documents from Daniel's archives.

In the morning, Chester, Daniel, Mike and I took one of
the Proxima Foundation vans up to Petulli's place. After
about 5 miles along a ridge, we passed through a gate, and
there was the Petulli mansion—massive and castle-like, made
with sandstone bricks. On one side was a large three-car
garage, on the other an observation tower that was topped
with a dome, presumably the observatory where Petulli kept
his telescope.

Daniel rang the doorbell. A surveillance camera peered
down at us. Petulli answered a moment later. He was 5'9"
with short hair, in his 60s but looking younger than his age.
We exchanged greetings and introductions. I wondered if
he'd seen my *Hot Reports* article on the Proxima Foundation
and what his impression was of me.

Mike and Chester headed immediately down the hallway
to a door leading to the basement.

Petulli looked over his shoulder at them. "Complete the
checklist, but don't turn anything on, not without me
present."

"Roger that. Safety first," yelled Mike before he and
Chester disappeared.

Petulli led Daniel and me down a long hallway, its walls
lined with old framed photos and awards. Many of the images
were of airplanes, some of him and his father in blue flight
suits and mirrored aviator glasses, posing in front of different
types of exotic experimental aircraft.

We entered a great room open to a large kitchen area with
granite counter tops. The walls of the great room were lined
with floor to ceiling shelves of books. Several plastic models
of rockets and airplanes were on a table in the center of the
room. No traces of a woman's touch anywhere.

A book caught my eye: *Ancient Aliens & JFK: The Race to
the Moon and the Kennedy Assassination.* I pulled the book out.

"You like books, Ben?" Petulli asked.

"Of course," I replied, pushing the book back and moving on to the next shelf. Petulli came over to make sure the book was pushed all the way back in, showing that he was the kind of man who needed everything in its place.

"I was about to have some nourishment; would you like some?"

"We'd love some," said Daniel.

A large tabby cat appeared and rubbed up against Petulli's leg. The cat meowed affectionately. "It's not feeding time yet, Mr. Snickles," Petulli said equally affectionately.

Petulli went into the kitchen and poured a frothy green substance from a large blender into three tall glasses, then returned, handing glasses to Daniel and me.

"This will put hair on your chest," Daniel said to me as he took a drink.

"More than that," said Petulli, "it will extend your life by ten years."

I looked at the glass of chalky green liquid in my hand and smelled it. It was odorless and tasted like raw vegetables and fruit.

"Soylent Green?" I smiled, thinking that Pettuli would get the science fiction reference.

"No, a synthetic mix of anti-oxidants," Petulli said in serious tone.

"Synthetic?" I was wondering if I should be worried about what I'd just swallowed.

"Proprietary blend of essential oils," he said.

"Just drink it, Ben," Daniel said, wiping his green mustache.

I asked Petulli about his photos and his experimental work in aviation design. He had 50 patents on designs and instruments. I also asked about the large observatory upstairs, and he suggested I return sometime for a tour and look through his homemade Dobson telescope.

We finished our "nourishment," and headed down to the basement. In the center of the basement room was a chair with a helmet with electrodes and a large Plexi-glass box with a sloppy array of tubes and wires attached.

"This is a transdimensional 3D printer or T3DP," Petulli announced. "Through Daniel's mediation protocol, we can focus intention and receive transmission intra-dimensionally from our EBE friends, and it prints what they want to send to us."

Alas, I knew what the secret the device was. "Wow. How did you know how to build this?"

"The EBEs sent the plans on how to build it. To Daniel. Telepathically," Chester explained. He was standing next to a large AC power switch on the back wall in a white lab coat with a pair of plastic goggles around his neck.

Did they really think the T3DP was going to receive something from aliens on Proxima b? "Does it work? Have you made anything with it?"

"Oh, it works," said Chester.

"You are going to witness a technological miracle today, Ben." Daniel added.

Chester handed me a pair of googles. "Its standard Personal Protective Equipment, in case there are any particulates or other unwanted objects that come flying out," said Chester.

"Unwanted objects? What would cause that?" I asked.

"Transient thoughts," Daniel answered, now in the chair and donning goggles.

Chester placed the helmet device on Daniel, Mike rechecked the wire connections, and Petulli readied things at the computer. Petulli motioned to Daniel that everything was a go, and Daniel gave Chester the nod to flip the power switch. Daniel closed his eyes and began to meditate. The overhead lights flickered and a strange hum resonated through-out the room, increasing in pitch and amplitude. Then the printer started, its nozzle moving at light speed and shooting resin in rapid fire. Within a minute, an object began to take form—an oblong, warped tic-tac shaped object about two feet in length and slightly larger on one end.

Looks like a giant penis, I thought, holding back a grin. Daniel's eyes were still shut, his forehead now glistening with sweat. After a few minutes, the printer slowed, then stopped. Petulli raised his hand, motioning to Chester to turn the power lever off. Daniel, looking exhausted, opened his eyes to behold the object. "It works!" Well hot damn! It works!"

"I knew it would," said Chester.

"What is it?" I asked.

Petulli removed the object from the printer housing and held it up for everyone to see. "It looks like you received a model of a Proximian space craft, Daniel."

Petulli handed it to Mike who handed it to me. I looked it over. Was this a technological miracle or a farse?

Petulli returned to the logs on the computer screen. "Daniel, you hit theta waves for nearly three minutes and the amplitude is off the charts. The bandwidth is incredible."

Daniel was still smiling. "Let's try again," he said.

Petulli, still at the computer, said, "I'll need to make a few power adjustments and make sure of the calibrations. If we are off, you could receive faulty plans and who knows what kind of danger that could cause."

"Like if they send the entire plans for a craft they want us to build," Chester added.

"Like in that movie *Explorers* in the 1980s," I blurted. "Several boys had the same dream about a technological device they built in a basement. It works, and they're shot up into the night sky where they rendezvous with a giant, adolescent alien." No one seemed to get the reference.

Daniel said, "This is no movie, Ben. I do believe that this technology will help get us to the moon, and well beyond. Interstellar space travel will be in reach in just a few years."

"Are you absolutely certain that this design came from the Proximians?" I asked Daniel.

"Certain?" He looked at Petulli. "Let's try it again, only a local test this time. Chester, hook me up." Daniel sat back and donned the goggles while Chester readied the helmet.

"Ben, concentrate on an object, any object."

"Any object?"

"Yes, anything that comes to mind, something tangible."

Tangible. "Okay, I'll give it try."

I slipped the goggles on and Chester flipped on the power. I tried to think of something tangible. At first, random objects came to mind—Nadine's statue of Quan Yin, the rubber duckie on my key chain, my laptop, the claw machine at Ramblin' Joe's—but my mind's eye came to rest on the face of a Proximian, staring me down with its black eyes. Now I couldn't not see it.

The printer came to life, moving slowly, then full tilt. I peeked my eyes open—everyone was stating at the printer. Except Daniel, who's eyes were shut.

When the printer came to a stop, Petulli removed a full-sized replica of a Proximian head and held it out for everyone. "Well there you have it. It works," he said.

I was both impressed and horrified. Either the head appeared by chance or it was an actual telepathic connection between Daniel and I. Either way, the thing gave me the creeps.

"How did you know that I was thinking about that?" I asked.

"Telepathy, Ben." He addressed Petulli. "It's time Robert. We need to let the world know about what we've accomplished here. Don't you agree?"

"I don't think we are ready for primetime just yet, Daniel. We'd better make sure that it's going to operate as planned," Petulli suggested.

Daniel nodded, then turned to me. "Ben, would you like to write a press release for the Proxima Foundation on this?" He probably saw my hesitation because he added, "The government can't stop us now, Ben. The Proximians can send us all kinds of transformative technologies, like a zero-point energy system. Once we get this out, there will be no way that they can shut us down. But we need to be calculated in how we release the information. Can you do it, Ben? Write a teaser release? We should do it right away."

"Okay, I'll do it," I said.

That night, Nadine gave me the go ahead to publish my abduction experience blog on the Foundation website. There were thousands of shares within an hour. I felt good about the blog—that I'd accomplished something. I also got to work on the intra-dimensional 3D printer press release, and sent it off to Daniel for approval when I was done.

20

THE NATIONAL PRESS CLUB

The National Press Club is more than just a conference center for Washington elites; it's known as "The Place Where News Happens." Daniel wanted that, and that's what he would get.

We had lunch in the Club restaurant and then headed into the main conference room. Daniel sat in front of a microphone at the center of a long table, his name displayed prominently on a large placard. To his left was Dr. Steiner, and to his right, Richard Mazzotti. Mike and I sat together in the front row and watched people trickle in—other UFO experts, government officials, and of course, the press. Cameras and photographers were lined up in back. Daniel's face was serious but glowing from all of the attention on him.

At exactly 1pm, Daniel cleared his throat. "Ladies and gentlemen, thanks for coming to this important briefing. For years, my esteemed colleagues and I have been advocating, for all of humanity, that the governments of the world release the truth about our alien visitors. Our federal government must take the lead. We the people demand it, which is why I've organized this press conference: to demand this release and share the truth openly with the people of the world. I've asked several experts to join me today to communicate to the government and public what we know to be fact—that the Proximians are no threat to humanity, and that the government has been staging alien abductions for more than two decades in order to scare the public and test new technologies on unsuspecting, unwilling participants."

Reporters began shouting questions.

"CNN News. So how long has the government known about this, if what you say is true?"

"It is true. Various departments and agencies of the government have known for 75 years. Isn't that right, Dr. Steiner?"

Steiner leaned into the microphone. "Yes. Everything that Mr. Byrne has said is true."

"What do their ships look like?" asked a reporter from NBC.

"We have been tracking two types: triangular ones, which we think are tactical in nature; and egg-shaped ones, or "tic-tac" shaped, as they've come to be known, which appear to be probes for surveillance. We've known about these since 2004. Tracked off of San Diego."

Once the press conference was over, Daniel was encircled with Mike at his side. I waited in the main lobby on the first floor, checking social media and the news. There were already reports about the press conference. Eventually, Daniel and Mike showed up.

"Sorry, Ben." Daniel said, "I was called to a special briefing with some government officials. Looks like our conference today did the trick: The government is definitely listening now. They want to meet with us at the Sheraton in 30 minutes to discuss disclosure strategy. Come on, we'd better get a cab."

At the Sheraton, we went to the top floor, Room 5601, where a man wearing a dark designer suit led us into the suite where two other men were seated, also in dark designer suits. Were these Men in Black characters? Daniel, Mike and I sat down on a large sofa facing the men.

Daniel smiled. "So where should we start?"

One of the two men was not smiling when he said, "We want you to cease and desist your public talks about alien visitation. We don't care about your UFO lectures, but you must stop talking about this fake abduction nonsense."

So these government men weren't there for Daniel's advice.

But Daniel was adamant. "You know that I can't do that. You can't stop people from learning the truth about MILAB operations."

The other man said, "Maybe you did not hear us clearly. You will stop all discussion about MILABs immediately, and you will stop building the telepathy device, do you understand?" He leaned forward, letting the gun tucked under his suit jacket become visible.

"Who are you guys?" I interjected, my heart racing. "Why don't you want him to talk?"

"Quiet, Ben, let me handle this," Daniel said confidently. He looked at the lead man. "You don't want the public to know the truth about what the government is doing, but I have a cache of information that I will give to the public if you try to stop me."

The lead man sneered. "Go ahead, release your cache, we don't care. But stop all press releases and social media about MILABs and your experiments." He looked at me. "That goes for you, too, Mr. Davenport."

"Or what?" said Daniel.

"Do you love your wife, Mr. Byrne?" said the lead man said calmly.

Daniel stood up, his face hardened. "Now you listen to me. If you lay a hand on her I'll…"

A quick scuffle ensued, but when Daniel was pushed out onto the balcony and against the railing, I stood to go to his aid, only to be pushed back onto the sofa. Mike looked like he was shitting bricks.

"Now, you listen to me," the man at Byrne's throat was saying, "you think that you are on top of this, but it takes nothing to make you fall. Am I getting through to you, Mr.

Byrne?"

Bone-chilling fear showed in Daniel's face. "Yes," he grunted.

"You remember what happened last time, don't you?" said the man.

"I do," said Daniel.

Daniel coughed and came back into the room. His composure regained, Daniel gestured to Mike and me. "Let's go," he said.

"See you around," one of the men said as we left.

In the elevator, I turned to Daniel. "Why didn't they stop you before you did the Press Club briefing?"

Daniel shrugged. "It's the federal government."

"Are you going to stop talking about the MILABs? What about the intergalactic 3D printer?"

"Go ahead and post the blog about the printer, and you might as well write one about what just happened here. Nothing can stop me from getting the truth out. I'm used to this kind of intimidation, it comes with the territory."

21

COSMIC WOODSTOCK

Daniel, Mike, Chester, and I took a Proxima Foundation van to the Missoula County fairgrounds late Saturday morning. There must have been two thousand people already there; families with children, cadres of teenagers, and lots of people in alien masks and costumes. A thousand more were expected for Daniel's afternoon appearance and the concert, and fireworks later.

We checked in with the festival program people and made sure that everything was all set. We inspected the stage area in the pavilion with its massive PA speakers and big screen TVs paid for by the Proxima Foundation. Daniel tasked me to help with the sound check and to keep up with social media updates throughout the event. Mike was the usual security detail, and Chester was to help with whatever else Grand Marshal Daniel needed.

During a break, I went to use one the many porta-potties and afterwards took a shortcut through the food vendor and beer garden area where I ran into Brenda working one of the booths. She had an apron over her t-shirt and black short skirt and black leggings. She asked me what I was doing in Missoula.

"I'm living and working here now at the Proxima Ranch."

"With the culties? Why?"

"A lot has happened, including something incredible."

"Oh yeah? I want to hear this. What happened?"

She removed her apron and suggested we sit at one of the picnic tables.

I took a deep breath. "I had an abduction experience about two months ago." I then told her the short version.

She looked at me like I thought she would. "Are you smoking some shit? You're fucking kidding me, right?"

"I'm serious, Brenda, it happened, and I can't fully explain it. I came to talk to Daniel Byrne about it. He's the expert, and I'm hoping that he can help me to figure out what it's all about. I'm just looking for the truth."

She stood up. "I need to get back to work."

"No, wait, Brenda. I'm not playing with you. Hear me out."

She sat down again. A few high school kids walked by in alien-antenna hats. "Do you really think he's going to have answers for you?" she asked, her sarcasm obvious.

"I don't know who else to talk to. I've researched everything I can find about fake abductions, and it's all the same conspiracy stuff that leads no closer to the truth. Something definitely happened to me, that, I know. It wasn't all in my head. It was physical—I mean, it felt physical, and someone or something made a mark on my chest, and sometimes I still have a ringing in my ears. Byrne has information. If it's true, then maybe he has some answers. Daniel really knows his stuff. He really does. He even knew about the exoplanet Proxima b before NASA did. I know that you probably think that I'm crazy."

She was glaring at me with her gorgeous brown eyes, "I can't believe that you are staying at the cultie ranch. So you're working for them now? Doing what?"

"They're letting me stay at the ranch, and in return I'm doing some office work and writing for them, press and social media stuff. It's just temporary until I figure out what to do next."

"Uh-huh, and who's that guy he has with him all the time?"

"Mike. He does security for him. He's here, somewhere." I looked around.

"Kind of weird, Ben. I wonder what's really going on there." She looked into my eyes.

I half-smiled. "Like what?" I knew what was coming.

"Maybe Byrne and his security are like, into each other. Something just seems off about it. Daniel is a married man always hanging around with a younger body builder guy. I'm just saying."

I suppressed a smile. "I don't think so. Mike's for security, that's all."

"Security? From who?"

"The government."

"And you believe that?"

"We were in D.C. for a conference and some feds roughed us up. It was real."

"What, like Men in Black?"

"It happened. I wouldn't lie to you," I said.

"Are you really sure you can trust these people? I think my aunt's murder has something to do with them, and so does my Uncle. You should have talked with my uncle before when you were doing your story. Why didn't you interview him or anyone else in town?"

I didn't have an answer. I felt bad about how I'd left Brenda high and dry, but all that mattered now was getting answers about what had happened to me in order to get my head straight.

Brenda got up. "Well, anyway, you better be careful. And yes, I do think you are imbalanced. Think about it. You're living on a compound with people who talk to aliens and charge people to look at drones and flares." She shook her head. "It's a cult, a scam."

"People can come and go as they please." I said.

Just then my handheld squawked. "Bravo Two, Bravo Three come in."

Brenda shook her head. I answered the call.

"Bravo Three. Bravo Two, go ahead."

"Where are you? We need you over at the stage."

"Okay, on my way. Bravo Three out." I looked up at Brenda. "I've got to go."

"Yeah, you've always 'got to go'. I thought you were going to help me figure out what happened to my aunt. What about the investigation? You said you would help me."

I stood up. "There's no investigation, Brenda. I'm sorry, I can't get involved in anything else right now. This is too big—They need me. I've got go."

She threw her hands up in the air and walked away.

"I'm sorry," I called out too late. I felt bad about not being able to help her solve the mystery around her aunt's death, but what could I do?

At the stage area, Mike and I tested Daniel's wireless. Half an hour later, Daniel was speaking, his voice booming over the audience still gathering. He did his usual routine about communication with the EBEs, and the progress he and the Proxima Foundation were making, including with the intergalactic 3D printer.

"And tonight," he announced, "we are going to do something exciting, something we've never done before. We're going to broadcast our viewing event on Facebook Live. For the first time ever, the world will be able to participate with us in real-time. We have a very special meditation planned, and if you have the iM4ET app, which I hope you do, you can track the EBEs with us."

Dozens of people pulled out their cell phones to download the app, including a young bare-chested dude with long hair standing behind me.

The announcer returned to the stage, thanked Daniel, and instructed the audience to assemble along the downtown streets of Missoula for the parade.

Daniel, Mike, Chester and I jumped into the classic 1964 Cadillac Eldorado Convertible, Sherwood Green and white walled tires of Daniel's friend Jim Bradshaw, Chester in the front seat, Daniel and me in the back.

"Where's Mike?" I asked.

"He's on foot behind us. Security," Daniel said. I glanced back. He was walking about ten yards behind us, his headset and sunglasses on. Serious face.

Bradshaw revved the Cadillac's 7-liter. "Ready, Grand Marshall?"

Daniel sat back and stretched his arm over the top of the white vinyl seat. "Let's roll."

We pulled out and moved to the front of the parade in the staging area. There were about a dozen home-fashioned floats and people dressed as aliens, astronauts, and characters from popular space-themed movies. We chugged along, trailed by the Missoula High School band. At the first corner a mom and her kids in alien antennas were waving at us.

"Wave, Ben," Daniel scolded me, "they want to see you too."

I waved.

Now on the main street, Daniel continued to acknowledge the crowd as he spoke to me. "Listen, Ben, I've been thinking. I don't think you need to come to the viewing event tonight. I know you are still nervous about things because of your abduction experience. I could use your help with setting-up and monitoring the live video feed at base station. That sound okay with you?"

"Sure, whatever you need," I said, relieved I was saved from going up the hill in the dark.

"Good. We've got a lot of people coming in for this one, and we expect tens of thousands on the livestream. No glitches, it's got to go smoothly."

We rounded a street corner. I saw Brenda on the sidewalk and ducked, hoping she wouldn't see me. *I can't believe I'm in this parade*, I thought. I couldn't help glancing over at her, and we locked eyes. The blood rushed to my face. Brenda shook her head in disappointment. I sunk even lower.

A few minutes later, we heard a loud boom, like gunshot. Daniel threw his arm over me and shoved me to the floor of the Cadillac. "Get down! Get down! It's a hit!" To Bradshaw, he yelled, "Go! Go!" Bradshaw looked back at Daniel, confused. "Hit the gas! Go! Go!"

As we accelerated, Mike jumped onto the back trunk. "You all right?"

We maneuvered around the marching band, causing the tuba player to trip. We drove two blocks to a Circle K convenience store parking lot.

"What are you doing?" Daniel yelled.

"I think it was fireworks, Daniel," Bradshaw said.

"I don't think so, it sounded like a .308 to me. You, too, Mike?"

Now on foot, Mike nodded, surveying the surrounding buildings and maneuvering in full tactical mode, pointing his Glock to the ground. We listened to the bottle rockets and firecrackers in the distance.

22

NOT SO GOOD SIGHTING

I set up the live stream connection, pre-synched the cellular
Wi-Fi for Mike's cameras, and then went to the cafeteria to
heat up some noodles for dinner. In the cafeteria, I ran into
some guests staying for the weekend. Robbie Spence was
there, and the fat woman I had met in the tent on the night
Brent and I filmed the hoax. Robbie came over to me with a
large smile.

"So you've come back to us?" he asked, shaking my hand.
"You going to join our meditation tonight?"

"Not tonight. I'm working here at the ranch. We're filming
tonight's event and streaming it live."

Robbie was definitely excited. "Daniel says he's expecting
a major sighting tonight. I've got my son and daughter, first
viewing event for them." He pointed to a small group of
people putting their daypacks on—two teenagers had the
same pudgy face as their father's.

I glanced out the windows at the clear sky. "Should be a
good night for it, I'm sure."

"Yep, and Daniel knows best," he said, putting on his
fanny pack.

I headed back to the basement office and ran into Mike on
the way.

"You good on the live stream?" he asked.

"Yes, all set up," I said.

"We're going live at eight-thirty sharp. Keep your radio on. I'll check in with you if I need to, got it?"

"Yeah, no problem."

"Thanks, man," he said, raising his palm for a high-five bro shake. First time he'd done that with me.

Back in the basement, I watched the clock. At eight-thirty, I went live, everything online and recording as planned. Mike radioed me once to confirm I was getting the feed. Daniel started in on his meditation at nine, loud and clear.

I watched as members of the group aimed their laser pointers into the northern sky, following Daniel's instructions. My iM4ET app indicated that others were online around the world—200,000 watching the live feed. Daniel would be pleased. I kept my eyes glued to the screen.

"There they are," Daniel said over the feed.

Mike's camera focused on three lights in the darkness, tracking them as they grew brighter.

"Major event, everyone, major event," I heard Daniel say.

"Oh my," said one of the women, "they are coming towards us!"

Then I heard a few muffled screams. The screen went white just before the connection dropped. I did what I could to restore it, resetting the feed, making sure that we were still connected to the Internet. Everything seemed fine on my end, but then my radio chirped. I waited and it chirped again, then went silent. *Mike must be keying the radio*, I thought, only there was no transmission.

I called out, "Base Station to Echo Tango One, do you copy?" Silence. "Base Station to Echo Tango One, do you copy?" No response. *What the hell is going on up on the hill?*

I checked my iM4ET app. There was a blip over Missoula. I waited a minute and then went outside to see if I could see anything in the sky. The night was still, stars shining bright. No sign of anything.

I tried the radio a few more times and another reboot, but

no luck. I was just as perplexed as I was excited. What was going on up there?

Just after eleven, the Proxima Foundation vans came down the driveway. Daniel, Mike, Chester and the guests got out. Some sat on the ground and fumbled with their cell phones while some crawled under the picnic tables. A few people were still hiding in the vans. Most of them appeared to be missing some of their clothing. I didn't see any daypacks.

"What happened?" I asked Daniel as he stepped out of the van. He looked distraught, his shirt was untucked, and his jacket and one shoe were missing. Silently, he headed straight for the house.

I asked the same thing of Mike and Chester.

"Something happened," Mike mumbled.

"What?"

"Abduction."

Chester's eyes were glazed over; he was undoubtedly in shock. He stumbled down the path towards our pod.

Mike followed Daniel to the house. Moments later, Nadine came out of the house to run damage control. The people sitting on or under picnic tables and in vans were in a daze.

"We're getting out of here!" yelled one of the men. "This is not what we paid for!"

"Everyone just calm down." Nadine said. "You are not safe out here in the darkness. We need to talk about what's happened. Let's go into the meditation tent, it's warm in there." Nadine looked at me. "Ben, don't just stand there. Get these people some blankets."

I went into the supply containers and grabbed as many blankets as I could carry. When I returned, everyone had moved into the tent. Mike rolled in a cart with hot chocolate and tea. I distributed the blankets and helped hand out hot beverages.

Nadine said. "Now, we all just need to collect ourselves and talk about this."

"Where's Daniel?" asked Robbie, his teenagers huddled

under a blanket near him.

"He's inside, making some calls to the FAA and his government contacts. He'll want to talk with you, too. He'll want to document everything." She looked at me. "Ben, start taking notes." She addressed Mike. "Get these gas heaters going, now!"

I went to the office and retrieved a yellow pad. When I returned, people were yelling.

"I want to go home! Give us our keys!"

When Nadine saw me she, whispered in my ear, "Ben, I need you to do the relaxation meditation regimen, now. Get everyone to calm down. Center them."

"I'll do my best," I said.

"Good boy," she said.

I proceeded with the mediation exercise. "Breathe in, now breathe out." It seemed to work. Some of the women were weeping.

Nadine returned. "Remember, everyone, it's important that we do not talk to anyone about what has happened until we understand more. Daniel is investigating this and will be providing more information tomorrow. You are free to do as you wish tonight, but I hope that you will stay with us until daylight."

It was after two in the morning when I retired to my pod. The lights were still on. Chester was in his bunk curled up in the fetal position with pillows pulled over his head. Seeing him in this state made me terribly uncomfortable. What did he and these people go through up on that hill with Daniel? My thoughts went to my own abduction experience. Were alien crafts over us? Would they come back? Or was this a government abduction operation, too?

Exhausted, I drifted off to sleep.

23

EVERYTHING HAS CHANGED

Nadine summoned me to the house in the morning. I'd overslept two hours and expected a tongue-lashing for not clocking in and manning the social media sites. I checked Twitter and Facebook on my phone as I hurried up the hill to the house. There were thousands of video views and comments about last night's live-stream footage.

Mike was in his usual tank top and blue jeans with strapped sidearm when he answered the door and directed me to the back porch. Nadine was in a robe in one of the Adirondack chairs with French press steaming by her side. She spoke in her usual warm country twang. "Have a seat, Ben. Would you like some coffee?"

"Sure," I said, relieved she didn't seem upset with me. She poured me a cup.

"I want you to know I appreciate your help last night. You did a wonderful job calming those people."

"No problem," I said. "Is Daniel okay?" I took the coffee and warmed my hands around the mug.

"He's still resting, but he wants to see you. He needs your help with a press release about the abduction last night. You have time today to help him, don't you?"

"Yes, of course," I said. I wondered what shape Daniel

was in and what his press release would entail.

"There are a few things I want to talk to you about before you go to see Daniel. You handled yourself so well last night that we think it's time for you to become a regular employee with the Foundation. It has full benefits, and we can pay a little more in salary than what we pay contractors. How does that sound to you?"

"That sounds great," I said, thinking I could use the money and health insurance coverage. Inside, though, I was unsure about the commitment. I hadn't planned on working for the Foundation long-term, but then again, I hadn't really thought it all out.

"Good. I'll have some paperwork for you to sign later today, tax documents, and such. The articles you've written— you're going to have to rewrite them."

"I am? Why? Because of what happened last night?"

"Yes. This whole story about the EBEs is unfolding in real-time, and we've got to get the narrative right. It is important that we have a unified message. There's a lot of important work ahead of us. Daniel will have more to tell you."

I expected more press releases, media inquiries, and likely a plan for more abduction research. All were things that my skills could help with.

"You've been through a lot, Ben, just like Daniel has." Her tone hardened. "And let me tell you, if we can show that the government knew all along about the alien presence and the risks, we can sue the pants off of them."

The only lawsuit I'd thought of was the possibility of one from the people traumatized under Daniel's supervision. "Do you mean a class action suit?"

"Yes, the biggest one in history, cosmic in size. But we don't have to worry about that just yet. Keep quiet about a lawsuit, we don't want anyone to know our hand just yet. Just help Daniel for now." She glanced at her watch. "Daniel is ready for you. He's upstairs, the master bedroom at the end of the hallway."

I set my cup down.

"One more thing, Ben. What were you doing talking to that waitress yesterday at the festival?"

A sharp sting of anxiety shot through me. Mike or Chester must have spotted me with Brenda. "Nothing. She recognized me, and I said hello."

"You should stay away from her. You don't need to get your priorities confused right now. We need you focused on your work here with us. Helping Daniel is more important than anything else. Comprende?"

"Yes, of course," I said.

"You know, Daniel thinks of you as a son. He feels that way about Mike, too, of course, but you are different. You and Daniel are a lot alike, both smart, inquisitive, and so committed to revealing the truth of things." She smiled. "I feel the same way about you. You're like the son we never had."

"Thanks," I murmured, embarrassed and taken aback.

She smiled again. "Now go and see Daniel. Scoot!"

I headed upstairs, thinking about Nadine's job offer and her apparent disdain for Brenda. I assumed it still had to do with her Aunt Sally snooping around the Proxima Foundation. Still, I got the sense again that there was something *personal* about it, but what? A possible class-action suit against the United States government! Could people molested during abductions come together and sue the government for damages? Maybe, but there would have to be undeniable evidence that the aliens are here to harm and the government covered it up.

Daniel was lying in a rustic four-post bed under a handmade quilt with multi-color patches, his head propped up by two pillows. The curtains were drawn so the room was dimly lit by one lonely bedside lamp. An oil diffuser on an oak dresser was spewing out lavender and frankincense. Quickly, I took a detour into the bathroom. Beside the porcelain claw-foot tub was a counter with marble his-and-her sinks in it. A contact lens box read, *Deep Azure Colored*

Lenses. They had to be Nadine's, which explained the glowing blue tone of her captivating eyes. *Not a big deal,* I thought. *A lot of people make enhancements.*

After my bathroom visit, I softly approached the bed. Daniel's eyes were closed, and the blue tooth earpiece in his ear flashed in standby mode. Was he awake? An odd metallic object about the size and shape of a grape was on a plate next to a glass of water on the bed stand.

Daniel's eyes opened. "Hello, Ben." His voice was weak. "Pull up a chair and sit next to me."

I grabbed the chair from a small desk by the window.

He propped the pillows against the wooden headboard and sat up. "Thank you for helping out with things last night in my absence. We had a lot of upset people, didn't we?"

"Yes. What happened exactly?"

"It's not good, not good at all. I need to do a press release immediately. We should do a video. Do you have your phone?"

"Yes, always." I pulled it out.

"Let's do it right here."

He straightened up, drank some water, and cleared his throat. I got him in view and waited for his okay before I hit record.

His expression was dour. "My friends, I have important news. Extraterrestrial Biological Entities from the Proxima system abducted me last night with a dozen other people completing my viewing workshop. These beings were not government MILAB fakes. They were black-eyed Proximians."

The mere mention of the EBEs and their dark, empty eyes triggered me. My hands began to shake uncontrollably. I steadied the camera, keeping Daniel in focus.

He continued. "While I was on their ship, they revealed their true intentions to me. They are not our friends. They have come to do evil. My warning is serious and real. This is no joke. We must cease our contact protocols and all experimental projects immediately." Daniel's voice cracked.

"I'm exhausted and still in shock." Tears were forming. "Terrible things they did to me." He took a deep breath and gathered himself. "I'll be making more announcements over the next couple of days. Thank you."

He nodded, and I saved the video. "Get that uploaded to our social media sites immediately."

"I will."

I sat back to take it all in. Daniel was abducted and completely flipped his position on aliens. No longer were they angels here for good; they were now demons here to harm. I thought about the Phoenix lights and my father's link to the Aurora Project and MILAB. Were they government fakes or Proximians? I also thought about the voices I'd heard that had said, *We will be back for you.* My stomach tightened.

"When did they say they would return?" I asked Daniel.

"On or before winter solstice this year. I'm to be their liaison—under duress. They said if I try to resist or hide, they will come for me." He shut his eyes in agony. "Oh, this is terrible, Ben. There must be people in our government colluding with the Proximians. They must have been doing it for years, since before the 1990s. It's going to be difficult to know now what was a fake abduction and what was real, who is on our side or with the Proximians."

"This is like the TV show and movie *V.*"

"Except this is real, Ben, everything has changed." He pulled the sheets and quilt up to his chin.

I picked up the metallic object and inspected it. "What's this?" I asked, passing the shiny object under my nose for a quick sniff. The scent of musk and cinnamon triggered me.

Daniel was watching me. "They implanted that in my rectum, Ben. I force passed it this morning. It's a monitoring device, I've seen them before."

Aghast, I set the object down. "What are you going to do with it?" I asked, wiping my fingers on my pant leg out of his view.

"Post images and information about it on our website to

warn others. We need to be careful to tell people to pass them naturally—we don't want to get sued if people try bleach or cut them out. They're not magnetic or metal and won't show up on X-ray. I'm going to have our app development company build a new scanning app." He sighed. "It all makes sense now. They wanted me because I had been communicating with them for years. They have been grooming me for this, Ben. I suspect they took you recently because of your connection to me."

More questions came flooding into my mind. "What about the others last night? They were abducted, too."

"As collaterals— I don't know. What I do know is that the EBEs want to psychically enslave us all, tap into our consciousness, suck our energy, turn us into mindless automatons. They'll use us for gene harvesting and conduct social experiments on a mass scale. It's going to be hell on Earth, Ben, and we won't be able to do anything about it. We will feel that something is wrong, but the truth will be outside our awareness. We'll forget what we knew in the past. Our history will be modified for their self-serving alien design."

"Why are they doing this now?"

Daniel shook his head. "There's going to be panic and chaos, Ben. We need to move fast to warn the people of the world and their governments. I got people into this, so it's my responsibility to help them prepare. Things may fall apart in the weeks ahead, and people may die. Riots, full societal breakdown." He nodded, deep in thought. "Our mission now is to educate others about the risks and dangers of abductions and how to prepare for impending alien psychic attacks."

"What about the government? What will they do? Do you think they will finally acknowledge that the aliens are here?"

"I briefed my contacts at the Department of Defense this morning. I suspect that they will make a full disclosure any day now."

My investigative journalist instincts were returning. "Who'd you talk to?"

"My contacts are deep and high, Ben. They'll be strategic

about it, but with so much bureaucracy, I'm worried." His face lit up. "We got it on film, didn't we? Shit, live-streamed on Facebook. It must go viral."

"It broadcast last night, and I recorded it. The Foundation social media sites have been on fire all morning."

"Good," he said, "post my press release with it. Hashtag *alienwarning*."

"Having video and witnesses is a big deal."

"Yes, it is. This whole thing is more important than anything else in the world."

"What are you going to do next?" I asked as questions spun in my mind.

"Well, I'm not going to sit on my back porch and whittle a stick while all of this happens. I'm going to do another press conference and speaking tour, and I want you to come along and tell your story through the lens of what we now know to be true. Are you up to this?"

"Are you sure that I should go with you? There's a lot for me to do here. Maybe we should do some research on this first." I was thinking that I could do some analysis of the others' experiences.

Daniel shifted. "I need to show you something." He unbuttoned his pajama top to reveal his stubbly chest. At the center was a hexagon, red, bruised, and the same size as mine was. "It's raised, just like yours. I was wrong, so wrong." He teared up again. "I'm responsible for what has happened to you and the others. But we have shared experiences now, and that connects us at a cosmic level. I need your help now, my son. Are you with me?"

My mind was muddled with confusion and uncertainty.

"I assume the trip to LA is canceled?" I said.

"No, we're still going to LA for the interview. It's going to be a *60 Minutes Special* with a studio audience and broadcast live. We've got to get the word out about this. So much to do."

How fast he'd switched from emotion to all business! And how things had already been arranged!

"Are you sure that it is a safe to travel right now? I mean, is there a risk of…"

"Abduction? Yes. I'm not going to risk an entire plane full of people. We'll drive, and we'll have video cameras and sensors on the van. And regarding your article, you'll have to update it with what we know now."

"I can add something about what I witnessed last night…"

"…and what I'm telling you. The more press on this, the better. Time is of the essence now. Planet Earth can't wait."

Daniel made sure I uploaded his video before I left him. I still wasn't sure how I felt about going on a press road trip, but how could I say no? It was my job per my contract, and now with the full employee offer, it would be difficult to say no.

Just as I stepped off the porch, Robert Petulli came tearing down the driveway in a green MG Midget convertible, parked and made a beeline to the front door, paying no attention to me. Petulli demanded to see Daniel. Mike yelled at him to stay outside and called for Nadine. A moment later Nadine came to the door.

"What's going on? What is Daniel doing?" Petulli asked Nadine frantically.

"Everything is under control," Nadine assured him. "Daniel had to tell the world about what's happening. This comes as a shock to everyone, Robert. We are well aware of the implications, but we must accept that everything has changed."

"Why didn't he tell me earlier?" Petulli looked genuinely hurt.

Nadine glanced at me and then signaled Mike to get me out of there. Mike came outside to me while Nadine pulled Petulli inside and disappeared.

"Petulli just saw Daniel's post," Mike clarified.

"I guess he won't be working anymore on the transdimensional alien 3D printer," I said.

Mike shrugged, and we stood in awkward silence. A minute later, a calmer Petulli exited the house, got into his car and sped away, stirring up a cloud of dust.

24

UFO CELEBRITY

We arrived in LA in the late afternoon, and went to the Ritz-Carlton ABC's producers put us up at. We freshened up, then took a limo to the studios where we were directed to the green room. Robbie Spencer was there too, with his wife.

Daniel spoke to me in the mirror as makeup artists worked on our faces and hair.

"Excited, Ben?"

"Very much," I said, smiling.

"Good. I'll take the lead questions, but feel free to share your abduction experience. The public wants to know. Tell it just as you experienced it. Don't let the host or producers try any tactics to get you to feel any doubt. They do that for the ratings."

"I know something about interview techniques."

He smiled. "Of course, you do. The message we are communicating tonight is the most important in modern history. We need to be careful about the take-aways. We don't want to create panic, but we also don't want to downplay the significance of all of this. The safety of the world is at stake."

The make-up person finished brushing his cheeks and started in on mine. "I understand," I said.

My stomach tightened suddenly. Here I was, about to go

on TV to talk about an impending alien invasion. One part of me believed it to be true, another part of me was unsure.

After make-up, I went to use the restroom one last time. In the bathroom stall, Jack Clark called to tell me that several anonymous UFO reports had come in from Missoula over the weekend, and that he had watched the abduction video on Facebook. He'd acquired updated FAA flight data for the Montana area and wanted to ask me some questions. I confirmed I'd been at the Ranch at the time of the group abduction and I was about to go on *60 Minutes* with Daniel.

"I won't keep you," he said, "but I've got to tell you this. It took me forever to get the FAA data, but all of a sudden, there it was. I'm still reviewing it, but I've already found some interesting stuff—a large object coming in from the north around nine o'clock. Whatever it was, it was big, and it disappeared from radar within minutes, similar to what the data showed the night of your abduction experience."

"From outer space?" I couldn't believe I was actually asking that.

"I can't be certain. The object appears and then disappears. We'd need to see more radar data to know the path of the object, but my friend said it wasn't available. The data's also sketchy in regarding altitude, but it seems to suggest that it was fairly low altitude, meaning less than 5000 feet. Missoula is just over 3000 above sea level, so it was *really* low. I've only seen data like this once before, and it was determined to be inconclusive. We never figured out what it was. But there is more. I looked back through the data to see if I could find other similar objects, and there's nothing."

"What about in April?"

"I don't recall seeing anything abnormal. What are you thinking, Ben?"

"Around the time Sally Jensen was murdered. She claimed to have seen a large triangular object with lights at low altitude, but it doesn't sound like the data supports it."

"Well, no, but I'll keep looking into it."

"Is there any way the data could have been tampered

with?"

"I've asked that question many times, Ben. It's not outside the realm of possibility that there could be omissions from the data, or additions. Conspiracy types have made those accusations since the 1970s. We know for a fact that the U.S. Department of Defense censors local flight data around Area 51 and a few other spots."

"So there could be a cover-up, if they wanted to?"

"Yes. But this is one of those areas where once you start digging, doors close fast. Everyone in the UFO business knows this. I'll try to get more information and I'll let you know what I find out. Good luck on your show. I look forward to watching it when it airs."

Back in the green room, Daniel asked, "You okay, Ben?"

"Yeah. Just some pre-show jitters." I didn't say anything about Jack Clark.

He smiled. "You'll be fine, just follow my lead."

Soon, an attractive production assistant with blond hair and red lipstick, in a white skirt and heels, led Daniel and I down a long hallway to the live stage and told us where to sit. The host, Gerald Bennett, came on set and shook our hands, and sat down. He was dressed to the nines with thick greying black hair and perfect bleached teeth.

I watched for the red light on the camera, worrying that my sweat would show through the make-up. Another production assistant hand signaled we were live.

Bennett started right in. "Tonight, we have Daniel Byrne, attorney and cofounder, along with his partner Nadine Byrne, of the not-for-profit Proxima Foundation, an organization that until recently, has been helping people make contact with beings from out of this world. Yes, extraterrestrials. We also have Ben Davenport, Pulitzer-nominated investigative journalist who wrote the article calling Daniel Byrne a charlatan but now claims to have had his own alien abduction experience. We also have Robbie Spencer, one of Daniel's students who is also an abductee. Just a week ago, Daniel and a dozen people attending one of his extraterrestrial viewing events were allegedly abducted, taken aboard a ship, and eventually returned to Earth, all of which was broadcast on live social media. The video has since gone viral. We will show you the clip in its entirety tonight." He looked at Daniel and me. "I understand this was the first time anyone ever live-streamed a UFO or alien abduction. Is that correct?"

"It is," Daniel said.

"So, Mr. Byrne, walk us through what happened on the night you claim to have been abducted."

"Thank you, Gerald, for having us on the show. As many of you may know, I have been teaching people for more than a decade now how to make contact with *benign* extraterrestrial entities by means of a specialized type of meditation. We've believed we were doing a good thing in connecting humanity with ETs—but I was wrong. They are not friendly."

"And you say this because of what happened to you the night you were abducted?"

"Yes. About a dozen of us were on a group-sighting event. Everything seemed like it had on other nights we had run the protocols, but then, well, we were abducted, taken aboard..."

"Hold on, Daniel, let's have a look."

A large TV monitor offstage lit up with the footage from that night. The backs of silhouetted heads crowded the bottom of the screen.

"Walk us through what we are seeing here," Bennett said.

Daniel followed the footage.

"I'd just given instructions regarding contact protocol. Here, we're waiting to see them appear."

The lights appeared, and Mike's camera focused as he tracked them.

"It looks like three—no, seven lights in the sky. Are those the ships?" Bennett asked.

"It's one large craft," Daniel said. "We watched it hover for a minute, then the lights got brighter and the wind gusted up. The giant craft moved towards us. See the three bright lights with a larger, red light in the middle? Then a beam of white and green light shot down, then came the swirling winds."

The video showed what appeared to be two people being lifted up into the light by a beam. People in the studio audience oohed and ahhed. Just then, a figure bathed in purple-white light appeared to be looking with interest at the camera.

Bennett looked at Daniel, then at me. "Is that an alien?"

"Yes, it is," Daniel said, "that is a grey from Proxima b."

The video went dark. Bennett looked at us. "This is not a hoax? This is the real thing?"

"This is the first ever live video recording of an alien abduction," Daniel said.

"What happened next? You were aboard their ship?"

"Yes, absolutely," Daniel said. "Next thing I knew, we were all on a large interstellar craft in a room with mirrored walls. Everything seemed to be moving in slow motion as if we were all swimming underwater."

"Then what? What did they do?" Bennett asked.

"Horrible things," Daniel said, for the first time avoiding the hosts' gaze. "I was separated from the others and taken somewhere else where they stripped me naked, strapped me down onto a table, then spoke to me, telepathically. They said I'd been selected because of my ability to communicate with them through meditation. They said they'd come again to destroy our current government and take our resources."

"You're serious?" Bennett asked.

"Deadly. This is real," Daniel looked not just serious but somber.

Bennett turned to Robbie. "You remember this?"

Robbie nodded. "Yes. We did the whole meditating thing, like normal. Then, I don't know, a few minutes in, we saw several bright lights that got closer. Then...I don't remember exactly, but it felt like something hit me on the side of the head. When we woke up, Daniel was maybe fifty feet away, putting his clothes back on."

The audience gasped, at last getting that this might not be TV fantasy.

Daniel looked out at the audience, though we couldn't see them. "Then we were returned to Earth. When I came to, I found myself, along with the others, on the ridge we'd been on in the beginning. My clothes were strewn about on the grass. We led everyone off the ridge and headed back to the ranch."

"Sounds traumatizing," Bennett said with some compassion, then turned to me. "Ben, you were watching the whole thing from the ranch?"

"Yes, I was controlling the social media feeds."

"What did you think was happening?"

Daniel's eyes were on me. I glanced at him for a second, then back to Bennett. "I saw what you just saw on the video. I was...Shocked."

"I can imagine," Bennett said. "And you've had your own abduction experience. Tell our viewers what happened to you."

After I told my story in brief, Bennett asked me, "What did the aliens look like? Were they the same?"

"They were humanoid greys with small, dark eyes, no whites to their eyes..."

"The Proximians, same species," Daniel clarified.

He looked at Daniel. "So for years you've been saying that the ETs are our friends and we should be communicating with them, but now you have completely reversed. You now feel you were wrong."

"Yes, I was wrong, but now I am now awake which is why I'm here tonight—to get the word out, even if it puts me at risk."

"At risk? What do you mean?" Bennett asked.

"There are parts of our government that want to keep me silent, but I need to warn the public. We must demand government action by all governments of Earth to disclose the threat that alien visitation means."

"Why do you think they haven't landed in force, like in the movies?"

Daniel sat forward in his chair. "That's a good question,

Gerald. They are intra-dimensional and can appear at will. I've always been right about that. The question is, how physical are they? Or are they attacking psychically?"

"They said they would return. To you, or should all of us be worried?"

"They didn't say when. Tomorrow, next year—we don't know yet. But their intentions are not good. They will experiment on us, and perhaps release an AI-run artificial virus to infect our brains and modify our DNA. You think previous infectious disease lockdowns were big—just wait and see what's coming. This is why I'm getting the word out now."

"And you've told the government about this?" Bennett asked.

"I've called my contacts. But like I said, not all of the government is open to making what's going on public. I can't emphasize this enough, Gerald; I need to warn as many people as possible. We are going to be doing a press release and social media campaign like we've never done before."

Bennett was shaking his head in awe. "Incredible, Daniel." He turned his attention to me. "Ben, you too were told you'd see them again."

"Yes, they said they would come back for me."

Bennett looked into the camera. "We'll hear more from Daniel and Ben after the break."

The break was a flurry of activities: makeup checking our sweat factor, lights and cameras being adjusted. Despite what Daniel was insinuating, it was TV as usual.

The red light on the camera lit up and the host was back at it. "I'm here with Daniel Byrne and Ben Davenport of the Proxima Foundation. Both claim, and have video to prove it, that aliens are visiting Earth and their intentions, they believe, are not friendly."

Somberly, Bennett looked at me and then Daniel. "So what's next? Are we going to be invaded? Are they going to blow up the White House? What can we do to prepare to defend ourselves, Daniel?"

Daniel looked into the camera. "We're studying the problem right now. I'm serving as a special liaison to the US government and consultant to the UN. The Proxima Foundation will be offering an Alien Preparation Kit. It will be available for download at our website. All proceeds go right back into research."

"What is in the Alien Preparation Kit?"

"An instruction manual, an infrared camera, and a spray."

"An alien spray?" Bennett enjoyed a moment of levity.

"A repellent," Daniel said without a sign of levity.

"Like for mosquitos? What is it made of?"

"Its ingredients are proprietary. We are wrapping up testing now. The infrared camera helps us to see them."

An image of the kit flashed on the screen, its logo a red circle with a large alien head in the center. The alien spray was new to me.

Daniel went on. "Abductees are of use to them. They've been coming here for tens of thousands of years. Like scientists injecting monkey brains with human DNA and making them smarter, we too could be a lab experiment."

"Like SIMs the video game," I interjected lamely.

Daniel didn't even glance at me. "They are interested in our evolution, watching our social behaviors, everything. Now I wonder: are they here to devolve us?"

"I assume the military and Department of Homeland Security now know about all of this."

"I've been in touch with the government, yes. I just hope they take me seriously so as to take the proper precautions."

"Well, Daniel, and Ben, this is a compelling story, and you have video, which now millions of people have watched. But you have your skeptics too, and David Ellis, editor of *Cynic* magazine, is one. I understand that you have a restraining order on him."

"David Ellis, like other so-called cynics, is a jealous person. I'm not a psychologist, but it seems that he may have some deep-rooted issues. I don't know what else to say, and I won't say any more, for legal reasons," Daniel said.

Bennett obviously could say a little more.

"A few years ago, Ellis challenged you to a televised debate right here on *60 Minutes*, and asked if you'd be willing to take a polygraph test. Would either of you be willing to take a polygraph test now? To prove to us that this is real, or that at least you believe it to be real," Bennett asked.

Daniel nodded. "Sure, I'd be willing to take one, under controlled conditions."

"How about you, Ben?"

Famous abductees had undergone polygraphs tests in the past—Travis Walton, Whitley Strieber. "Sure," I said.

"Any chance for peaceful co-existence with the Proximians?"

Daniel paused. "I wish there was, but no, there isn't."

"Wow, Daniel and Robbie and Ben, this is incredible. You've all been through a lot and have awakened to the true intentions of these aliens. I want to thank you for sharing your story with us."

"Thank you, Gerald," Daniel said, smiling into the camera.

After the show, Spencer returned to his family while Mike, Daniel, and I had beers in the hotel bar. We clinked our together and Daniel announced, "Now the world knows about what has happened. This is big."

I nodded. "How many people do you think will watch this?"

"Twenty million," Daniel said, placing his hand on my shoulder. "You're famous now. You'll probably be getting a lot of calls."

I wasn't looking forward to that. "Are you serious about doing the polygraphs?"

Daniel took a sip of his beer. "Sure, but it's not necessary. We have a preponderance of evidence. We just have to keep getting the word out."

I wanted to ask Daniel about David Ellis, but I was afraid he'd become irate. Later in my room, I did an Internet search for Ellis. I listened to a few podcasts where he argued against theories of pre-Ice Age advanced civilizations, Big Foot, and alien presence on Earth. According to Wikipedia, the white-haired middle-aged publisher had a Master's degree in history and had been adjunct faculty at the University of Oregon. He seemed to have been quite a celebrity up until three years ago, apparently when the Byrnes got the restraining order on him. There were a few references to articles he'd done about Daniel Byrne and the Proxima Foundation, but the articles themselves were gone, wiped clean from the Internet. *Cynic* magazine published print versions up to about three years ago, but apparently their finances tanked after the Byrne's lawsuit. I found an image of a cover whose headline read, "Here We Go Again: Cosmic Guru Lures Followers, and Their Wallets, to Mountain Top."

David Ellis was clearly Daniel's nemesis, and although Nadine and Daniel were successful at muzzling him with a restraining order, he still seemed to be under Daniel's skin. I didn't see any jealousy of Daniel, just disbelief.

25

PSYCHOTRONIC

Somewhere between LA and Bakersfield, Jonathan Mahue called. Mike glanced at me in the rearview. I spoke as softly as I could. Jonathan said he'd seen me on *60 Minutes* and had intended to call me weeks ago but was too busy being a father and husband. I asked him if he ever got around to looking into the iM4ET app.

"I did, and I looked at the code. It's really strange: the app seems to have the ability to access the transmitter on phones. I can't really tell what it's doing."

"What does that mean exactly?"

"It means the app can be controlled remotely to transmit signals at variable frequencies. I've seen this only a couple times in special engineering applications that require FCC approval. I'm just not sure why this kind of app would need such a feature. Do you have any idea why?"

"It's supposed to detect the presence of alien craft. Maybe they designed it to transmit a beacon or something. But accessing the transmitter…Can the transmitted frequencies be harmful?"

"In theory, yes. I have no way to tell how much power it can transmit with the equipment I have. You'd need a specialized lab. There are limits to how much energy it can transmit, though; the FCC regulates it—*specific absorption rate* or the *SAR*, it's a measure of how hot your brain becomes when using a phone. Your phone transmits when you call someone, but someone else controlling that feature, maybe at high energy levels…I wouldn't want to be too close to a cell tower, either."

"Cancer risk?"

"Not just that. All kinds of studies prove that electromagnetic frequencies are harmful to the human body—mess with brain frequencies, sleep, tweak DNA—those kinds of things. Remember all the conspiracy stuff about the 5G rollout? There's real science behind millimeter waves. Why would they use the SAR if there wasn't an effect on the body? To cut to the chase, Ben, if it was my phone, I'd uninstall that app immediately. I've never heard of these developers—*Such and Such LLC.* Any idea who they are?"

Daniel looked back at me from the passenger's seat. "Everything okay, Ben?"

I nodded. "Just talking to a friend who saw us on TV last night." I rolled my eyes, to show just how annoyed I was by my newfound celebrity.

Daniel returned his eyes to the road. I resumed but spoke softer than before. "Jonathan, I think the primary developer subcontracts the development out, but I'm not sure."

"Might make sense to figure out who exactly they are," Jonathan said. "I'll see what I can find out."

"Thanks for telling me about this."

"No problem, my friend. Interesting times we're in, and it looks like you are right in the middle of the whole UFO thing. It's getting crazy with the preppers here—the toilet paper is flying off the shelves. You really think aliens are coming? Government hasn't acknowledged it yet."

"I don't know. I really don't, but there is definitely something going on."

I ended the call and tried to make sense of why did the Proxima Foundation's app had access to the phone's transmitter. How did it get approved? Was the app causing my headaches? Was it messing with my mind, maybe causing hallucinations? Was this why I felt better when I wasn't around my phone or when it was powered off?

I thought about Jonathan's question about if I believe the aliens are coming. I had said *I don't know* spontaneously, which made me think that this was my real thought about Daniel's alien arrival, regardless of what I said under the bright lights of live TV the night before. One thing was for sure; *Something had happened to me on the ridge, and my perception of reality had been altered since.*

We stopped for lunch at a truck stop. After we got our sandwiches, I took the opportunity to ask Daniel about the iM4ET app.

"You mentioned on the show that you've been working on updating the iM4ET app. When will it be ready?"

"The developers are working on it. They should have it done in a couple days, and we'll get it up on the app stores by the end of the month."

"Who are the developers? Do you trust them?"

"Yes. It's the same developer company we used before. They're building the new app to my specifications. Petulli is helping, too, as are a few other experts I know. Nadine handles the contracts with the developer. I can't think of their name at the moment. Nadine has taken care of everything."

Of course. Nadine was in charge of the business side of everything.

Mike had his eyes on me. Only half-joking, he said, "He's sounding like a reporter again."

I plowed ahead. "How do we know that all of the people who downloaded the iM4ET app have removed it or received the software update? If someone didn't get your message or is in an area without a network connection, aren't they at risk of calling in the Proximians?"

"The auto-update should take care of it, Ben. That's what the developers told me when I asked them the same question." Daniel turned to look at me. "Are you worried?"

"Maybe a little," I said, noticing Mike still had his eyes on me.

"Well, that's another good reason why we need to get in as many conferences and radio shows as possible, and as soon as possible," Daniel said. "And let's get those updates on social media tonight. Got it, Ben?"

"Sure thing," I said, sitting back, wondering if I could find out about the app developer from Nadine. My concern about its transmission effects on me was increasing. I wanted answers.

Before sunset, we stopped for the night outside Portland. After dinner, I went online in my room's Wi-Fi, not for social media updates, but to research mobile phones and mind control. I found an article published by MIT on psychotronics, directed energy technology for sending beams of electromagnetic energy directly to people's brains and bodies for purposes of control. In the 1970s, the Soviet Union tested "radiosleep" whereby an entire military unit was induced into sleep by directed radio waves. The US Department of Defense tested a similar system during the First Gulf War in the early 1990s to command thousands of Iraqi forces to surrender. I found a reference to something called "voice-to-skull" technology tested by the US Army, and the US patent for it. US Representative Denis Kucinich had introduced HR2977 in 2001 to force the President to engage in negotiations to ban psychotronic weapons. Nothing had come of it. Interestingly, Kucinich claimed to have witnessed a UFO above the Puyallup River near Mount Rainier in the early 1980s. His political career had basically ended after he came out about it during a presidential debate in 2008.

An article in *Scientific American* about how low-level radiation from cell phones could alter brain waves and thus behavior struck a chord. Several studies showed that electromagnetic fields emitted by GSM mobile phones, under experimental conditions, impacted working memory, slowed response times to tasks, and even impacted short-term memory. Another study from 2008 showed that cell phone radiation would not only disrupt brain-wave patterns during a phone call but for a long time after a phone was shut off. I turned my smartphone off and decided to get one of those pre-paid flip phones that didn't have any apps on them. I discovered EMF shielding hats—the "tin foil hats"—curtains and other materials to line your home with to keep radio waves out. A couple studies stated that the shielding hats actually worked. I got onto Amazon and found one called DefenderShield EMF Radiation Protection Beanie. The description said it could block up to 99% of wireless EMF & 5G radiation up to 10 GHz. The reviews were 4.5 stars. I ordered one to be shipped to an Amazon Locker in town. I also ordered some xylitol gum and a three-pack of Hanes boxer briefs too.

Exhausted from our day on the road, I reached for the light when the room's phone rang. It was Nadine.

"Ben, why is your phone off? I've been trying to contact you."

"The battery was low and I… I'm really sorry."

"You need to keep it on, Ben, especially now with all that Daniel has going on. I also need you to be monitoring the social media feeds. That is an expectation for your employment with the Proxima Foundation. No slacking when on the road. Don't let it happen again, okay?"

"I understand. I'm really sorry."

Her voice softened. "Oh Ben, what am I going to do with you? You need to post what Daniel tells you to, every day. Do you understand?"

"Yes, ma'am, I'll make sure everything gets done."

She knew I had the power off. *How did she know?* Probably because the phone wasn't transmitting. Was that why she was so insistent that I keep it on all of the time? For tracking, or something even more sinister?

26

TOILET PAPER

Back at the ranch, I went to work on press releases, updating
social media, and creating online advertisements for Daniel's
new apps and alien repellent kits. I snooped around the
Proxima Foundation network folders to see what financial
files I might find on the iM4ET app. I found some old
invoices, most of them related to grounds maintenance, the
big circus tent, and some bids for work around the
compound, but no documents related to the app or anything
else suspicious. But why would I? Nadine and Daniel
wouldn't leave something like that out in the open for some
employee to discover. If there were records, they'd likely be
locked away in Nadine's private office or in the Proxima
Foundation vaults.

Nadine dispatched Mike and me to the big box store in
town in the morning. She had an extensive list: wine, toilet
paper, rice, beans, canned food—obviously preparation for
alien arrival or social unrest, whichever came first.

The store was packed with preppers.

"We should have done this before we did the TV show,"
Mike said jokingly, handing me a walkie-talkie. "I don't want
to stay in here any longer that we need to. We still want to get
to the gun shop."

So Mike went to the dry goods, I to the produce and wine section where I ran into Brenda in her t-shirt and jeans, her raven black hair in a ponytail. Miniature dream catcher earrings hung from her ears.

"Hey, Brenda."

"Well, if it isn't the UFO celebrity," she smiled. "Going to sell me some of that alien repellant? Maybe recruit me into your pyramid scheme?"

I grinned. There was that Brenda snarky attitude that turned me on so much. "I have some information. Do you have a minute?"

She slung a case of Bud into her cart. "I don't have any time for bullshit. What is it?"

I looked over my shoulder for Mike. Luckily, the water and toilet paper were on the other side of the warehouse. I told her about my conversation with Jack Clark regarding the FAA radar data.

Right away, she got defensive.

"So you don't believe my aunt saw something? You think she was crazy?"

I rolled my eyes. "I didn't say that. I'm just saying that according to Jack Clark, the data is inconsistent, like it may have been tampered with."

"By who? The government?"

The radio chirped before I could respond. "No toilet paper," Mike barked. "We're going to have to stop at Home Depot."

I pulled the radio from my pocket. "Copy."

Brenda smirked. "Should have stocked up for the mind-control alien invasion, when you had the chance."

"Listen, Brenda. I'm still trying to figure things out."

She eyed me suspiciously. "So you're back to being an investigative journalist now?"

"I think what happened to your aunt is important to figuring out this whole UFO thing." I told her what my friend Jonathan Mahue had said about the iM4ET app and its apparent ability to cause cell phones to transmit on alternate frequencies.

"So?" she asked, shoving a second case onto her cart.

"I did some research and found evidence that the frequencies used may have to do with brain functioning, cognition, hallucinations, and maybe mind control. The technology may have something to do with the strange things that have happened to me and your aunt."

"You think the alien app is causing people to believe that they are seeing UFOs and aliens?"

"I know it sounds crazy, but I think there's something important about these frequencies."

She paused and reflected for a moment, then said, "You should talk to my uncle. I've been researching things, too. Maybe we can meet up and I can show you what I've found."

I was interested in what her uncle had to say, and in seeing Brenda again. "I would like to talk with him, if you can arrange it."

Mike interrupted on the radio again. "Where the hell are you? I'm going to the check-out, I need the card."

"Copy, I'll be right there." I looked at Brenda. "I've got to go."

"Of course, you do. Muscle boy needs you." She smiled.

"When can I see you again to meet your uncle?"

She threw one more case of beer into her cart. "I'm off tomorrow. Why don't you meet me back here in the parking lot at noon? You can follow me out to his place."

Fleetingly, I thought about Nadine's warning regarding Brenda. "I'd have to come up with some reason for being in town again. They're prepping and have me working extra hours. They might get suspicious if I come back too soon."

"Say you need to come back to town for something you forgot to get. You're a smart guy. I'm sure you can come up with something."

I looked at my cart, then pulled out the bottles of wine and put them back on the shelf. "Okay, I'll meet you here at noon. Let me give you my new number." I pulled out my new flip phone.

"What's with the flip phone?" she asked.

"No apps, no tracking, and no weird frequencies, just in case." I sent her a text so she'd have my alternate number, then left for the checkout line.

Back at the ranch, Mike and I unloaded the supplies, then I retired to my pod to work on more social media updates and a refresh of the Foundation Wikipedia page. Nadine called me to her office an hour later.

"Ben, where's my wine?"

"I forgot. I'm really sorry. The stores were crowded, and Mike insisted we needed to get going to Home Depot for toilet paper. Stuff is selling out fast."

She sighed. "It's no surprise. We have an impending alien invasion on our hands."

"I'll go back to the store in the morning for the wine. I need to get an oil change anyway. Do you need anything else from town?"

"No, but go with Mike, and take Chester with you. He needs to get out more. And don't be in town for too long, we'll need you back here in the afternoon. Daniel has more work for you."

That evening after dinner, Mike, Chester and I discussed plans for the next day. Mike had ordered an AR-15 from an online dealer, and the required two-week waiting period was up. He wanted to pick up his rifle, and then have a red-dot sight fitted. Chester wanted to go with him. I'd drop them off and do my errands. I figured with a long line of preppers at the gun shop, I'd have plenty of time to meet with Brenda and her uncle.

27

CROP CIRCLE

I dropped Mike and Chester off at the gun shop the next morning, grabbed the wine, picked up the EMF beanies from the Amazon Locker, and then met up with Brenda in the big box store parking lot. She insisted on taking one vehicle, so I climbed into her Jeep Cherokee stick-shift 4X4.

"What's with the beanie?" she asked.

I pointed to my new hat. "Oh, this? It shields EMF frequencies."

"A tinfoil hat?" she smirked.

"Call it what you want. It really does block all kinds of frequencies bouncing around. I researched it."

She glanced at me as she pulled out. "Is it working?"

"I think so. I got you one too." I pulled her hat out of the packaging and placed it on her lap. "Maybe try it on later?"

"Sure. Well, I found something out, too. I looked into the escaped con who supposedly killed Aunt Sally. Department of Corrections records are publicly disclosable, so I requested them. His name is Jimmy Durst and convicted for killing his wife and a business partner. He was transferred to a federal facility up in Toole County, Montana a day after my aunt was murdered. He couldn't have done it." She pointed to a stack of papers on her dash. "Take a look."

I shuffled through the documents. "Holy shit, Brenda, this suggests he was a patsy. They didn't cover this up very well."

"I told you there was something not right about it. But it doesn't explain who killed her." Her voice cracked a little as she turned onto the highway.

"Were you close to her?"

"Not really," she said, wiping her eyes with the palm of her free hand. "We'd had some disagreements over the years. She didn't get along with my mother at all. They were opposite personalities, I guess. My family is pretty upset, though. I wish she'd never gotten so obsessed over the UFO thing."

"I'm interested in what your uncle has to say. Will the kids be their?"

"They are with my mother today. My mom and I have been helping my uncle." She down-shifted and turned onto another road. "What's it like living out there on the ranch, anyway? Do you all sleep on bunk beds in those shipping containers?"

"We don't have bunk beds. I do their press releases and social media, stuff like that. It's pretty normal, I guess."

"And you're free to leave when you want but worried Nadine Byrne is suspicious of you going into town. That should tell you something."

"You mean it's like a cult?"

"It is a cult."

I hesitated. "Nadine doesn't want me associating with you. She says you are…" I paused, realizing my words might offend her.

But she was already offended. "What does she know? I'm not just some going-nowhere small-town waitress. I'm about to graduate from U of M with a pre-law degree and dual major in psychology. I'm supposed to go law school next year. I killed the LSAT and am just sticking around for a while to help my family and save some money. Then my aunt was murdered. That's why Nadine Byrne doesn't want you talking to me and asking questions because the culties had something to do with her murder. Something's not right about the Byrnes. You should be investigating them. You work there—you're in the perfect position to do just that. You call yourself an investigative journalist, don't you? That means you research stuff. Get to the bottom of it."

In a way, I was already doing what Brenda was saying—digging for information—finding sources—asking questions. I was a Pulitzer Prize-nominated journalist with more than twenty investigative stories under my belt, a Master's degree in journalism from Northwestern, and a press pass, for whatever that was worth.

She pulled onto a dirt road leading to her uncle's property. On one side were grazing horses, on the other an expansive view of rolling hills. A late model maroon Ford F-150 was parked out front of a modest single-story ranch house. We got out of the jeep and Brenda rang the doorbell. A moment later, Mr. Jensen answered. He was in his mid-forties with a beard and a cane. He'd thrown his back out and was now on disability. We sat in his living room, drinking soft drinks. His voice was country gentlemanlike with a bit of a smoker's rasp.

"So how do you know my niece?" he said, popping the top of a Coke.

"We met at Ramblin' Joe's a couple of months ago. I was doing a story on the Proxima Foundation. Maybe you read it?"

"Yeah, I read it. I was always suspicious of those UFO people, just like Sally was."

I glanced at the framed photo of his deceased wife standing next to a horse and smiling in jeans and riding boots. He followed my eyes.

"Sally loved horses, but she had developed a fascination for UFOs too—an obsession really."

"How long had she been investigating UFOs?" I asked.

"Ever since we saw one, right out there." He pointed out the window, "a late evening last summer. We had just come in from feeding the horses when we saw a formation of lights drifting across the sky, then moving off to the west at super

speed. We'd never seen anything like it. Then with those
UFO people in the area, she started investigating. Like I said,
it became an obsession. She'd investigate on her own time,
but was worried about being ridiculed at work. She was very
professional."

"I saw some of her reporting online. She was good," I
said, hoping to cheer him up.

He nodded. "Damn FBI. I don't understand it, why they
kept everything so secret about the investigation. I think they
were out here to seize what they could, not to investigate.
Doesn't seem right to me."

"Brenda mentioned they took your computers. Why do
you think they did that?"

"I don't know for sure. Maybe they were looking for clues
as to whom she might have been connected to. Funny thing
is, Sally had this theory about electronic interference. She'd
been complaining about a strange humming sound. She was
fascinated by the connection between UFO sightings in the
area and a facility up on Solomon Mountain, over in Lolo
Forest," he said.

"Facility?"

"Yes, an old Air Force installation. About a year ago, they
took down the old radio tower that was there and put up a
camouflaged cellular phone tower—you know, the ones that
look like trees. Never seen it myself, but a few guys I know
who hunt in the area say it's there. She thought it might have
something to do with the humming sound."

"Did she describe what the humming sound was like?" I
asked.

"A buzzing, kind of like crickets in late summer, up in
pitch at times. I thought she was coming down with tinnitus
or a neurological problem. She went in to the doctor a couple
times, but she checked out fine."

Was there a connection to what I'd been hearing? "When
did she start hearing this buzzing sound?"

"Last summer, after the tower went up."

I glanced over at Brenda. "Did she ever meet the Byrnes?"

"She did. She went over there one time to talk with Daniel Byrne. She wanted to ask some questions about UFOs. His wife—what's her name?"

"Nadine," Brenda answered.

"Yes, Nadine Byrne told her to get the hell off the property. She must have known that Sally was going over to that area at night. Sally was found about five miles east of the ranch. I don't think she'd been over there before, but she was chasing after that light she saw in the sky. I don't know what she saw, and I don't think it was a hoax, regardless of what the news people say."

"Did Sally ever used an app called iM4ET from the Proxima Foundation?"

"Not that I'm aware of." He thought for a moment. "Come to think of it, she did mention something about an app on her phone that had something to do with UFOs. I'd let you look at it but the police never returned her phone to me. Why? Is that important?"

"I don't know yet. It's something that I'm investigating."

"Did Brenda share that phone message from Sally with you? The one where she was chasing the light?"

"She did," I said.

"That was the last message from Sally." Mr. Jensen held an absent gaze for a moment. "She was a good woman, and a good reporter, too." His voice cracked. "This shouldn't have happened to her." He drew a deep sigh. "Brenda said you might be interested in seeing where they found Sally. Maybe it would be helpful for your investigation."

I hadn't really thought about the crime scene since I visited the sheriff's office. I looked at Brenda.

"I'd like to see," she said, looking at me. "You have the time?"

I checked my flip phone. It was almost two. "I've got an hour or so."

"You can follow me so you won't have to come back here," her uncle said. "You need the four-wheeled drive."

We followed Mr. Jensen down into a valley, up on a high

plain, and then along a ridge on a gravel fire road. At the top, we exited the vehicles. He pointed east. "It was over there where they said they found her. Best you walk from here."

"You coming, Uncle John?" Brenda asked.

"No, this is far enough for me. I'll wait here. You go on." Brenda and I walked a few dozen yards up a grassy road until we found yellow crime scene tape still wrapped around two trees. Brenda stopped near the tape. I could see the grief in her eyes, so I gave her some space. I continued to look around, inspecting the area and imagining where Sally Jensen had her last breath. On the far edge of the area, a trail of flattened grass went over a knoll, possibly a deer or elk run. Curious, I headed down the trail.

"Where you going?" Brenda shouted.

"I want to see where this goes. Maybe I can get a view of the Air Force installation across the valley," I said.

Brenda followed me. Over a knoll and ahead was a massive circular clearing about 30 yards in diameter. Brenda came to a stop behind me. I must have been in a daze for a minute or longer, transfixed by what I was beholding.

"Is this what I think it is?" she asked.

"Appears to be a crop circle," I said. I kneeled down and touched the grass. It was pushed over in a perfect spiral—too perfect. I walked part of the perimeter, then cut across to the circle's center. Was it here when they found her, or was it a hoax played by locals? I pointed to the east. "Over there somewhere is where the so-called facility is."

Just then, the wind gusted up and my ears began to ring. It grew louder and increased in frequency. I felt a powerful zap to my head, as if a migraine switch had been flipped. With the palms of my hands at my temples, I bent over—a futile involuntary reaction to the now fierce, pulsating pain.

Brenda, saw my distress. "What's wrong?"

"I'm not sure. Something's not right," I groaned. "I think we should go."

She helped me stand up and restore my bearings. We backtracked to the vehicles where I vomited. By the time

Brenda got me to my car, the ringing was gone.

"There's something up with the cell tower and the mobile app," I said, reaching for my flip phone.

"Who are you calling?" Brenda asked.

"Jack Clark. Maybe he knows something about this."

Jack answered. I asked him if he knew of the link between electromagnetic energy and UFO sightings.

"There have been stories about UFO sightings around power lines and power plants, sure. Nuclear power plants and nuclear missile silos, definitely. You remember the famous story about Maelstrom Air Force Missile silo, don't you?"

"Something about a UFO shutting down the missile?"

"Shut down ten ICBMs. Scared the shit out of a lot of people back then."

"What about cell towers? Any link there?"

"Not that I'm aware of. Why are you asking?"

"A cell tower near the Valley of the Moon is supposed to be on old Air Force installation or something. Know anything about that?"

"There were Cold War era early warning facilities all over the country. I don't know about one out there." He paused. "Wait a minute. Where did you say this tower was located?"

"On the north side of Solomon Mountain, just south of Valley of the Moon Road."

"Hold on just a second," he said. We could hear him shuffling papers. "I'm looking at a book called *The Confidential Frequency List* from the early 1980s. It says it right here: AFG10 Air Force Station, Missoula. What are you thinking, Ben?"

"Sally Jensen reported seeing lights in the sky out here and thought it might have something to do with the facility, which apparently has a new cell tower on it."

"Interesting, Ben. I'll look into it."

I thanked Jack and ended the call, then looked at Brenda. "Your aunt had the iM4ET app, too. I told you there was something going on with it."

"Maybe you should find out who developed it."

"I asked Daniel about it. He said Nadine handled the business side. The credits say Such and Such, Inc. I looked it up and didn't find anything."

"Follow the money. Someone had to pay for it, right? Either it was the Foundation or someone else," she suggested.

"Daniel said Petulli was involved with the app development. Maybe he bankrolled it."

"Can you ask him?"

"We're supposed to go up to his place to get the Transdimensional 3D Printer. He seemed really excited about showing me his Dobson. Maybe I can get some time alone with him."

She smirked. "To see his Dobson?"

"It's a telescope."

"And what is a transdimensional 3D printer anyway? Are they selling plastic alien artifacts in the gift shop or what?"

"Daniel thinks he can send and receive things from across interstellar space telepathically."

"Well, can he?"

I held a straight face as best I could. "He received what appeared to be a giant penis."

"An interstellar cock? I bet he did," she laughed and so did I.

When we made it back into town, she pulled up next to my car. "Why don't we find a way to get together in a few days?" she suggested.

"It will have to be next this week. Daniel, Mike and I are driving to Las Vegas for a conference."

"Driving all the way to Las Vegas?"

"Daniel is afraid to fly. He's worried about getting everyone abducted while in the air."

"Well, have fun in Vegas with Alien Man and Muscle Boy." She smiled. "What happens in Vegas stays in Vegas."

"Ha, ha," I said, "I'll call you when I get back. Remeber to use this number from now on. I don't trust the regular smartphone." I looked at her one last time before getting out of the Jeep. "You sure you don't think I'm crazy?"

She grinned. "Maybe a little."

28

DR. PETULLI

The next morning, Daniel sent Mike, Chester and me up to Petulli's to retrieve the Transdimensional 3D printer equipment. Petulli let us enter. His hair was a mess, suggesting we'd awakened him.

"The lab is unlocked, do what you have to do," he said sleepily.

We went downstairs and surveyed equipment we needed to haul out. Mike gave the orders, and we went to work. Petulli sat on one of the office chairs and watched. After a couple of loads out to the van, I asked Petulli if he was still willing to show me the Dobson.

He paused for a moment. "I suppose I could."

We headed out of the basement lab and ran into Chester and Mike on their way back down.

"Mr. Petulli is going to show me the Dobson. Will only be a few minutes. Daniel said it was okay," I said.

"Don't be too long, we've got more work to do when we get back."

I followed Petulli down the hallway to the large stairway leading to the second floor. Just as we began our ascent, his tabby cat came shooting down past us.

"Watch out, Mr. Snickles," Petulli called.

"So how long have you known the Byrnes?" I asked.

"We go way back. Nadine represented me in a case almost a decade ago. I met Daniel through her, and we've been friends ever since."

"What kind of case?"

"A patent issue with one of my inventions, the Quantum Vacuum Oscillator. The Patent Office said that the Department of Energy already had a claim and that mine wasn't possible. Nadine helped me prove that my design was unique. She's been my lawyer on such matters since then."

"What's a Quantum Vacuum Oscillator?"

"The QVO is a device used for creating anti-gravity fields. A propulsion system."

"I see." Now I knew what their connection was, and that Nadine must have some expertise in technology. "You must be upset about us having to destroy the 3D printer—all the effort you put into building the thing."

"Nadine and Daniel have convinced me that it could be dangerous. I trust Daniel on this. He's concerned that the Proximians could bring in a Trojan horse weapon."

I thought of the phallus-looking device they'd shown me—hardly a weapon of mass destruction. "Could they do that, anyway? I mean, just drop something down through the atmosphere?"

He looked at me inquisitively. "But what if they had tricked Daniel? We could have finished the device and found out that it was really an interstellar transport device for a planned invasion."

"A Star Gate?"

"Exactly. Nadine asked me to help make the modifications to the new scanning app and the alien detection app. It got my mind off of it."

"So you're helping to fund it?"

He looked at me. "This is serious work. The Byrnes are going to save the planet from disaster."

"Do you think the app will work? Alert the presence of aliens?"

"I do. It uses a special electromagnetic field to detect ships. I'd been working on the technology for years. Now it has a real-word application."

"How does it work?"

"The software uses the receiver in modern cell phones to detect fluctuations in the electromagnetic field of radio transmissions in the Sub 6 GHz Band. By using my machine learning algorithms, we've taught the software to detect patterns and filter out natural fluctuations of those caused by human-made objects such as airplanes, helicopters, and even drones. It is the first time that such technology can be in the hands of everyday people. The 5G networks have made it possible, and it came just in time. Now we just need to get it out to everyone."

Petulli led me into the observatory that was in the south tower of the mansion. There was a large telescope in the center of the room.

"This is my 42-inch Dobsonian. I built it myself. It's motorized and has a precision optics lens. It's a spectacular telescope."

I began examining its features. "How far can you see with this thing?" I glanced out the windows, seeing Daniel's ridge and the Lo Lo forest peaks to the south.

"It's not how far, but how long back in time. Most of the stars that you see in the sky gave off their light millions of years ago. I've taken photos of objects that existed 10 million years ago. The skies aren't quite as dark as they used to be in this part of Montana, but not bad."

I smiled. "Ever seen a UFO with it? What about the craft from Daniel's viewing events?"

"This is for looking into outer space, not terrestrial viewing. And yes, several times. I got a few of the Oumuamua object when it came through. NASA said that it was only visible with infrared, but that wasn't true. They also said it was the first known object entering the Earth's solar system from interstellar space. That's not true either."

"Was it a ship of some kind?"

"Yes, a mothership, passing through. That is what Daniel thinks, and I do, too. It looks a lot like the craft that Daniel received through the E3DP device."

"Did you take any photos of it?"

"Of course, I did. You are welcome to come over here at night sometime when I'm viewing. I can show you the photos, too."

We shook hands. I stepped outside and Mike was waiting.

At the ranch, he pulled the van into one of the large garages.

Daniel came out to give instructions regarding the Transdimensional 3D Printer.

"Destroy it, boys."

Mike and Chester grabbed sledgehammers and smashed the device into smithereens. Pieces flew across the dirt.

Back at the pod, I spent some time looking at Google maps, trying to place the location of the suspect cell towers. There was a pattern: the location of Daniel's viewing spot was in the exact middle of a triangle, Petulli's to the North, The Proxima Foundation Ranch to the east, the Station to the West. A perfect, equilateral triangle! There had to be a link to the cell towers, the iM4ET App, Sally Jensen, my headaches, UFOS, and maybe even abduction experiences.

29

USEFUL IDIOT

The 37th Annual UFO Conference was at the luxurious Marriot Resort and Spa Las Vegas. We checked in, and after a fresh-up, went to the main talk. Daniel, Dr. Mazzotti, one of the Navy aviators from the UFO sightings in the 2000s and I sat in chairs on the stage. Priscilla Mense, a conference organizer and our panel moderator, introduced us. I gazed out at the audience of more than three hundred, consumed by stage fright plus embarrassment about the entire UFO thing. *60 Minutes* had been bad enough, but this live audience was huge. And I was more conflicted than ever about my experience. Was it really an alien abduction, or was it a psychotic state induced by electromagnetic waves emanating from the iM4ET app?

Daniel kicked off the discussion, covering the need to take precautions and his role as liaison with the Proximians. Mazzotti talked about alien probes, and the aviator about the sightings off the East and West Coasts. Everyone agreed there was a link between the military sightings and Daniel's warnings about imminent alien arrival. Reluctantly, I spoke about my own abduction experience and my work at the Proxima Foundation.

During the Q & A session, a plump middle-aged woman

in glasses stepped up to the microphone. "This question is for Mr. Davenport. Why do you think they abducted you and were you ever abducted before?"

"I have no idea why I had this experience," I said. "I've never been abducted before—that I'm aware of, anyway."

Daniel leaned to my ear and whispered, "Tell them about your connection to me and your work at the ranch."

I stared out at the bright stage lights and mumbled, "I've been helping Daniel with his work, so that might have something to do with it."

"Its most definitely why," Daniel said, "and Ben witnessed to the Phoenix Lights back in '97. We know now it was the Proximians over the American Southwest that night, and he was likely scanned and identified then, if not earlier. You see, the Proximians are very selective about who they commune with. They need to know who they can trust, who is capable of understanding them, and who can work with them. Who they choose to abduct and communicate with is intentional and calculated."

Another woman asked Daniel, "Does the alien repellant really work, and where can I get some?"

"From the Proxima Foundation website, and yes, it works," Daniel said.

"I'm wearing it right now," Priscilla added.

A person in the front row dressed in a giant green alien suit with antennae pretended to be gagging and choking. She slumped dramatically in her chair, and half the crowd erupted in laughter.

Daniel was not pleased. "This is a serious matter, everyone. They are coming, and we must prepare ourselves."

Daniel went into more detail regarding preparation and what the Proxima Foundation was doing to help the government. I noticed that my inner voice, the one that I'd not heard from in months, was starting to question Daniel's story about the Proximians. His pushy sell of Proxima Foundation products, and focus on himself as the one with all the answers about the off-planet entities smelled like bullshit. But why were former government officials, seemingly credible and reputable, on board with his story? And, not one person from the audience was challenging him, no inquisitive press, no unconvinced scientists—no one. I was conflicted. Loyalty to Daniel, something had happened to me on the ridge outside Yakima, but what?

That evening at dinner, documentary film producer named Mark Brunsky and Priscilla joined us at our table in the hotel restaurant. Daniel introduced me and we ordered appetizers and drinks. Brunsky looked excitedly at Daniel through his shaded glasses. "The documentary's going to be huge, Daniel. Netflix just got in on it, which means we can spend more on production."

"Release before December?" Daniel asked.

"Yeah, it's doable. Summer is the best time for documentaries, but the holiday season is second best. I've been working on some story boards I'd like to show you." He pulled out a notebook. "We want to do a re-enactment of the group abduction—it will be a great visual."

"No," said Daniel firmly, "no reenactments."

Brunsky was surprised. "Why not? It will be great!"

"I've never seen them done well, not in *Communion*, not in *Fire in the Sky*. I want this to be a think piece. What you don't see is more frightening than seeing it. You know what I mean?"

Brunsky nodded. "Sure, like Blair Witch. So what scenes are you thinking of?"

"Visuals of the aliens, close ups. Do you know any good CGI people? It's got to look like the real thing."

"Yeah, we can do that. We should do some wide shots with you walking on the hills in Montana. We'll use drones." He flipped to another page of sketches.

Daniel looked over the sketches. "I like it. We can have some dramatic music here, maybe analog synthesizers, maybe some crossfades."

"Sure," said Brunsky, "interviews too, I presume with some of the folks who were up on the ridge with you."

"Mike, of course." Daniel looked at me. "And you too, Ben, you're in it as well."

"Great," I said, although I had no interest in being in his documentary.

"If we can get the film out at the same time as the book, all the better," Daniel said.

"Doable," Brunsky said. "We'll wrap up preproduction this week and get everything ready to ship for the shoot. I'll have my people set up a time to start when it's good for you."

Daniel nodded. "Excellent. Whatever Nadine says will be fine."

I couldn't help thinking about all of the Armageddon religious cults selling videos and books about the end of the world for $19.95. If the end is nigh, why bother making a profit?

The next morning, I checked out and waited in the lobby for Daniel and Mike, going through my messages.

A man in cream-colored khakis and a blue sports jacket over a checkered white shirt appeared out of nowhere. "Hi Ben, may I join you?"

"Sure," I said automatically. It was David Ellis, editor of *Cynic* magazine. He plopped down on the sofa across from me and we stared at each other for an awkward moment. I was unsure what to say and worried about Daniel's reaction if he saw me with his nemesis.

Ellis smiled. "So you are in deep now with the Byrnes. How's that going?"

"Fine, I guess. What are you doing here?"

"I like to attend these conferences from time to time, keep up with all of the latest claims, reveries, and ruses of the UFO community. Couldn't miss this one, not with all the buzz about an alien invasion."

A light bulb went off. The tone of his voice and choice of words were very similar to the anonymous McMinnville phone call.

"It was you, wasn't it? You called me when we were in McMinnville."

"Me?" He smiled even more. "Yes, it was. I was at that conference too, in background, like I was at this one. I made the call because if I hadn't, you'd be writing part of your story about me. You probably know about the defamation suit and restraining order. Maybe I wanted to add a little mystery, like Deep Throat in Watergate. I was expecting you to dig more than you did, but at least you got the hoax on film. That was impressive. Did you look into the locals who did it?"

"What locals?"

He raised his eyebrows. "Sounds like you didn't investigate like an investigative journalist should. I'm willing to bet that if you find out who they are, and who got them up to it, then you'd know more about who's behind all of this."

I thought about the men who had roughed us up in DC and my questions about Congressman Young. "So you're saying there are more involved than just the Byrnes? The government?"

He looked around. "There's always conspiracies hovering around government UFO fakes. I suspect this is bigger, and yes, it involves the Byrnes, but I can't say exactly what they are up to."

"What do you think about Daniel's announcement? Do you think…"

"…aliens are coming?" He smiled. "Every regime in power has its chimera. They use whatever unseen threat they can conjure to control the population to achieve their ends. Funny how whatever crisis there is seems to dissipate or be conveniently resolved at just the right time—until the next threat is fabricated."

Ellis's cynicism about the government was sounding like Daniel's months before. "So this Proximian alien thing is a false flag?"

He shrugged. "Maybe it is, maybe it isn't, but a man-made crisis seems a lot more plausible than humanoid life forms coming from a planet 4.24 light-years away to commune with a washed-up lawyer."

"Daniel thinks you work for the CIA. Any truth to that?"

He chuckled. "I've been accused of being on the CIA's payroll many times. No, that's complete and utter bullshit. I'm just an independent journalist and publisher, a truth seeker, and truth teller, like you."

"Why didn't you do the story?"

"I think you know the answer to that, Ben. If I'd published a story involving the Byrnes, I'd be in serious legal trouble. You see, a lot of people hate me because I expose bullshit. It can cost them money. But the truth is those same bullshitters need me. Having someone like me criticizing them gets them attention, and the publicity is good for them. It feeds their egos and can make them more money. The Byrnes are no different. But you are in a position to get to the bottom of this, unless you signed a nondisclosure agreement. Did you?"

"I might have." I was embarrassed, knowing I should have paid more attention to Nadine's contracts, but I saw no harm in asking questions now. "Jack Clark suggested I talk to you, and I probably should have months ago."

"Jack Clark—he's a good man. A shame he stays neutral—he could be exposing more of the bullshit than he does, but he has to keep the MUFON coffers fed with memberships. He's forced to fake his interest in every late-night call from a lonely farmer, truck driver, or crackhead who's got a sighting report to file. Sure, he has to be selective about some of it—it would hurt MUFON if they published data on every bullshit UFO sighting. Some years back, I got Jack to share all of MUFON's UFO report data. A colleague at the University of Michigan and I tested some machine learning prediction models to see if we could find any patterns in decades worth of data. You know what we found?"

"What?"

"Nothing. In fact, the only thing we found was that people were more likely to report spaceships and alien beings similar to the latest blockbuster movie that year."

"So, you don't believe in aliens at all, even with the Navy videos and all the stuff that's come out recently?"

"I don't know what those pilots saw, but what I do know is that the military, ours or someone else's, tests new weapons. Maybe those pilots weren't briefed on it." He leaned closer to me. "Ben, who's to say government contractors aren't testing some new tech on their own in international waters? Just think about what we do know they are testing, like the Northrop Grumman X-47 drone, the new B-21 Raider stealth bomber, and hypersonic weapons. Now think about what we don't see, yet. These objects could also be the Russians or the Chinese. We know that the Chinese have used laser technology to project images into the sky. Or better yet, our foreign adversaries are deploying drones in order to get our military to turn on radar and other sensing equipment so they can gather intelligence on its signature."

"It's a possibility," I said. "What about Congressman Young? Know anything about him?"

Ellis smiled. "Now you are going deeper into the rabbit hole." He spoke softer. "The Congressman is most definitely linked to black projects involving the Aerial Threats Program and Space Force. Interesting isn't it—the connection between the Congressman and your so-called abduction experience? What do you think?"

"I was doing a story on cell towers and the Congressman's involvement in the Yakima Reservation lands. I'm wondering if there's a link, perhaps with 5G technology and effects on human brains for mind control. Do you have any opinions on that?"

He paused. "The government has played around with weapons like that for decades, and so have companies like Raytheon and Lockheed Martin. Are you thinking there's a link to the Byrnes?"

I pulled up the image of the 5G tower from the Lo Lo forest. "Ever seen one of these?"

He glanced at it. "Yes, I've seen a few of those images. Where is that?"

"Montana. The Valley of the Moon. I got it from a reporter who's dead."

"You mean Sally Jensen?"

"Yes. What do you know about her?"

Ellis shrugged. "I read the news. She had an interest in UFO sightings, and I'm willing to bet she had to have come across the Byrnes."

I kept a lookout for Daniel and Mike. "What the news didn't report was that she also had an interest in a mysterious cell tower located on the edge of the Byrne ranch property. Maybe she thought there's a link with the UFO sightings. It's just too much of a coincidence that she was investigating these things and then ended up dead so close to the Proxima Foundation land."

Ellis thought. "Interesting. Sounds like you are back to being an investigative journalist. It would be interesting to know more about the cell tower. But if it is there, wouldn't it be registered by the FCC?"

"It's not. I checked. It appears to be military, not commercial."

"Where are you going with this tower thing, Ben?"

"Maybe it is making people hallucinate—on purpose."

"CIA mind control?" He snickered. "*Nuit d'apocalypse?* Do you know what that was?"

I had come across the story in my Internet searches. "Yes. In 1951, the Special Operations Division of the CIA tested LSD on the village of Pont-Saint-Esprit, hiding it in their bread flour."

Ellis nodded. "It was the MKNAOMI biological warfare program. Hundreds of people experienced the same hallucinations, and seven died."

"So what do you think about the possibility of a mind control operation here involving cellular technology?"

"I'm not saying there isn't some truth to your theory, as history demonstrates, but who needs sophisticated mind control technology like that when there's social media? Control what people see and don't see and use psychology and dopamine rewards for their clicks, shares and likes of disinformation. The masses of everyday people are unwitting useful idiots to the corporate elites."

"I suppose you're right," I said, "and combined with the mainstream news media…"

"…it's full-on propaganda bombardment every day, whether people are aware of it or not. It's brilliantly sinister, if you think about it."

Something caught Ellis's attention across the lobby, his face turning sober. Daniel was at the front lobby desk and Mike was behind him with the luggage.

"Well, I should be going," Ellis said. He slid to the edge of his seat and extended his hand. "Nice to meet you in person, Ben, and good luck, especially if you find a link to Sally Jensen. It won't be easy, though. Go down the UFO alien contactee path and no one will take you seriously, although, the media narrative has changed in favor of aliens as a threat."

"Can I call you if I have any questions?" I asked him.

"Sure. You can find my office phone number on my website. Leave a message. I don't have a cell phone."

Ellis slipped out the hotel entrance with a stream of tourists and conference attendees.

Daniel and Mike approached. I could tell by Daniel's flat expression and eyes on me look that he'd seen me with Ellis. "What were you doing talking with him?"

"He sat down next to me, I didn't plan on it," I stammered.

Mike dropped the bags and stared me down while Daniel continued. "What did you talk about?"

"Not much. He just asked about how things were going— what we were planning to do next."

"And?"

"I mentioned that we are planning a couple more conferences. Doing more press and things."

"What else?"

"That's it," I said.

"That man is an asshole," Daniel said, "stay away from him. We still have the active restraining order. Looks like he just violated it. Wait until I tell Nadine. She's going to be pissed."

"I'm sorry, Daniel, I didn't know who he was until he started talking to me. He seemed a bit off. I want nothing to do with that guy."

"He's strange, all right, not trustworthy at all. A fake journalist and a hack." He gestured to Mike to grab the bags. "Come on, let's go. We have a long drive."

30

THE PLEDGE

Brenda's doublewide was fifteen miles from town, surrounded by foothill grasslands and nestled in a valley. The sun shone bright above in the crisp air.

"Come in," Brenda said at the door, her hair in a ponytail. "I was just making some tea. Would you like some?"

"Sure," I replied. A strong desire to hug her came over me, but she slipped into the kitchen before I could.

"Make yourself at home," she said over her shoulder.

I removed my shoes, coat, and EMF shielding beanie, and went into the living area. Soft music played on a Bluetooth speaker, and a peppermint-scented candle flickered on a scratched-up coffee table.

"Do you take milk with your tea?" she asked over the sound of the teapot's whistle.

"Straight will be fine." I let my eyes snoop about while she fixed our beverages. Books on a shelf, a laptop on a small desk, a few family photos in frames, and to my delight, no sign of a dude anywhere. I went over to the bookshelf, kneeling to inspect the books—Hobbes, Locke, and Emerson. Impressive. I pulled out the Emerson and opened it to where she'd placed a bookmark. Illusions.

She came out with two mugs and saw me with the open

book. "Ever read that?"

"No. Should I?"

"You should," she said.

I joined her on the ragged old sofa, setting Emerson on the table. I filled her in on what I'd learned from Petulli about the iM4ET app developer, and how Daniel made us smash his transdimensional 3D printer.

"I told you," she said. "They have him fooled like all the rest of those people that hand over their money to them." She sipped her tea. "What else have you found out?"

"Can I see your laptop?" I asked. "I want to show you something."

I pulled up Google maps zooming into the Valley of the Moon and the fuzzy spot where the tower station would be. I ran my finger along the outline of the triangle, point to point. "Your aunt was found right here, on the edge between the ranch and where the tower station is. She knew the humming in her head had something to do with the cell tower, and your uncle said she had the iM4ET app. I'm certain there's a link, and it's affecting people's minds. People have been talking about electromagnetic mind control experiments for years. Even Daniel knows about MKULTRA. You know about MKULTRA, don't you?"

Still looking at the Google map, Brenda said, "You mean CIA mind control experiments from the Sixties, right? If there was something like that going on, wouldn't Byrne be manipulated too?"

"I don't know yet, but I'm leaning towards the possibility that he is under control, just like everyone else. In the original MKULTRA program, the CIA programmed words to subconsciously trigger people into doing things. Maybe they are using electromagnetic waves to cause hallucinations and as triggers. What other plausible options are there?"

"Well, there's either a secret CIA mind control operation going on, or aliens are coming to Earth to fuck us all up, or the Byrnes are con artists. It seems like the Byrne con is the simplest explanation."

I agreed with her logic, but not quite.

"But all things are not equal as far as the evidence goes. We've got proof there's something going on about the iM4ET app, and we know there's something going on with the cell towers. Even your Aunt Sally thought there was something going with the cell towers, remember? And then there's my abduction experience. Maybe it was just a hallucination. I'm just starting to think that maybe I've been a victim of a mind control experiment too. And the voice I was hearing in my head—maybe it was to spook me into going to the Byrne's ranch. By the way, that EMF hat I bought—it seems to be working. The ringing in my ear has all but left. So what does that say about electromagnetic experiments around here?"

"But if mind control electromagnetic waves were transmitted on a mass scale, wouldn't the effects influence the people doing the influencing? It's just like those chem trail conspiracies—why would the world elites manipulate Earth's atmosphere if they and their families have to breathe in the same air?"

"Because they can direct the electromagnetic waves locally with mobile devices so only people in the immediate proximity are controlled. It could be that both smartphone apps and cell towers are being used—phones for single person influence, and cell tower beams for groups of people. It's possible."

"But you don't have any hard evidence yet, certainly nothing that would hold up in court." She sighed. "One thing's for certain: control and manipulation of others is behind all of this, no matter which scenario is the truth."

I looked at her. "I ran into David Ellis in Las Vegas."

"Who's David Ellis?" she asked.

"The *Cynic* magazine guy, the person the Byrnes have a restraining order on. He suggested that if I found out who paid off those kids who were blamed for the UFO hoax, then I'd know the answer. I should try to interview those kids, if I can find them."

Brenda thought for a second. "My uncle probably knows who those boys are. He knows everyone in town. I'll call him."

She was right: he knew the name of one of the boys and where both lived.

"I'll go with you," Brenda said, "The boys might trust me more than they trust you."

"And you are hot and we are talking about teenage boys here," I added.

She rolled her eyes.

I had another idea. "Let's talk to the manager at your aunt's TV station. He may know something, too."

"Good idea," Brenda said. "I'd like to know what the station shared with the investigators that wasn't released to the public."

We talked for a while longer about various topics, including future plans and our families. We had some things in common: Brenda grew up without her father around—just a stepdad whom she didn't relate to at all. And like me, she was an only child. I wondered if that had anything to do with her strong-willed independence and the loneliness I sensed. Her eyes lit up when she talked about finishing college and going on to study criminal law. She wasn't sure where she'd end up living after law school, but she knew she'd eventually have to leave Missoula. Her loyalty to her family impressed me, and so did her steadfastness in getting to the bottom of Aunt Sally's murder.

She asked me why I became an investigative journalist and if I enjoyed revealing societal injustices. I told her that I didn't get into it to be become an activist: I was a journalist because I believe in the *Fourth Estate*. Uncovering wrong doing and corruption for the benefit of society is what drives me, not other political objectives. She nodded in approval.

I told her about what little I remembered of my father and how his life and connection to what was happening to me now remained a mystery. I remarked on how strange it was that Brenda and I crossed paths and how we shared a twisted connection to the Byrnes. It felt beyond good to talk with her so openly, and I was inescapably falling for her.

Our meeting came to an end all too soon and we agreed to meet the following weekend.

As soon as I returned to the ranch, Daniel summoned me to the camera studio to produce a new video.

Daniel cleared his throat and began; "Greetings, my friends. I am taking a pledge that I hope you will take with me. I pledge to advocate for and acknowledge all lived experiences and identities of every earthling and alien life form, intelligent or not. I pledge to devote myself to ongoing self-reflection, education and knowledge-sharing to better myself and our communities here on Earth and everywhere. I pledge to be an example of establishing open and inclusive environments. I pledge to constructively share all experiences and information gained from others, including our off-Earth comrades, to inform the way I interact with all others. Thank you."

I stopped the camera as he smiled widely.

"That felt good, very good."

As I put the equipment away, I wondered about Daniel and his commitment to his beliefs. A *Don Quixote of La Mancha*?

31

PRANKSTERS

I met Brenda in the Home Depot parking lot and got onto her Cherokee. The first boy's house was a rundown two-story on Missoula's east side. Blinds covered the windows and a four-foot rusted chain link fence enclosed the small yard. When I knocked, I could hear a huge dog barking ferociously from inside. A beer-bellied middle-aged man in a t-shirt opened the door holding fast to a pit bull's collar.

"Is Jared here?" I asked.

"Who's asking?" he growled.

"I'm Ben Davenport, a journalist, and this is my assistant Brenda. We're doing a story on UFOs sightings and I…"

"He's not interested in talking with you," the man said, ready to shut the door.

"Who is it, Dad?" a squeaky pubescent voice said from inside the house.

"No one," the man shouted, the dog still straining to get past his legs to get at Brenda and me.

"I just want to talk to your son about the UFO hoax story," I said. "He's not in trouble or anything. I want to hear his side of what happened."

"Did you not hear me the first time? We're not interested to talking to any more reporters."

"It will only be a few minutes," Brenda said.

"No!" He slammed the door.

Brenda and I then went over to the second boy's house, fifteen-year-old Jared Simpson in a nicer part of town. His mother answered the door.

"Yes?"

"I'm Ben Davenport, a journalist doing a story on UFOs. I'm hoping to talk with your son Trevor about the UFO hoax incident he was involved in. I'm just trying to get some information about how they did it for a story I'm working on."

"We're not looking for any more publicity. He's gotten enough already."

"What if I told you that I don't believe he was behind the incident reported in the paper?"

She paused and looked me and then Brenda. "What newspaper did you say you were with?"

"We're independent," Brenda said.

I pulled out my press credential card and showed her.

"Look," she said, "my son has already talked to the local news channels about the drones. I don't think this is good for him, you know what I'm saying?"

"I understand, ma'am, but I'm hoping for just a few details. I don't think the local press did a very good job with the story."

She stared at me. "You're the guy who was on the TV show with that Daniel Byrne, aren't you? And you did that story on the UFO hoax."

"Yes, that was me."

"I don't think it's a very good idea for us to be associating with you. All of this crazy UFO stuff. I don't need my son getting involved in this anymore than he already has. I'm sorry. Goodbye, Mr. Davenport."

Brenda and I headed back to the car. "My first attempt at interviews in more than three months and failure," I said. "Maybe I can try again in a week. Journalistic persistence often pays off."

We were half way back to the Home Depot parking lot when my phone chimed. It was an Facebook message from Jared.

Saw you at my house. I want to talk to you. Meet me at the Skate Park near the river in 30 minutes.

I showed Brenda the message. "He must have heard me and his mother and found me on Facebook. Do you know where this skate park is?"

"Yeah, all the kids hang out there after school. Let's go."

When we got to the park, we waited on a park bench. I watched for a teenager who resembled the image I'd seen online. At last, a tall, skinny blond kid rolled up with a backpack slung over one shoulder.

"Are you Jared?"

He kicked up his skate board and held it. "We weren't even out there that night. We were here."

"So you weren't even there? Someone must have told you to say it was you, right? Who was it?"

"Two dudes in a jeep. One of them gave us a thousand dollars each if we said we did it."

"What did they look like?"

"Short hair."

"An East Coast accent like from Boston? Body builder?"

"No."

"Skinny? Blonde hair with sunken eyes?"

"Nope, two dudes, man, lookin' like they were in the Army or something."

"Had you seen him before or since?"

"No. When I asked, he just said he wanted to mess with those people who watch UFOs."

"When and where did they approach you?"

"Right here. We skate here all the time." He dropped his skate board on the ground and kicked it up again. "I'm only telling you because I saw you on TV. Are you really sure the aliens are coming?"

"I don't know," I said, "We're trying to figure some things out."

"I gotta go. Promise not to tell anyone that I told you this."

"We promise," I said.

He threw his board down again and rolled off into the darkness. I looked at Brenda. "Well, I guess Daniel was right: Someone from the government wanted me to think it was a hoax. But why?"

"Maybe to get you more involved," Brenda said. "It's getting late. Why don't you come out to my place later this week? We can discuss this more."

We made arrangements, then she returned me to the Home Depot parking lot. Not long after I arrived at the ranch, Nadine called me up to the house. I hoped to hell she hadn't found out about Brenda and me investigating.

I stood in the doorway of her office as if reporting to a military commanding officer. "You spent a lot of time in town this weekend. Is everything okay?" she asked.

"I just had some errands, oil change and stuff."

"You seem distracted lately. Is something on your mind?"

"Maybe I'm just nervous about the Proximians coming. I wanted to stock up on some medications and things, too."

She nodded. "That's understandable. Everyone is on edge right now. Daniel needs you more than ever, and I need your head in the game, representing the Foundation and all that we do for humankind. You can do that, right?"

"Yes, ma'am, I'll do my best."

She smiled. "I know you will." She slid a small cardboard box across the oak desk to me. "I have something for you."

I opened the box and removed the packaging. Inside was a Blue Tooth headset, identical to the one Daniel used.

"For your phone, Ben, so you can stay connected while you work. You can keep it all of the time."

"Thanks," I said. "I'll get it set up right away."

She smiled widely. "Good boy. Oh, I do have some horrible news."

"What?" I felt whatever it was in the pit of my stomach.

"Remember David Ellis? The police found his car

abandoned on a highway just outside of Las Vegas. They found his body this evening. It appears to be suicide," she said coldly, watching me closely.

I was in shock but trying to seem unfazed. "That's terrible news." Did he really kill himself or was he killed?

Nadine sighed. "The guilt must have finally caught up with him. May his soul rest in peace."

When I got back to the pod, I looked for news articles about Ellis's death. One AP read, "Skeptic David Ellis Found Dead in Desert." His body was found in a rural, area of Clark County, on the edge of Death Valley National Park. His wife reported him missing after he didn't return from the Las Vegas conference. A handgun was found with his body, but no suicide note. From my journalism experience determining suicide as cause of death can take weeks or months. It didn't seem right. I went over the conversation I had with Ellis in the hotel lobby. Did he really shoot himself or was he snuffed out? Why drive hundreds of miles to a UFO conference and then shoot yourself on the way home? I shot Brenda a text with the news:

(Brenda) *Did he seem depressed to you?*

(me) *He seemed level-headed when I met him. But I think he may have been killed. CIA?*

(Brenda) *Or he killed himself because of the lawsuit. The Byrnes wrecked his career.*

(me) *But why now? Doesn't feel right. I think there's more to it.*

(Brenda) *Maybe, but you never know what someone's internal mental state is.*

I knew she was right. How do you really know what's going on inside someone's head?

32

SALLY JENSEN

Nadine had me make a run to the FedEx store to drop off some packages the following day. Given that Brenda and I hadn't had time the day before, I stopped at the Channel 4 TV station on the way back and asked to see the station manager Robert Shaw, about a story, flashing my press corps ID. The station had reported the boys drone hoax, so I figured he'd be interested in more. Shaw was paged, and a few minutes later a middle-aged man in a tweed sports jacket was shaking my hand. "What can I do for you, Ben?"

"Remember I called you earlier this year about Sally Jensen?"

"Yes, I remember. I also saw you on *60 Minutes.* Interesting story."

"I'm still on the Sally Jensen story and want to ask you a few questions, if that's okay." I searched his eyes for any signs of apprehension. If there was a government cover-up of Sally's murder, maybe they'd gotten to him.

"I'm not going to be in the story, am I, Ben?"

"No, sir, this can be completely off the record. I'm just trying to understand what Sally Jensen was doing with all the UFO stuff. As you know, I'm interested in the topic."

He nodded. "Well, she asked about doing a story on the

Proxima Foundation folks. We were not interested in covering UFO stories at the time, but she kept pressing on it. We let her do one short report a year ago. I don't know why she was so obsessed." He looked at me to measure my reaction.

I grinned. "I suppose if you experience something otherworldly, a person can get a bit obsessed. Do you know if she ever went out to the ranch? Maybe to do an interview?"

"Not that I'm aware of. But I think she met Daniel Byrne at a coffee shop called Bigfoot Java in town."

"When was that?"

"Last fall. She used it as background for the story she did."

"What about cell towers and mobile apps? Did she have any interest in that?"

He looked perplexed. "Cell towers? Come again?"

"You know, 5G technology."

"I don't think so, Ben, why do you ask?"

"One of her family members said she had an interest in cell towers. Maybe as background for her story on UFOs?"

"That's new to me," Shaw sighed, "but we'll never know, will we? She was a good reporter. The Montana Morning Magazine hasn't been the same without her. We really miss her here at the station."

"What about Jimmy Durst, the convict the police say killed her? Did she have any connection to him that you know of? A story, maybe?"

Shaw looked me in the eyes. "Not that I'm aware of. Why did he take her up onto the ridge and torture her like that? Maybe he had his reasons, but it doesn't make a whole lot of sense to me."

"I've been thinking the same thing," I said.

We talked for a few minutes more about Sally. Then he walked me out to the lobby. "Do you really believe in this UFO stuff? The contact with extraterrestrials?"

"I'm not sure. I'm investigating. Do you believe in it?"

He scoffed and smiled. "Not really. I think it's all just a cover-up for technology the government is testing. Drones. I don't know."

When I got out to my car, I called Brenda.

"You're not going to believe this," I said excitedly. "The station manager said Sally met with Daniel for an interview. They met at a coffee shop in town."

"What coffee shop?"

"Bigfoot Java. Know it?"

"Yes. Holy shit, she met with Daniel Byrne? She didn't tell my uncle about it. I wonder why?"

"I'm going there now to see if anyone working there saw them or knows anything else about her meeting with him."

"I'll meet you there. I can take an hour off."

When I arrived at the coffee shop, Brenda was already in line. We ordered lattes. I asked the barista if she had been working there last fall. She had, and after a moment she recognized me. "Aren't you the guy who was on TV with Daniel Byrne?" She smiled. "You were abducted by aliens, right?"

Brenda and I exchanged glances. I could hear her calling me UFO celebrity now.

"I was abducted, yes, then invited her to sit down with Brenda and me for a moment. She agreed, so we three sat at a table with our lattes.

"Did you ever see Daniel Byrne in here?" I asked.

"Yes, a few times, but not for a while."

"Alone or with someone?"

"He'd meet with some blond woman. I don't know who she was."

"When exactly?"

"Late last year, winter mainly," she said.

"Was this her?" Brenda pulled out a photo of her aunt on her smartphone.

"Blond, pretty, wearing a lot of makeup. It looks like her," she said, "I'm not sure."

Brenda found another photo. The young barista inspected it. "Looks like her, but I can't be certain. Sorry."

"They were together more than once?" Brenda asked.

"Yeah, a couple times," she said.

"Did they seem like they were just talking?"

"I guess. Honestly, it looked like they were dating or something. You know, joking and laughing, affectionate-like." She glanced over her shoulder. "I've got to get back to work. Hope that helps." She got up and left.

Brenda turned her attention to me. "That bastard was meeting with Aunt Sally."

"You don't think they…"

"An affair?" She shook her head. "I don't think she'd do that to my uncle."

I sipped my latte. "We need to find out what the relationship was. It's not like we can just ask Daniel, though." I also knew we'd already taken a big risk in interviewing people about Aunt Sally. If word got back to the Byrnes, I'd be toast.

Brenda looked pale as a ghost. "Fucker," she said, then sighed and stood up. "I should get to back to work."

I looked at my watch. It was after two. "Shit. I've got to get back to the ranch." I stood up. Brenda left her latte untouched. "Want your coffee?" I asked.

"No," she said. I could tell she was still in shock about her aunt and Byrne "Joking and laughing."

We walked outside and stood by our vehicles. "I'll see what else I can figure out about all of this," I said. "Brenda, I'm going to help you solve this, I mean it."

She hugged me close. It felt good, and holding her close got me a bit excited.

33

DIGGING DEEPER

The camera crew arrived on Tuesday and began filming long-shot scenes for the big documentary. Daniel had me tag along in the golf cart to take photos and video of the shoot for "behind the scenes" bonus material.

I spent most evenings scanning the Internet for information about cell towers and electronic mind control, diving deeper down into the rabbit hole with every click. A journalist named Jessica Cassidy—a journalist graduate of my alma mater—had been a member of Journalists Without Borders but had gotten into trouble a few years back after being accused of releasing classified information about a new directed energy weapon system the US Department of Defense was developing. She was now living in Costa Rica, surviving as a freelance writer with a hit podcast called *Proof Pudding*. I made contact with her via a secure messaging app. She was familiar with my work and had seen the *60 Minutes* interview I had done with Daniel and Mike. I was worried the secure app wouldn't function given the possibility of a government conspiracy at play, but it worked. We set up a video call over the same secure app when I knew I'd have some time alone. She wore a silver beanie and dark glasses.

"I have some questions I'm hoping you could help me

with," I said, "regarding Congressman Matthew Young and his possible involvement with a black project involving 5G. Have you heard anything about this?"

There was a long pause as she sat thinking, maybe worried about government surveillance or my intentions. At last, she said, "Everyone knows he's on the Senate Armed Services Committee and supporting DARPA, possibly the secret program called Operation Mindscrew that involves electromagnetic transmitters and mind-altering frequencies. The buzz about this a few years ago went dark after the Presidential election."

"Would Mindscrew involve DARPA technology that's able to cause mass hallucinations?"

"Delusions, hallucinations—you'll find all kinds of stuff on the Internet about how the CIA is using 4G and 5G microwave towers for directing mind-control frequencies at targets. No one has confirmed this, though, and Young never mentions it."

"Is the program still active?"

"I don't know. Journalists, myself included, who've tried to find out have been called crazy and 'canceled' from social media. No one employed will touch the topic now."

"What about testing on Indian reservations in Washington and Montana?"

She paused again. "It's possible. You'd have to test towers with a specialized radio spectrum analyzer to determine what frequencies they're emitting. But with evidence, it's not like you can do anything with it to convince the public that the government is up to no good. No one will take you seriously, and mainstream journalism is just disinformation and spin for manipulating the masses. Try to report the truth and you get accused of being crazy and then buried. The world is fucked. The best thing you can do is get away from high population density areas and shield yourself the best you can."

I held up my beanie.

She removed her hat to reveal a beanie similar to mine. "You should be wearing it."

I slipped my beanie on, then told her about the iM4ET app and what I'd learned from Jonathan Mahue. I asked her what she knew about using electromagnetic fields to target specific individuals.

"There's a professor named Dinesh Trivedi in India who's an expert on this," Jessica said. "I contacted him when I was doing my research on the directed energy story. He specializes in nanotechnology. You should talk to him. I'll give you his secure chat link."

"That would be great," I said, "I'm planning to get to the bottom of this."

"That's what a journalist is supposed to do. Let me know what you find out about this app thing and UFOs. Maybe I can have you on the podcast sometime."

Chester was at the door, so I ended the call as he entered and hid my EMF beanie under my pillow. We chitchatted about the events of the day, then turned in. Apparently, Daniel had begun extra-long meditation sessions during the evening, and Chester and Mike were assigned additional security duties around the ranch compound.

The next evening, I located Dinesh Trivedi, PhD from Stanford and MD from All India Institute of Medical Sciences in Delhi. I sent him a message, telling him that I was a journalist researching for a story on nanotech. He responded the next day and we made arrangements for a call that night.

"How can I help you, Ben?" He asked in thick Indian dialect.

"I'm trying to learn more about how nanotechnology could be used to cause hallucinations. Is this possible?"

"If nanotubes can be used to carry psychotropic medications, they can be used to cause hallucinations, absolutely," he said.

"I saw that you are conducting research with nanobots controlled by radio waves."

"Yes. The nanobots are armed with radio transceivers for remote control. They can be turned on or off, commanded to release chemical compounds, and remotely reprogrammed. This technology has been in development for more than two decades."

"Could cellular phone transmission be used to control these nanobots?"

"Why not? Cellular bandwidth extends to high frequency radio waves. Nanobots would need to be synchronized and calibrated to appropriate brain frequencies. If you wanted to target just one person at a time, from space, you'd have to keep people apart by six feet or so."

"Is the United States government testing this technology?"

"Oh yes, the U.S. Army, for medical applications, biotech corporations, university labs, my lab here, of course, DARPA. Nanotechnology is the hottest issue going."

Congressman Young was a big supporter of DARPA, the Defense Advanced Research Projects Agency. There had to be a link. "So, it's conceivable that 5G millimeter waves could be used to control nanobots."

Dr. Trivedi seemed surprised that I was putting it all together.

"Most definitely. I can send you pictures of a nanobots if you like—quantum dots, fullerenes, origami nanotubes..."

"Yes, please."

He sent me photos via email.

Images included hexagons, strange objects with antennas or feet like insects. The hairs on my arms stood up, and my skin began to itch. Were these entities under my skin? Floating in my veins? Attaching to my optical nerves?

"Hexagons?"

"Hexagonal lattice structure. The hexagon appears everywhere in nature. It's a very strong structure. High-resolution transmission electron microscopy is essential for photographing these nanoparticles made of silver ions less than 50 nanometers. We have to use X-ray diffraction to see and measure them."

"Could you control someone remotely with nanotechnology?"

"They have successfully controlled lab rats, so possible, yes."

"Could nanobots cause ringing in the ears?"

"If they are hit with a very high energy source and at the correct frequency, certainly. Why do you ask, Ben?"

"How do nanobots get into the body?"

"Injection, possibly breathed in. Nanobots can easily cross the blood-brain barrier."

Breathed in, possibly ingested. I thought about the day I was with the Congressman. We had chicken, wine, and apple pie. Nadine was always serving apple pie and had me drinking tea. Daniel was always eating her pie. Or maybe it was in the oil diffuser. She'd given me one, and there was one in their bedroom. Petulli had one too.

"Could the nanotech be in food?"

"Yes. It is completely invisible to the human eye. One billionth of a meter."

"How can we know they're in us? Blood test, x-ray, or something?"

"A blood sample would work if the nanobots are in your blood stream, but you need a lab that knows what to look for and has the right equipment to detect them."

"If someone had these nanobots in them, how could they get rid of them?"

"Detoxing, cleanses, possibly magnetism—I'm interested in where your story is going, Ben."

"I just want to know everything I can about the technology, Dr. Trivedi. Good journalists make an effort to really understand so as to know what questions readers might be asking. What about testing food and drink?"

"Like I said, a lab would need the right equipment. I suppose a food lab could test for compounds, forensic lab for poisons..."

I checked the time, knowing that Chester would be back any minute. "Thank you for speaking with me, Dr. Trivedi. Is it okay if I contact you again if I have follow-up questions?"

"No problem, Ben. When will your article come out?"

"Soon." I said, "I'll send you the link."

I sat back to take in all that I'd learned. Why hadn't I thought of this earlier? Was I part of an experiment? Could nanoparticles controlled by electromagnetic beams from mobile apps and cell towers be used to create delusions and hallucinations? Perhaps a program was specifically targeted at reporters and journalists. Mass hallucinations controlled by whomever controls the technology, like the shadow government? Suddenly, I was sure that there was a CIA or DoD front testing nanotechnology's uses for mass hypnosis and hallucination. I was a guinea pig and others were, too, including Daniel.

I did a few more searches on the Internet, reading articles and scientific papers that confirmed what Dr. Trivedi said. I also looked into what might make some people more susceptible or resistant to mind control. Turns out there is an entire corpus of scientific literature about hypnotic susceptibility and its association to personality types and psychiatric conditions. Some studies estimated that about ten-percent of the population is highly susceptible to hypnosis, and about twenty-percent cannot be hypnotized, with everyone else falling in between. Where was I on this scale? I certainly don't believe I'm a person who's easily hypnotized and influenced. I also thought about Jack Clark's interview question about being fantasy-prone. That didn't seem like me either. But what about susceptibility to mind control caused by technology involving radio-controlled nanobots?

An EMF shielding hat wouldn't be enough. I needed to purge the nanobots. It was time to get serious, but how? Who knew how to do this? A pharmacy with Ipecac and ex-lax? I'd order a nice EMF shielding ski hat for Brenda and a tactical one for my buddy Brett.

Mike rapped on my door.

"Ben, Daniel wants to see you. He needs you to help with another video."

"Now?"

"Yeah, now. He says it's important. Nadine and Daniel

have been texting you for thirty minutes."

I threw on a jacket and jumped in the golf cart Mike had arrived in. Daniel was waiting for me in the video production room.

"Ben, this is a special video. It's ten o'clock in Asia, they will see it first."

"What's it about?" I grabbed the video camera.

"The Proximians have contacted me again. Are you ready with the camera?"

"Yes." I hit record.

Daniel looked into the camera. "My friends, for the last several weeks, I've been meditating, pleading with the Proximians to show mercy on us humans, and to let them know that we want to work with them for mutual benefit. Well, tonight I received a message from the Proximians. They are coming here to the ranch to meet with me. I realize that making this video and announcing this historic event will cause all kinds of attention, which we don't need because we must not intimidate or threaten the Proximians in any way. If they sense any hostility, then any possibility for me to make a deal will be off. They have assured me they are coming out of good will. I will be inviting just a few trusted government officials and scientists, and select members from the press corps, to the Valley of the Moon Ranch for the arrival. I cannot tell you when they will come—that remains secret. But I have arranged for a lottery that you can enter at our website where I'll be providing updates as things progress. I thank you for your trust in me. Good night."

He nodded, and I stopped the video.

"You know what to do, Ben. Get this out, right away. The phones are going to be ringing off the hook tomorrow." He sighed. "I'm exhausted, completely exhausted."

"Are you sure about this? The Proximians are coming here? When?"

"Of course, I'm serious." He looked at me. "You don't think I'm serious?" He sighed. "Perhaps I can make a deal with them—find some mutual ground."

"When?"

"I'll brief you later. We have to maintain operational security on this. We don't need a bunch of yahoos showing up with shotguns and potato guns."

A bit too late for that, I thought. "What about the military and the government? Won't they take this as a threat? Thousands of people are probably going to show up here. Isn't that going to cause problems?"

"Likely. So we'll block off the entrances. The Sheriff's Department will help. The ranch is more than 175 acres. It will be secure. All the attention will be good. We need people of the planet to be paying attention to what is happening, and to not panic. We're already seeing things get quite crazy out there."

"You mentioned leaders and scientists. Who are you inviting?"

"I can't tell you that yet either. In time, Ben. For now, we have to start preparations. Mike will be in charge of setting up the arrival area, and security, of course. And remember, you can't tell anyone about this, not until I give clearance."

He put his hand on my shoulder as we walked out of the production room. "I'm going to need you to help with the press, as usual. And don't worry, you're invited to the arrival event, you'll be at my side, and meet the Proximians in person. I know it may bring up some trauma for you, as it will undoubtedly for me, but we have to be strong. We're representing planet Earth here. Are you with me?"

"Of course I am," I replied, unsure of what else to say to a man who, whether under mind control or not, believed he was the only person on the planet who could make friends with beings 4.24 light-years from Earth.

He smiled. "Good, my son, now let's get to work."

34

BRENDA

The Proxima Foundation social media feeds were on fire by morning. Daniel's Twitter account skyrocketed past one hundred million followers for the first time, outpacing Lady Gaga and second only to Barack Obama.

My Twitter followers also hit record levels, but I wasn't feeling good about it. A wave of negative emotion washed over me, muddling my mind with confusion and hopelessness. Was Daniel Byrne just another in a long line of prophets and seers, from Emanuel Swedenborg, to Aleister Crowley, to the nut job from Heaven's Gate? Was he a tool of Deep State CIA mind control technologies ushering in the New World Order? I felt like a fool for believing in him. Why had I been so susceptible to his manipulation? What was wrong with me?

I pulled myself together and went to the pharmacy for ex-lax and Ipecac for my nanobot purge. Once I started, I went full bore, drinking buckets of water to flush everything out, from vomiting to unbearable shits. I wanted those little bastards out of me in any and every way I could.

The following morning, I dragged myself out of bed, showered, and after breakfast, told Daniel I needed to go to the pharmacy again. I dropped by Brenda's and filled her in on Daniel's Proximian delegation announcement.

"Sounds like another bullshit publicity stunt to me," she said. "What do you think?"

"On the surface, yes, but I'm convinced there's more to it." I told her about what I'd learned from my journalist friend and the nanotech professor.

"Operation Mindscrew? MKULTRA? You mean it's even crazier than I thought?" she said.

"I think your aunt got too close to something and she was killed."

"The Byrnes, you mean?"

"I don't know. If this is a CIA operation, then it could have been government operatives or a contractor. We need more information. If we can prove that a secret operation is going on here, we might be able to link it to your aunt's killer or killers."

"I have something I want to show you," Brenda said, opening her laptop to the State of Illinois Bar Associations web page. "Nadine is licensed here in Montana but was licensed in Illinois fifteen years ago under her maiden name of Brewster. So I kept searching and found a Melda Brewster from Canton who was born September 14, 1967. Take a look." She showed me a black and white photo of 18-year Melda Brewster with curly brown hair and mid-1980s hair spray bangs. "It's Nadine. She changed her name when she was eighteen. She's not who she says she is. And look at her eyes. Do they look odd to you?"

I inspected the photo closely. "You mean the colored contact lenses?" I read the caption. "Voted most bossy. That makes sense too." I looked at Brenda. "Why is she's hiding her past?"

Brenda clicked to State of Montana real-estate licensure website. "She also has a real-estate broker's license in Montana and in Washington." She looked at me. "Is she involved in any real estate you know of?"

"Just the Valley of the Moon ranch that I'm aware of." I sat back to think for a moment. Why hadn't I done a thorough background search myself months ago? It would have led me down a completely different path on my first article about the Byrnes.

I leaned into her laptop and searched for Daniel's yearbook site. In the Spring Valley High School, Peoria Illinois, Class of 1985 page there was a photo of a slender Daniel Byrne with shoulder-length ginger hair and glasses. The caption read, Biggest space case. "Kind of a geek, huh?" I said to Brenda.

She smiled. "You think?"

At the Harvard yearbook site, we found both Nadine and Daniel. "Well, they were telling the truth about Harvard," I said, "but Daniel said they met at a law firm in Chicago. I wonder about Congressman Young. He was a Harvard grad and is around the same age as the Byrnes." And there he was, in the same class. Nadine and Congressman Young had been in the Harvard freshman debate club.

"Well, I'll be, damned!" I said, "they all knew each other! They lied!"

"Did the Byrnes ever mention knowing the Congressman?"

"Daniel said he was involved in DARPA dark projects and fake UFO abductions. That's all. So there's a connection between a government black operation and the Byrnes, but it's not enough evidence to prove it. We need more."

"Like documents or an admission."

I thought for a second longer. "Nadine keeps files on her financial dealings in her office. Maybe there's something there."

"Why would she keep files like that onsite?"

"She's a control freak. Locked file cabinets. Maybe I can gain access. Mike has all the keys to the ranch facilities. I should be able to get them from him when he's at the gym. I should have enough time to look for the files and return the keys."

"What if you get caught?"

"We need the evidence, right?"

245

"But even with evidence, what then? It's not like you could take it to the FBI."

"I don't know yet. Maybe I'll write an op-ed and send it to the New York Times or the New York Post. Someone's got to pay attention."

"Maybe," Brenda said, "but you can't really trust them, either, can you?"

"I'll blockchain the documents to spread them all over the Internet so there's no way to censor them once they are out there."

"Maybe start your own podcast, too. Everyone has their own news channel these days on YouTube. You are already a celebrity, of sorts, and with your journalism skills, I'm sure it would be a hit."

A podcast. I hadn't thought of that. "That's a brilliant idea, Brenda, like Joe Rogan—You know, whenever I'm here with you, I feel so good."

She smiled. "Maybe it's because there's no cellular signal out here."

I looked her in the eyes. "Do I seem of sound mind to you? Like I'm not some kind of conspiracy nut."

She smirked. "Yes. Everything we've talked about makes sense. My aunt Salley wasn't a crazy conspiracy type either. She was onto to something."

I shook my head. "I feel like such a fool for not digging into the Byrnes months ago. I should have known."

She looked at me with those big brown eyes. "You were manipulated. It's not your fault."

"Do you think if I was still under mind control influence right now, I'd know it?"

"If it was working, you'd be completely oblivious or in denial, wouldn't you?"

I nodded. "I'm aware that I'm questioning whether I'm under mind control, therefore I must not be."

She smiled. "I don't think you are either, if that makes you feel any better."

I turned toward her and our knees touched. I decided to

go for it. I leaned in and kissed her lips. They were softer and sweeter than I'd even imagined. She was responsive, so I leaned in and kissed her again. We kept kissing, and soon I was touching her breasts and she was rubbing my leg, driving me to a frenzy.

"I can't believe I'm making out with a cultie," she said softly.

"I'm not a cultie," I said equally softly, "but I'm going to have to go back tonight."

"I know," she said, our lips nibbling at each other. She smiled, and before I knew it, she led me to her bedroom, pulled the drapes and released her raven black hair. We undressed and fell onto the bed. It was the best sex I'd had in a very long time, and from the sound of her moans, it was for her, too. What a high.

I thought about us as we lay in each other's arms afterwards. She was beautiful, sexy, witty, sharp as a tack, and she seemed genuinely supportive of my career as a journalist—what more could I want? Could we have a future together? Sure, she still had graduate school and I didn't see myself living in Missoula long-term, but perhaps it could work.

On the way back to the ranch, still feeling high, I contemplated the podcast idea. It would be a show about understanding truth and how our own biases keep us from it. Maybe two episodes a week, the first few focusing on truth, journalism, and conspiracies. I'd be candid and completely honest about my own errors in judgment. Maybe I'd have guests on and make enough money to cover health insurance and my cost of living. I'd call it *Sciencecaster*. It would be a hit; I was sure of it.

I was also sure I was no longer under the influence of a mind control technology. I'd done everything I could to make myself immune—I was adhering to the purging regimen and cleansings. I was meticulous in what I ate. I hadn't had any alcohol in weeks. I'd avoided EMF as much as possible, wearing the shielding hat, and keeping my smartphone

shielded or off. I avoided those Blue Tooth ear buds that
Nadine gave me. And most importantly, I had full force of
mind. Not only did I have an objective reference of the
soundness of my mind from Brenda, I knew I was in control
of my thoughts. The ringing in my ears had subsided, along
with the hallucinations and the uncanny voice in my head. My
mind was clear and sound. I was centered—not going to any
extremes. I was finally able get to the bottom of all of this
with my bullshit detector tuned and fully operational.

35

SIT DOWN WITH NADINE

What happened the following day took me by surprise.
Nadine came by the office just as I was completing the social
media routine for the day. She pulled up a chair. "I was
thinking, Ben. I know I was hard on you before about seeing
that girl Brenda. You are a young, strapping bachelor, and
you need to make up your own mind on who to associate
with. And I'm sure you really put the razz on her berries,
being a big-city journalist and all. We have such important
work to do here at the Foundation, especially now, and I was
just looking out for you. So I was thinking, I'd like to meet
her in the flesh. Why don't you invite her over for tea on
Sunday? We'll have a nice sit down. Besides, I think that's
what she wants. What do you say?"

"Really? Now?" What was Nadine's real motive? What
would Brenda say? What could go wrong?

"Why not? At two?"

I thought for a quick second. I was nervous, but I wasn't
sure how to say no. "I'll call her right after I finish up here
and see if she's available."

"Oh, I'm sure she will be." She tapped my knee and stood
up. "I'm looking forward to it."

I went down to my pod and called Brenda right away.

"Nadine invited you to the ranch on Sunday, for tea."

"For tea? Why?"

"She made it sound like she wants to meet you in order to make amends with me. She knows we've been seeing each other."

"Make amends? She must have some other reason. Do you think I'll be at risk going there? Are the culties going to attack me or something?"

"I don't think so. We can tell others you are here and if anything happens, you know, a…"

"…deadman's trigger, right. Do you want me to come?"

"It's up to you. You can say no." I was still apprehensive about the meeting, fearing things might go bad if Brenda pressed with too many questions.

"I'd like to meet her face to face and see what she has to say. When did she say she wants me there?"

"This Sunday at two. We don't want to give it away that we are on to them. The last thing we need to do now is poke the bear."

"No shit. I've got questions. She's a lawyer and I'm pre law, remember? I know what I'm going to do."

"Maybe don't eat any food she serves. There could be nanobots in it."

"Should I bring something? Something to eat or a gift?"

"The gesture would be nice. No meat, though. They're vegetarians."

"I'll figure something out. I'll meet you there then, on Sunday at two."

On Sunday afternoon, Brenda arrived at two in a skirt and blouse, her hair curled and flowing, with a plate of shortbread cookies she'd made the night before. I was too nervous to hug her. I was certain we were being watched.

"Are you sure about this meeting?" I asked again as we headed to the house.

"I came all the way out here, didn't I? I'm sure."

"Remember, don't…"

"…poke the bear, I know. Relax, Ben," she said as we

passed the giant tent and newly constructed Learning Center. A pair of Nadine's horses ambled up to the fence to watch us.

"Beautiful horses," Brenda said, "expensive too."

From the main house, we caught a glimpse of the metal shipping container huts in the hollow. "Are you going to show me your pod afterwards?" she asked, half smirking.

"I'm sure Nadine would love that."

Nadine met us at the door. "So you must be Brenda," she smiled, her country twang in full swing.

Brenda presented her cookies. "Shortbread. My grandmother's recipe."

"They look delicious, so nice of you."

In the living room, Brenda and I sat together on the sofa with Nadine across from us in a large leather chair. On the coffee table was a silver tray and a teapot of steeping Earl Gray tea, three cups, and a platter of apple fritters, to which Brenda added her shortbread cookies. I felt like I was bringing my first girlfriend home to meet my mother.

"So sorry Daniel can't be here to join us. He's busy working on some very important things right now. No grass growing under the feet of that one."

"Thank you for inviting me," Brenda said in calm tone.

"So tell me, how did you two meet?"

"We met at Ramblin' Joe's when I first came out here," I said.

"Do you enjoy working there, Brenda?"

"It's okay, I suppose. Just temporary."

"Going back to college soon?"

"Yes, in the spring."

"At Montana State, I presume?"

"Yes. They have a good pre-law program."

Nadine smiled. "And affordable. So you want to be a lawyer?"

"Yes," Brenda said, returning the smile. "You went to Harvard, didn't you? Must have been expensive."

I gave Brenda a quick eye. Watch it!

"You know my educational background? Yes, Harvard. An Ivy League education isn't cheap, but it helps when running a major not-for-profit like our foundation." She began to pour. "How do you take your tea, dear?"

"Straight is fine," Brenda said.

Nadine poured out tea and set the teapot down. "Apple fritter?"

"Yes. Thank you," Brenda said, taking one onto a plate.

"How about you, Ben?"

"Sure." I took one and nibbled on it, knowing I was going to have to hit the ex-lax later.

Nadine sipped her tea. "I'm terribly sorry about what happened to your aunt, Brenda, you must have been devastated. And those young children. Bless them."

Brenda nodded. "Yes, it's been difficult for my entire family, especially my uncle. What do you know about my Aunt Sally's death?"

"Just what has been in the news. She was killed by that terrible man who escaped from the penitentiary. God rest her soul."

"Did you ever meet my Aunt Sally?"

Please don't go there, I thought. I could feel the rising tension in the room.

"No, but Daniel talked with her on the phone once. Your aunt wanted to do a story on alien contact and our Foundation. Did you see her story?"

"Yes. I'm not absolutely sure she was killed by the convict. Couldn't it have been someone else?"

I felt the tension about to break.

Nadine stared at Brenda. "Who else could it have been? The police did a thorough investigation, especially the FBI. If we can't trust them then who can we trust?"

Brenda held her ground. "He couldn't have killed her. He wasn't even in the state at the time. I did a public records request."

Nadine glanced at me. "But why would the police make up a story like that?"

"Maybe a cover up?" Brenda said, sipping her tea.

Nadine chuckled. "A cover up? My dear, I'm sure that the FBI knows what they are doing. What are you insinuating?"

"I'm not insinuating anything. We're just talking about some discrepancies in what the public was told."

"What do you mean by discrepancies?"

"Beside the Department of Corrections report, wasn't it odd that Aunt Sally was found on the edge of your property?"

Nadine shrugged. "We have curious people trying to sneak in all of the time to watch the viewing events. I can't say whether she was ever on our land or not. We have over 175 acres here. What I do know is that the location of her…well, she was on federal Reservation land. That's why the FBI is involved, isn't it?"

Brenda's was becoming upset. It was time for me to speak up.

"This is a difficult topic for everyone," I said. "Brenda just wants to know more of the details that the media and official documents didn't cover."

Nadine glanced at me, then back at Brenda. "I don't blame you, Brenda. The media did a piss poor job of reporting."

But Brenda wasn't done. "You said your husband only talked to my Aunt Sally once on the phone. Are you sure they didn't meet in person?"

Nadine stiffened slightly, no doubt realizing that Brenda was interrogating her. "We share everything."

"Someone in town said they'd been seen together at Bigfoot Java."

"Who said that?"

"Someone who works there. They said they were seen more than once."

"Are you sure about that? Daniel has meetings with editors and reporters all the time. I'm sure that is who he may have been seen with. Who at Bigfoot Java told you this?"

"I should stop," Brenda said. "I'm just trying to figure out what was going on before she was killed."

Nadine relaxed a little. "Darling, you've every right to be

searching for answers. It's such an unfortunate and horrible tragedy. It must be so confusing for you." Nadine glanced out the double bay window, then back to Brenda. "Do you like horses, Brenda?"

"Yes. I suppose so."

"I love watching them run free in the pastures here. Powerful, beautiful, and so smart. I ride year-round." She smiled at Brenda. "Would you like to come out for a ride sometime?"

"That's nice for you to offer," Brenda said, "but I thought aliens are supposed to be coming here any day now. Isn't that going to change a few things for everyone?"

Nadine smiled. "Daniel's working on it. Just because our world is about to change doesn't mean we can't or shouldn't enjoy simple things while we can. What kind of world would we be in if you weren't allowed to do any of the things you are passionate about?"

"But if they're coming to do harm, control the planet or something…"

"I'm more than confident that Daniel will lead us out from under alien threat and preserve our rights as inhabitants of this beautiful planet." She looked at me. "Ben too has confidence in Daniel—don't you, Ben?"

"Absolutely," I said.

We talked a while longer until Nadine's large yawn. "Oh my, excuse me. I feel like a Sunday afternoon nap."

"I guess I should be going then," Brenda said, "thank you for the tea."

"My pleasure, and thank you for the cookies. Any friend of Ben is a friend of ours."

We all stood up.

"I'm going to walk Brenda to her car, if that's okay," I asked.

"Well of course it is. Such a gentleman you are," Nadine said.

I walked Brenda to her Jeep Cherokee.

"She knew about Aunt Sally and Daniel. I guarantee it,"

Brenda said.

"Are you sure? How do you know?"

"I just do. Call it woman's intuition. She's covering for him and she's got him wrapped around her finger. I wonder what else you'll find when you look through her files, maybe credit card statements or something." She shook her head. "And those were definitely colored contact lenses and that was a fake country accent if I've ever heard one."

Her comment about Daniel around Nadine's her finger gave me a thought. "Maybe Nadine is Daniel's handler. That was a thing in MKULTRA you know. Someone would be the handler of the mind-controlled person, and the handler would be mind-controlled too—a pyramid of handlers controlling victims handling more victims."

"So you think The Congressman Young or someone else with black project ties is handling Nadine?"

"Maybe. I'll look for evidence and take a photo if I come across anything. Okay?"

She nodded. "She didn't even try my cookies."

"I hope she doesn't give me a hard time about the sit down. Text when get home, okay?"

"Sure," she said, "I'll see your pod next time, all right?"

I watched her drive away, then started back to my pod when I heard Nadine call my name. I walked toward the doorstep. "Yes, Nadine?"

She handed me my unfinished apple fritter on a napkin. "Don't let this go to waste, and after dinner, go see if Daniel needs help with press releases. Don't let him do all the work."

"I will, thank you," I said, nibbling at the fritter. While heading down the trail, I tossed the rest of the fritter into the bushes.

36

LAST SUPPER

I reported to the Byrnes for Thanksgiving dinner at five-thirty. Mike and Chester were there, along with Mr. Petulli and Mark Brunsky the filmmaker. A large presentation easel was setup in a corner, cloaked by a cover. I assumed it had something to do with planning for the Proximian arrival event.

I sat between Chester and Mr. Petulli for the vegetarian dinner of Tofurkey, mashed potatoes, stuffing, vegetables, and the wine I picked up at Costco a few weeks prior. When we finished the main course, Daniel wiped his mouth with a napkin, tapped his wine glass for attention, and then stood. "My friends, in less than thirty days, the Proximians will be here in the Valley of the Moon. It will be the biggest day of my life, and the most important day ever for all of mankind. I want you to know how much I love each of you." He looked at everyone in the room in turn, resting his eyes on me for an uncomfortable moment, and finally his wife. Tears formed in his eyes. "You are my family, and I want to let each of you know how important you are to me."

Nadine clutched her hands over her chest and looked at him with doting eyes.

Daniel cleared his throat. "Nadine, the love of my life.

Ever since we met in law school, you've been the apple of my eye. Thank you for guiding and supporting me over the years."

Nadine smiled and wiped a tear.

I felt nauseous.

"And Mr. Petulli, your support has made this foundation what it is today. Without you, none of this would be possible. Thank you."

Petulli responded with an expressionless, subtle nod.

"And Mike, you've been my rock by my side. We've traveled the world together, from the South American rain forests to Europe and the Hawaiian Isles. Your dedication and commitment have been unwavering. Thank you, my friend."

Mike raised his wine glass to Daniel.

"And Chester, you've been a great addition to our family. You've been through so much, and I believe, with the bottom of my heart, that it was destiny for you to come and work with us at the Foundation."

Chester rendered a salute.

Daniel saluted back then looked at me. "And Ben, I'm so glad you came to us, both times. Your journalism and social media skills have helped us get our message out to the masses in ways we could not have done on our own. It means so much to me that you are here now for this historic event."

The unsettled feeling in my stomach worsened. I felt like it was the Last Supper, only with Tofurkey and Costco Chardonnay.

Daniel got up and went to the demonstration easel. "We have a lot of work to do to prepare for the arrival in three weeks." He flipped the first page to a hand drawn map of the compound with a hexagon in the south field. He pointed to it. "This is where our visitors will arrive." He moved his finger east. "Here is where our guests will be, including select members of the press." He then pointed to the edges of the map, drawing a perimeter with his finger. "We are going to set up some surveillance cameras, and Mike, assisted by

Chester, will lead security and keep the inner parameter clear of unwanted guests. We don't need another flash mob showing up. I've already arranged for additional security just in case."

"Copy," Mike said. Chester leveled his eyes on me. "What about him?"

"Ben will be in charge of social media leading up to and after the event, and he can assist with camera setup. We'll have our digital cameras on batteries, too, just in case we lose power or Internet." He moved his finger up on the map. "And Mark, here is where it may be best for you and your crew to be. Ben, I need you to focus in on the craft and me when it first appears. Mark will get the wide shots for the documentary. We had to scratch the drone shots: the Proximians don't want anything in the sky." He then pointed to a spot next to the hexagram. "This section will be for our VIPs." He smiled, looking at Mr. Petulli and Nadine. "We are expecting the Governor to join us. We only have a month to prepare, so we'll need everyone's head in the game."

"We are with you, Daniel," Mike said.

"You know it," Nadine said.

"Good," Daniel said, "any questions?"

"I've got one," I announced. "How much press are we inviting?"

"A select few, using the lottery system. We want only the best," Daniel said.

"And the Proximians will be okay with them and everyone else being here?"

"Oh yes," Daniel said, "as long as everyone stays in their designated area and keep electronic devices off. I suggested to the Proximians that it would be important to have the media present to assure the public it is all real—Oh, that reminds me. I've drafted a program for the event. Ben, I'll want you to review it for me."

"Sure," I said.

"Now, let's all meditate," Daniel continued. "May the cosmic power entrusted in me empower me to communicate with the Proximians, let them know that we mean them no harm, and that they should mean us no harm. Our hearts our open to them, as we are wrapped in the same cosmic destiny. Our fate is their fate, and their fate is ours. Let us work together in unity."

Daniel opened his eyes and thanked each of us for coming to the dinner. He hugged and kissed each of us on the cheek as we exited. He placed his hand over one side of his mouth. A toothache? He stopped me at the door and handed me a stack of pages stapled together. "Read through it and give me a good copy edit. Okay? Then, help me to get it formatted in that program you use?"

"Microsoft Publisher, no problem," I said. "What's with this?" I gestured to my jaw.

"Oh, just a filling that's come loose. I need to get it taken care of." He smiled. "Let me know when you are done with the program."

That evening while in bed, I flipped through the pages of the program draft. The first section described the Proxima Foundation and Daniel's story, highlighting his accomplishments towards alien disclosure and contact with the Proximians. The next section described the Proximians, where they were from, their history, and what they likely wanted from us and our planet. The third and final section described a list of dos and don'ts during the arrival, with special instructions for the press corps. Daniel had spent hours on the program, and he was obviously confident that the Proximians were arriving on Winter Solstice. If this was a mind control operation, the event was going to be one brazen and risky experiment with all of the press and other witnesses on site. If this wasn't about group hallucination mind control, and an alien race was actually coming to the ranch, it would undoubtedly be the most important event in modern history. If neither happened, it would be the biggest farce of the century.

37

QUAN YIN

The opportunity to search Nadine's private office came on Wednesday when Nadine and Daniel went into town— Nadine for her monthly Botox and collagen refresh, and Daniel for the dentist. Mike and Chester asked if I was going to join them in the gym. I told them I had some urgent social media announcements to attend to. They seemed to buy it. I estimated they'd be working out for at least forty-five minutes, and if they used the sauna, I'd have an hour. I'd have longer if they smoked a joint afterwards.

I slipped into the locker room, and found Mike's pants hanging on a hook. I took the keys from his lanyard, and went quietly to the vault, my heart pounding in excitement. I dug deep into the cabinets, pulling out files and skimming them for relevant information. There were bundles upon bundles of real estate records. It appeared that the Byrnes had acquired additional tracts of land in the area around Missoula and up along Interstate 90. In another drawer I found lease documents for cell towers. They were bringing in some serious money from the leases, more than $150,000 a year. How did they acquire so much land? I kept digging and found some banking records, showing loans to the Foundation. It appeared to me the Byrnes were acquiring land and leasing it to cell towers companies. The Proxima Foundation had to be a front for the CIA or whoever was behind the mind control operation. It made sense. Cloak the experiments in a UFO cult so that victims of the mind controlling hallucinations would believe they were seeing spaceships and having encounters with extraterrestrials.

As I began to take photos of the documents the door flew open. It was Mike, still in workout shorts and tank top, his face glistening with sweat. He had a handheld radio in one hand, his Glock in the other. I instinctually threw my hands up, the one with the cell phone nearly knocking the statue of Quan Yin off her shelf.

"What are you doing in here?" he shouted. Veins pulsed on his forehead as he held me in the pistol's sights.

I stuttered and spewed out the first explanation that came to mind. "I'm looking for some paperwork Nadine asked me to work on. Routine stuff."

"Oh yeah? Routine? Like what?"

"Just some accounting stuff."

"Bullshit!" Mike moved closer. "You're not authorized to be in here. Keep your hands up where I can see them."

My mind scrambled for what to say next. I started to put my hands down.

"Keep your fucking hands where I can see them!" he shouted.

I threw my hands back up. "Relax, Mike, no need to point that at me."

His eyes glued to me, he called on the radio. "Code Red. Nadine's office."

Chester responded. "What? Who is it?"

"Hurry your ass up here," Mike commanded.

Mike sat on Nadine's desk, Glock still on me. "What are you doing, man?"

I still had hope that I could weasel my way out of the situation and hightail it out of there. "Like I said, Nadine asked me to review some files."

"What files?"

"None of your business, Mike."

"It is my business. I'm Chief of Security. You're lucky I didn't cap your ass when I walked in on you. You've got some explaining to do."

Chester arrived in sweatpants and half out of breath. He swung an AR-15 from around his shoulder and pointed it at me. "What's he doing in here?" he huffed.

"That's what I want to know," Mike snapped, still pointing his gun at me.

"Come on, guys, is this necessary?" I asked. "I'm just doing my job. You need to talk to Nadine when she gets back. She'll explain this."

"I knew you couldn't be trusted. Fucking journalist," Mike said.

"Not too smart," Chester added, "the room is alarmed."

"Hand over your phone, Ben," Mike demanded.

"I'm not going to do that," I said quietly.

Mike shoved the Glock into my face. "Chester, take his phone."

Chester slung his rifle and grabbed my phone. I pulled it away. He gripped my arm. Mike's Glock was now inches from my brow. "Hand it over or tap tap."

I yielded the phone to Chester.

"Wait until Nadine finds out. She's going to be pissed," Chester said.

"Go ahead and call her. You know she's getting her face done."

"You're a dumb fuck," Mike said. He waved the barrel of his gun towards the door. "Come on, let's go."

They led me downstairs and out into the backyard. Mike made me sit on the ground while he phoned Nadine. To my unfortunate surprise, she answered. Mike told her that I'd been caught snooping around in her office. Mike asked about Daniel, but apparently Nadine wasn't going to tell him about the situation right away.

After several more yes ma'ams, Mike ended the call and ordered me to get my ass up.

"Where are we going?" I asked.

"You'll find out soon enough," he said.

They led me around the back of the house into the horse stables. In the back was a Conex container for Nadine's equestrian supplies.

I eyed the box in terror. "You're not going to put me in there. That's unlawful imprisonment."

"Oh yeah, I am. Nadine said she doesn't want you running off. Get your ass in there or I'll put you in there!"

Chester opened the door and shoved me. "Yeah, get your ass in there."

The odor of tanned leather whipped my nostrils. I looked at Mike and the Glock one last time before he closed the door.

There were saddles and tack along the walls. I felt around until I found the string to the light. I paced and thought about how I was going to get out of this situation. Were they going to drug me and then kill me? Bury me somewhere in the valley?

Twenty minutes later, the door opened. Nadine stood before me, hands on her hips, Mike and Chester at her sides.

She shook her head. "What in tarnation do you think you were doing, Ben? Snooping around in my files? What are you looking for?"

I stood up. Mike stepped forward, hand on his gun.

"That won't be necessary, Mike, let's hear what he has to say."

"I was looking for information about the Phoenix Lights and my father, that's all."

"What exactly, Ben? You know you can just ask Daniel for information. We are not trying to keep anything from you, and I know you know that. So level up. What were you really looking for?"

"I think it's time for me to go. Can I have my phone please?"

"Want me to make him talk?" Mike asked.

"You know this is unlawful imprisonment. You need to let

me go."

"Darn it, Ben, you are lucky Mike and Chester didn't shoot you. We've had people breaking into our offices before, looking to sabotage Daniel's work. Now, tell me what in tarnation you were looking for? You have pictures of our real-estate records and other financial records. Why, Ben? These are all private Foundation documents."

"Yeah? We'll why don't you tell me what is going on with the cell towers?"

"What about them?"

"You tell me," I said.

"All right, you got me. We've been buying up land and leasing it out for new cellular towers. So what? No crime in that. Its just a good investment." She shook her head.

"Are you sure that's what it is?" I asked, my hands were shaking from fear. I knew they could kill me at any moment, but something was driving me to demand the truth.

"What else would it be?" Nadine asked.

"What about the iM4ET app? Why is it transmitting on non-FCC-approved frequencies? What's up with that?"

"I have no idea what you are talking about. Have you lost your mind? The app was approved by the app stores and is fully compliant with all laws. Where are you are getting this information? The Internet? Come on, Ben."

"I know that something is going on here and I know you are not who you say you are."

"Well spit in my eye and call me a liar!" said Nadine. "Ben, you're blinded by the effects of the Proximians. Don't you see it?"

"No, I'm not blinded by anything. I'm thinking clearly, and I know you're hiding your true identity. You and Daniel were at Harvard together, why lie about that?"

"What do you mean? We met in Chicago. We found out later that we were both at Harvard at the same time. You're wasting your time fishing for the moon in the water. You've let us down, Ben, we trusted you like our own son. But now trust is broken. I have no choice but to let you go."

"He's going to write another crap article," Mike warned.

"No I'm not. I'm just ready to move on. Can I go please?"

"And don't forget you have a legally binding employment contract and nondisclosure agreement with us," Nadine said.

"Should we go and get Daniel?" Mike asked her.

"No, I'll tell him later, it will just upset him. He doesn't need to be distracted by this foolishness; he needs to focus." She headed out of the stables. "Mike, Chester, take care of this. I don't have time for him anymore."

They grabbed me by both arms and took me out of the barn and down the hill toward the pods. I struggled to free myself from their grip. Were they going to take me out back and beat me to a pulp or just shoot me?

When we got to my pod, Mike shoved me in. "You need to pack your shit and get out. You're lucky I don't just shoot your ass."

The two of them kept their eyes on me while I packed, then they followed me up to the parking lot to my Jetta. As I set my bags down to open my trunk, Mike kicked me in the ass and threw my phone at me. "Asshole," he said.

"Fuck you, Mike!" I replied, picking up my phone.

As I turned the car around, I saw Daniel on the back porch. He stood up from his Adirondack, his reading glasses on and stared at me through the screen. I wanted to wave, do something, but I couldn't see any point in it. Relieved I was still alive, I hit the accelerator and drove out of the Valley of the Moon and straight to Brenda's where I paced around her living room, livid from what had just transpired.

"They locked me up in one of those shipping containers, pulled guns on me. Assholes! I should sue them!"

Brenda convinced me to sit down. I told her about the altercation with Nadine and what I managed to learn about the cell-tower land leases. I looked for the document photos on my phone, but they were gone. "They wiped the photos off my phone."

"Of course, they did," Brenda said.

Just then, the iM4ET app chimed. I shook my head. "I

don't believe this; that damned iM4ET is on my phone again!" I held up the cracked screen with the app icon to prove it to Brenda, and then uninstalled the app. "The Proxima Foundation is obviously a front for a CIA mind-control program. Why else would they have a stake in the towers and why this app?"

"That's been your hypothesis for weeks, but we still don't have any proof."

"I called Nadine on it too. I asked her what they were doing with the cell towers and who she really was."

"What did she say?"

"Denied it of course, called me crazy. I'd like to know what else they have hidden in those files. If only I hadn't gotten caught."

"What are you going to do now? It's not like you can actually sue them. Probably best you are done with them. You're lucky to be alive. They could have killed you."

She was right.

"What about your aunt? We can't prove who killed her."

She put her hand in mine. "It's all right, we'll think of something else. By the way, Happy Thanksgiving." She smiled at me. "Hungry?"

She heated up some real turkey leftovers from her Uncle's while I sat at the kitchen table with her laptop, checking to see what news media were reporting. A story was circulating about an increase in UFO sightings and Daniel's alleged contact with aliens.

"I bet they are raking in the dough now," Brenda said.

I was more irked than ever that I'd failed to find any smoking gun.

We sat down to eat, Brenda poured some Merlot while I stared at my plate, thinking about what to do next.

"Get some rest tonight," Brenda said while eating. "Maybe you can get a start on the podcast we talked about."

"That's a good idea," I said, picking up my fork.

The next few days, I camped in Brenda's trailer while she went to work at Ramblin' Joe's. I tried to write an article and set up a YouTube channel for my new podcast, but I had temporarily lost my way. Instead, I spent hours on social media, reading Twitter posts and checking the social media feeds from the Proxima Foundation. I was restless, waiting for Brenda to come home, sometimes after two in the morning. I found myself drinking a bottle of wine per night. Not good.

On Tuesday, my phone chimed with an email message. It was Marcus, my old boss at *Hot Reports*. He wanted to know if I'd be interested in doing a contract investigative story, and if so, whether I could come to the office on Monday to discuss it. I thought it over, my head cloudy from alcohol, I wasn't employed, I hadn't made any progress on the podcast idea. I thought for a moment more, then emailed Marcus that I'd see him on Monday.

I told Brenda about the call from Marcus the next morning.

She looked at me for a moment. "What about the podcast?"

"I can't concentrate. I need the structure of writing an article."

"And the cell towers? You can't stop now."

"No one said I was stopping. I just need some structure and money."

"Are you coming back?" The old distrust reared its ugly head in her face.

"Of course. I want to be here for the Solstice arrival event, for sure. I just need to get my head on straight."

I tried to hug her, but she pushed me away.

"If you need to go, then go!"

On Friday, I packed up the Jetta and headed for Seattle.

38

RETURN TO SEATTLE

Friday night in Seattle I was having a second round of beers with Brett at Jonesy's. Brett belched and asked me why I wasn't shacking up with him and not Brenda.

"I needed to get out of there," I said. "I'm not sure she really wanted me hanging around, anyway." Was that true? I wasn't sure, but didn't want to get into it with him.

Brett sipped his beer. "She's hot, man. You're crazy."

Maybe he was right about me being crazy, but I needed to clear my head after all I'd been through with the Byrnes.

"What's with the beanie? No mountain to ski on in Ballard, man."

"It's EMF shielded, made out of silver. It's supposed to block ninety percent of microwave frequencies."

"You sure it works?" Brett asked.

"I think so. I watched some tests on YouTube."

"Well, if YouTube says so." Brett leveled his eyes on me then removed his Carhart cap and flipped it upside down, revealing its tin foil lining.

I smiled. "No way! How long have you had that in there?"

"Since 2010, after I got back from Iraq."

"Shit, dude, I had no idea." For some reason, it made me

feel better.

"You've got to design it right or you'll end up making it work more like an antenna, causing a buildup of radio energy. It will fry your brain."

"I know," I said, "I saw it on YouTube." I grinned at him. He looked at me with a little smile.

"Of course, you did. Let's do a shot," Brett said, hailing the bartender.

The TV above the bar switched to a live special report about a UFO sighting over Seattle. A large formation of lights had been tracked over the ocean, then come down the coast before flying over Vancouver and then Seattle before flying over the Washington state capital in Olympia, then down the Oregon coast. Everyone at the bar had their eyes glued to the screen.

"You think it was real?" A young woman at the end of the bar asked her friend reading Twitter feeds on her phone.

"Probably the new Air Force bomber flying down from Alaska," Brett said to me, his eyes still on the screen.

"Maybe," I said, "or maybe it's not real at all. Can't trust mainstream media."

The bartender topped off our glasses with Patron Silver.

Brett looked at his glass. "Well, hair of the alien ball sack," he said, taking the shot, then slamming the glass onto the bar.

I rolled the shot glass between my fingers. "This will help my nanobot cleanse, right?" I threw it back.

At closing time, we headed out into the cold drizzle. "You're not still freaked out by the windsock man, are you, man?" Brett asked as we headed down the alley past the windsock.

"Not going to happen," I said, pulling my beanie tighter.

At his building, Brett embraced me in a drunken bro hug. "Good to see you again, man."

"You too," I said. I meant it. Brett was a good friend for letting me shack up at his place again until I figured out what to do next. That night, I drunk-dialed Brenda.

She let the phone ring a long time. "Did you just get off

shift?" I asked, trying to sound like everything was okay between us.

"Are you drunk?" she asked.

"I've had a few. I wanted to hear your voice and say that I think I love you. I really do."

There was a pause. "Really? I can't believe you are telling me this. You took off. I thought you were going to... Never mind. I don't know why I waste my time on you."

"Hold on," I pleaded, "I mean it. I love you and want to see you again."

"Yeah? When?"

"I'm not sure yet."

"What about the arrival event on the Solstice? Did you forget about that? What about your investigation?"

"I'm going to meet with my old editor at *Hot Reports* on Monday."

"Maybe a story about The Lochness Monster?" she sneered.

"I love your sarcasm, I really do."

"Whatever, Ben. I've got to go."

Drunk-dialing never works out.

I went downtown to the *Hot Reports* offices. Marcus met me and shook my hand, then led me to his office.

"What's with the beanie hat?" he asked, sipping his Starbucks and inspecting me through his hipster glasses.

I pointed to my EMF shielding hat. "This?" I was hesitant to mention my reasons. "It was really cold out in Montana."

"Interesting look," he said. "Listen, Ben, I've always had an interest in UFOs, but now with all that's going on, I'd like to do another in-depth investigative story on the Byrnes and the Proxima Foundation."

I was suspicious. Did he want me to do the story because I was the story—the journalist who went to work for the very person I'd discredited for being a hoax, who claimed to be abducted by aliens, then went back to the people I'd exposed for guidance?

I scratched an itch under my beanie. "Why not ask

someone else to do it? You've got some good writers on staff."

"But you worked closely with the Byrnes—you'd have a unique perspective. There's no one who's had the experiences you've had."

"So it's not about me, but the Byrnes—what it's like being part of their organization?"

"Something like that. And since you are no longer their employee, you're free to do a story. I think our readers would be quite interested in hearing what you have to say, based on your experiences."

I was curious. "How did you know I no longer work for them?"

Marcus smiled. "A little birdie told me."

I stared at him. "My non-disclosure agreement could be an issue."

"I can have our attorney look at it. No problem."

I was still suspicious. Was something more nefarious at play? Was his request part of a propaganda campaign? Was Marcus under EMF mind control influence, too?

"What kind of author's freedom would I have with this story?"

"Full. I guarantee it. Of course, I have to review it. Do we have a deal?"

"Can I get that in a contract?"

"I'll have the attorney draft it today, no problem. And we can pay you ten thousand for the story. Three-week deadline. Can you do that?"

Ten thousand for three weeks of work. Not bad. I needed the money.

"What about some of the things that I know about the Byrnes business dealing?"

"If it's contextual, sure. What specifically are you referring to?"

"I have some info about their land deals and with cellular towers. They own a bunch of land with cell tower leases, new 5G towers, and they're involved in testing some new technology involving cell towers and a mobile app."

"What do you mean, new technology? What does it do?"

"Generates mind-altering frequencies."

He looked at me curiously. "Mind control?"

I nodded. "Yeah, mind control." I kept my eyes on his face.

He rubbed his chin. "Interesting. You have evidence?

"Of course."

"I've taken an interest in this 5G thing myself since the Yakama article. I was about to put someone on a new story, but for some reason I didn't. Go ahead and write what you want to write on this one. I look forward to seeing what you come up with."

"So let make sure I'm hearing you correctly. You will let me write a story about anything I want related to the Byrnes?"

"As long as it isn't defamation or violate the nondisclosure you have. It's all fair game."

"Full control over what I write?"

He smiled. "Yes, Ben, though now I'm wondering what you have in mind."

"I'll do it," I said excitedly.

We shook hands.

I couldn't believe it. He was giving me full control. *Hot Reports* prided itself on publishing articles that were controversial, even to questioning government and corporate actions and programs. They prided themselves on being an independent publisher, which is why I went to write for them to begin with.

Over the next week, I forgot my suspicions and wrote the article. I dug deep into the possible link between cell towers and sightings of UFOs. I showed it to Marcus.

"You have evidence?"

I handed him the flash drive will all the data I'd compiled.

"Are you sure about all this and the 5G mind control stuff?"

"Yes, as far as I can tell."

"Go ahead and send it to the copy editor. We'll get it queued up in the next issue. Yours will be the front story." I was ecstatic.

That afternoon, I received a letter-sized Fed Ex package with a Missoula P.O. Box as the return address. It had to be from the Byrnes, probably another cease-and-desist or death threat. I opened it. Inside the outer envelope was a second envelop made of copper foil. I carefully opened it and removed a one-page typed letter on standard office paper.

You've been selected by random drawing to attend a special event at the Proxima Foundation Ranch. Daniel Byrne will be communing with a delegation from Proxima Centauri b. Due to sensitivity of the Proximians, and at their request, there will be no cell phones, cameras, or electronic devices of any kind allowed. You must bring this invitation and present at the gate on the day of the arrival.

There was also a QR code with instructions to log onto a website on a particular day when a secure message would tell me the exact date and time to arrive. I made the list!

My thoughts were all over the place. Was it a trap? Were they trying to lure me back to kill me? Mike and Chester had pointed guns at me and locked me in a shipping container. Why would I put myself in danger? Besides, wouldn't they have already of killed me if that was what Daniel wanted to do? They had the perfect opportunity to do so when I was locked up in Nadine's shipping container. Plus, they'd have to know that I'd tell others where I was going, right? I thought for a moment. What would Pulitzer-worthy investigative journalist do? Was it worth the risk to be a part of Daniel's arrival event?

I went to Marcus. "Look what I just received—an invite to the Proxima Foundation arrival event."

I handed the copper invitation to him, and he inspected it.

"You should go. Could you take a camera or recording device?"

"I don't think so. It says right here in the invitation that they are prohibited. Mike has an EMF sniffer thing."

"Didn't you have a friend help you the last time you filmed the hoax? Maybe you can film it from the outside?— Well, consider doing it."

During Thanksgiving dinner, Daniel had mentioned hidden cameras and a security detail. I wouldn't put it past Mike and Chester to shoot someone.

Marcus went on. "I heard back from our attorneys. You're good to go on the story."

That night, Brett and I went to the bar, and I filled him in on the Proxima Foundation invite. After a second round, I brought up the possibility of a repeat of what we'd done before.

"Hell yeah," Brett said. "I could do surveillance with my drone."

"They may have electronic fences, sensors and cameras. I don't know where or how many, but Daniel said they were going to put in extra battery-operated cameras."

"What about stuff in the air? Helicopters? Drones?"

"I don't think so. Daniel said the Proximians don't want anything in the air."

"That doesn't mean the government won't have something up there, but we can deal with that. When exactly? Are we talking day or night operation, or both?"

"The invite said I'm supposed to log into a web site to get the exact date and arrival time, but I already know it's on Solstice."

"That's in three days! But if this is a mind control operation, aren't you worried about that? Are you sure these EMF hats would be enough?" he asked, sipping his beer.

"Well, I haven't had buzzing in my ears in months. I'm pretty sure the technology they're using has to do with the mobile app and towers. Plus, I've been purging for weeks."

"You are looking a bit thin," Brett said.

I finished my beer and stood up. "I read somewhere that once you are aware of mind control, it no longer works. What do you think?"

"If you are asking if you are crazy means you're not crazy."

"Are you sure?"

Brett stared at me. "Do I look crazy?"

"Not at all," I said.

"But this could be state-of-the-art technology, Ben. It doesn't care what you think." He finished his beer and stood up. "I'll pack up the jeep in the morning. This will be fun."

"Thanks, man," I said. "We can stay at the Motel 6 and park in the back parking lot."

"You going to see that chick?"

"Brenda? I don't know. We've had a falling out."

"Too bad," he said."

I checked the Proxima Foundation website that night, still no information about the ETA. On social media feeds, speculation about the arrival had gone viral. On Twitter, Solstice was indeed the day. I could hear Daniel now, ordering Mike, Chester, and the cadre of for-hire security to patrol the ranch parameter.

In the morning we packed Brett's jeep and headed east on 90. We hit snow on Snoqualmie Pass and had to put on snow chains. Finally arriving at one a.m., we were exhausted and checked into adjacent rooms at the Motel 6. We planned breakfast at Ramblin' Joe's, which meant seeing Brenda.

39

THE PLAN

I rolled over and glanced at the clock. Nine-fifteen. I'd overslept. Into the shower and out the door to get Brett. I rapped on his door. No answer. Boot prints in the light dusting of snow led in the direction of Ramblin' Joe's. *Bastard*: he was over there, flirting with Brenda. A few hundred strides and there was Brett, entertaining Brenda as she refreshed his coffee and giggled at one of his offhanded jokes.

"What's up?" I asked as I approached the booth.

"Here he is," Brett said, "bright-eyed and bushy-tailed."

Brenda and I made eye contact. I went for a hug, but she turned away. Not the warm welcome I was hoping for.

"Coffee?" she asked.

"You read my mind," I said, scooting in on the banquette across from Brett. I scanned the restaurant, then looked at Brenda. "Anyone from the Foundation in here?"

"No culties or out-of-towners, except you," she said.

"I told Brenda about what we're doing here," Brett said, "I hope you don't mind."

She looked down at me, steaming coffee pot in hand. "So you're back to being a journalist again?"

"My old boss is giving me an opportunity to write a story on the Byrnes and the arrival event. I got an invite, so I'm going in while Brett films it from the outside."

"Sounds dangerous," she said.

Brett looked at me. "We should go over the plans."

Just then, two men and a woman came into the restaurant. They were obviously not locals, and by the woman's plastic appearance, she was likely a cable news reporter.

"Let's go somewhere else," I muttered sotto voce.

"He's right," nodded Brett, "not the best operational security. Let's go out to my Jeep. Map's out there, anyway."

"I want to see this," Brenda said, taking off her apron, "someone else will seat them. Follow me out the back."

We followed Brenda through the back and out into the parking lot. Confident we would remain unnoticed, Brett spread the map out on the back gate of his Jeep. "I'll park three miles to the east on an old fire road and hike onto the ridge, south side of the Lolo National Forest about a half mile from the Proxima Foundation ranch." He pointed to a spot on the map. "There's a clearing here where I can launch and land the drone. This is public land, so I shouldn't have to worry about any rancher throwing a hissy fit about me trespassing."

"Drone?" Brenda asked.

"Check this out," Brett said, pulling back a canvas cover in the back of his Jeep to reveal a large black box, tactical pack, and a cross-bow. He lifted the latches on the box, and there was a high-tech quad drone about three feet wide. "It's the model 3100 with a custom configured 4K camera and night vision mode. Streams live to a mobile app. Flies fast, too."

"What if you lose the drone?" Brenda asked. "Aren't drones supposed to be registered with the FAA? If it crashes, and they find it, they'll figure out who owns it."

"Not this one. I never registered it. Besides, I won't lose it. It's got a multi-frequency transmitter for radio control. It would take a pretty sophisticated jammer to take control of it. Some military units have them. I'll fly in, get video, and fly out. We did this all the time in Afghanistan for Taliban surveillance. Easy-peasy."

"What's your plan for confronting security?" she asked.

"I'm a wildlife photographer, which I am."

"Who knows Ben Davenport," Brenda added.

"I won't get that close. I'll get a look from across the ridge and fly the drone after dark," Brett said, then looked at me. "She's sharp, doesn't miss much."

I looked at Brett. "Just get the hell out of there if anything goes sour."

"Got it, man, nothing to worry about. It's *you* I'm worried about."

Brenda and I made eye contact. "I'm going, too," she said, "I'll help film it."

"I don't think that's a good idea," I said. "Daniel has security with guns. It's too dangerous. Just think about what happened to your aunt..."

"I know what happened to Aunt Sally, that's why I'm going. I want to see this for myself. Besides, there's going to be a lot of people at the ranch, right?"

"They're expecting about two hundred or so, mostly media. Are you absolutely sure about this?" I knew I wasn't going to change Brenda's mind, but I still wasn't happy with it.

"Yeah," she said, "I'll ride with Brett."

"I could use help with the cameras. It's cool," Brett said, looking back and forth at the two of us.

"You'd better wear an EMF hat," I said to Brenda. "Do you still have the one I gave you?"

"Yeah, I've got it," she said.

"I've got one, too," Brett grinned. "We'll be fine."

"So we get the footage—what are you going to do after the event is over?" Brenda asked me.

"I'm going to get the hell out of there, that's what. And if we have footage, Marcus said he'd let me run it. I'll post it on the Internet."

"You trust him?"

"Who, Marcus? Yeah," I said. "*Hot Reports* is known for breaking big stories."

Brett addressed Brenda. "So meet me at the hotel at three this afternoon?"

"I'll be ready," she said.

"All right," Brett said, checking his watch. "Are we are clear on the mission?"

"Crystal clear," I said.

"I'll have the kitchen cook up some breakfast and bring it over to the motel," Brenda said.

I wrapped my arm over her shoulder and pulled her in for a hug. I didn't care what she thought about it. "Are you sure about this tonight? I don't want anything to happen to you."

"I'm fine," she said, pushing me away. "I want to help, and I need to do this for Aunt Sally."

I gave her my room number, and Brett and I went back to the motel to finish our prep and wait.

Later that afternoon, as I drove into the Proxima Foundation Ranch, I pondered the depravity of what was going down. The Byrnes had sent copper foil envelopes and invitations to select people they thought were worthy to attend the inter-dimensional arrival of extraterrestrial beings from a star system 4.24 light-years away. How could anyone believe such a thing unless they were under the influence of mind control? This might also be Brenda's opportunity to get to the bottom of her aunt's murder, or was I just putting her in danger? My mind flashed through a speed reel of apocalyptic scenes—orange-tinged lighting, sulfurous wasteland, MILABs and all.

What if the government was testing some new EMF mind control on the crowd of onlookers? Would my precautions and my resistance to the effects of the radio wave-controlled nanotech continue to work? What if Mike and Chester were mind controlled and opened up on the crowd with their AR-15s? I thought about the risk my buddy Brett was taking. Sure, he was a bit post-war crazy, but he knew what he was getting into, and if anyone could carry out the mission, Brett could. I felt about him being out there with Brenda, and them together watching me below. Maybe they'd be able to go for help if needed, or at least live to tell it if everything went south in the Valley of the Moon.

40

THE EVENT

I rolled up to a fortified security gate manned by two men I assumed were the hired guns Daniel had mentioned. Or were they government agents? I rolled down the window and handed one of them my copper foil invitation. They directed me to a makeshift parking lot about one hundred yards from the main house. Dozens of vehicles had already staked out their ground there, but I quickly found a spot alongside the sundry SUVs and sedans with government plates. A stab of the lock button, and off I went toward a path to another gate marked by yellow security tape. Chester, armed with a holstered pistol, checked the invitation and my ID as if he'd never seen me before, and proceeded to run a handheld scanner over my body. Finding me clear, he handed me Daniel's arrival event program and let me enter the grounds. I walked toward the main house, flipping through the glossy pages of the event program I'd proofed for Daniel just weeks before.

Daniel was off to the side of the house in conversation with John, the documentary director. Mike was at Daniel's side, his sidearm strapped and a radio piece in his ear. A cameraman, sound guy, and a couple of assistants were scurrying around setting up equipment.

Daniel and I made eye contact while Mike gave me a good once over and said something to Daniel. Smiling, Daniel approached and shook my hand, cupping his other hand over mine. "I'm glad you came, Ben."

"Thanks for inviting me," I said, feeling uneasy with Mike's eyes on me. Was he still stewing over my second betrayal of his trust? I reminded myself that if he didn't want me there as part of the press corps, he wouldn't have invited me.

"I wish that I could spend more time with you, Ben, but when I get done with the film crew, I need to meet with a few folks from NASA. But feel free to take a look around and mingle. I'm sure you'll recognize some of the guests." He was already stepping away. "Nadine has a nice spread of food and hot drinks up at the tent. We've also opened the new Learning Center building. Check it out."

"I will," I said. I felt awkward about our cursory meeting, but I was there on a mission, not to regain his friendship or make amends. I was there to witness and prove, without any shadow of a doubt, that the entire event was a government mind control operation. I was going to pull the poles on this circus tent and shed light on the truth as an investigative journalist.

I ambled up to the tent and the new Learning Center where thirty or so people were gathered. Some were touring the freshly painted building; others were standing or sitting under gas heaters around the tent where coffee was brewing in BUNNs, and yogurt bars were neatly stacked on biodegradable plates. I estimated that half of the visitors were press, with the other half a mix of government types and local luminaries, including several City Council members and the mayors of Missoula and Clinton.

I made my way through the few exhibits on display—artist renderings of large-headed Proximians, star maps, retro sci-fi film posters from the Fifties. To my surprise, Jack Clark was there, inspecting one of Daniel's 3D-printed models of a Proximian spacecraft. With an arrival event program securely tucked under one arm, he lifted his free arm to tip his Stetson-style hat at me.

"What are you doing here?" I asked, shaking his hand.

"I got an invitation at the last minute. I couldn't say no to this." He grinned. "This may be my chance to finally see a UFO."

"I thought it was only going to be press and government types."

"Well, I made the list." Jack opened his program. "Says here that there's a giant landing strip in the form of a hexagram. Have you seen it?"

"No, but I heard they put it out on the south pasture."

"Let's go take a peek before it gets dark. What do you say?"

"Why not?" I wanted to see it and assess whether or not Jack was under the influence of mind control.

We synced strides on our southerly trek beyond the main house. A giant hexagram made of river stones was spread out in the grass, surrounded by yellow barrier tape, apparently to keep onlookers out of the area. Extra reams of tape delineated a second area, set aside for the press corps. A mess of scaffolds, bleachers, and a portable PA system rose up on one side. On the other side, more bleachers, and stretching across the crux was what appeared to be a VIP box about twenty feet wide, screened in by Plexiglas. The entire scene reminded me of a smaller, more intimate version of the arrival platform on the backside of Devil's Tower in Close Encounters of the Third Kind.

"Interesting shape for a landing strip, don't you think?" I asked, to assay Jack's opinion on it.

"It's not a landing strip. It says on page 3 that it's an interdimensional portal," Jack explained.

My hope that he was free from mind control was fading. "Do you believe all of this, Jack? That the Proximians are coming here to deliver a message through Daniel?"

He grinned. "Don't you?"

His excitement wasn't like him at all. A knot formed in the

pit of my stomach. I was reluctant to utter any doubts for fear my words would get back to Daniel. "I guess we'll find out."

He smiled. "My entire life, Ben, I've felt like a cat chasing the little red dot of a laser toy across the floor. Every time I thought I'd caught the answer, it moved. I got to the point where I wondered if the answer I was chasing was real at all. But now I'm convinced I'm going to have the answer."

"Are you worried at all about this? I mean, what if it doesn't go well?"

"Oh, I'm sure it will be fine. If the Proximians wanted to destroy us, they would have done it already."

Strange comfort.

Jack continued. "Do you think that there will be convincing evidence collected tonight?"

"I've got a couple other MUFON guys with me and volunteer observers and field investigator crews on alert in five states." He smiled widely. "This is going to be incredible, and we've got the best seat in the house."

I knew then that he was gone—three sheets to radio-controlled nanotech. I felt sorry for him. He'd been a good friend during my abduction ordeal and investigations that followed.

We returned to the Learning Center and the circus tent. I mingled but refused the refreshments. I didn't want to risk ingesting anything that would set me back after the past month of careful purging, heavy metal detoxes, and intense mental focus exercises. My mind was clear and loyal to the truth, and I intended to keep it that way.

By 4 p.m., the number of visitors had doubled. A special entourage arrived and headed to the VIP area of the landing zone. I didn't see who it was, but assumed it was someone from the government or perhaps one of Daniel's celebrity followers. It wouldn't have surprised me if it was Brad or Tom.

At five, Mike, wielding a megaphone, commanded the crowd to gather at the landing zone in the south pasture. I had a fairly good view of the VIP box from my position.

Sitting in it were Nadine, Mr. Petulli, the mayors, and to my surprise, Congressman Young! I knew he was involved, and his presence there that night proved it! I was hoping that Brett and Brenda were zooming in with their cameras this very moment.

Mike flipped the large lights on as soon as the sun set, illuminating the giant hexagram in a pale glow. A half-moon rose in the east, just as Brett had said it would. He needed it for the night vision cameras and goggles.

Daniel took to the PA, speaking in a cool, confident tone. "Thank you, everyone, please take your seats. Soon, our Proximian comrades will arrive. Do not panic. They will speak through me, until they speak directly. Please refer to pages six through eight in the program."

People shuffled through their programs.

Still positioned on the outside of the hexagram, Daniel announced that the arrival was imminent. He ordered everyone to stow their programs, face the center of the hexagram, and go down on their right knee as a show of humility. The crowd complied without hesitation. Jack looked up at me, and I went down, too.

Daniel stripped naked and headed into the hexagram center. He settled into a full lotus and began to mumble words inaudible from my position. Everyone had their eyes on him and were eerily silent. I hadn't really thought about it until then, but the whole scene resembled a ritual. Daniel was about to make a deal with preterhuman intelligences who were to appear through an interdimensional portal. Brenda was right in calling them *Culties*.

Daniel's meditation went on for several minutes. I kept glancing up into the moonlit sky. Nothing seemed to be happening. Suddenly, Daniel threw his head back and flung his arms wide. Seemingly to welcome something appearing in the sky. He then shifted into the kneeling position like everyone else.

The crowd let out a gasp in strange unison, everyone's gaze fixated on the space above Daniel. More gasps and awe.

A few people laughed and giggled out of joy or nervousness. I scanned the skies. I saw nothing. Mind control! Everyone was under the influence except me! Were Brett and Brenda getting all of this on video?

Daniel turned and looked at me, gesturing for me to join him in the circle.

"He's calling you," Jack whispered.

"I see that," I whispered back. Had he noticed I wasn't affected by the radio beams? I stayed down on my knee. There was no way that I was going to be part of this.

"He wants you to go out there," Jack said. "You'd better go."

Daniel gestured to me again. I could feel eyes on me. The silence of the crowd and their stares were overwhelming. Jack gave me a nudge. I gave in and walked out to Daniel. When I got within a few feet, he turned to face me. "Sit with me, son," he said softly, his pupils dilating, the whites diminishing before my eyes. "Take off your clothes," he said, pointing upward. "They want you to."

I unzipped my jacket slowly, thinking, what have I gotten myself into? A churn of emotions welled up: anger, sadness, even pity.

"Your pants, everything," Daniel said, "and kneel."

I stopped. "Daniel, I can't do this."

"Ben, you have to. The Proximians are here. Don't you see their craft? It's beautiful." He pointed toward the sky. "Strip down and kneel with me. They're about to exit their craft and appear before us to deliver the message they want us to share with the world."

My heart pounded. I glanced up and then back at Daniel. "There's nothing there."

Daniel's eyes were fully dilated now, all black. He gritted his teeth. "Do it now or there will be severe consequences for us all. They command you."

I stood, frozen. I saw Nadine erect against the Plexiglas of the VIP section of the bleachers. Around her, an army of eyes had me scoped in the crosshairs. My head said, Make a run for it, but my feet stayed nailed to the earth.

"No Daniel," I shot back, "I'm not doing this." As I turned to walk away, a wave of fear surged over me, and I felt myself slipping, legs shaking, my body. I cursed the sensation off and reclaimed my physical self. Nerves could be dealt with later. I strove to focus.

Mike and Chester bolted at me and grabbed me by both arms.

"Bring him over here, strip him and make him kneel," snarled Daniel.

Mike put me into a walking head lock.

"No!" I yelled, struggling. Chester began ripping at my clothes.

"Strip him bare and make him kneel," Daniel repeated.

"I'll snap your neck if you don't do it," Mike said into my ear.

Suddenly, a black object darted out of the dark sky and slammed into Daniel's back, thrusting him face forward onto the ground. He let out a yelp, and Mike and Chester pivoted their attention to him. Pieces of drone fuselage spewed in all directions. I broke free and made a dash for it, heading west in the direction of Brett and Brenda up on the ridge. Before I made it to the edge of the hexagram, the kneeling crowd of reporters leaped up in unison, as if commanded to stop me. I pushed through the zombie press corps and sprinted across the pasture to the tree line with Mike, Chester, and a cadre of security close behind.

I charged into the dark woods and began the ascent up to the ridge. What had Brett's map shown? Luckily, memory served and I made it to the small clearing and escape point. A few minutes later I found Brett and Brenda crouched behind the stump of a fallen ponderosa, Brett kitted out in winter tactical clothes with his tactical pack and crossbow strapped over his shoulder, his face camouflaged by black and white face paint. Brenda was in her white winter jacket, ski hat and boots, digital video camera in hand.

"Did you get it on film?" I pressed, trying to suck in

enough oxygen to keep from passing out.

"Yeah, we got it," Brenda said.

"What in God's name was going on down there?" Brett asked.

"Crazy time," I said, catching my breath. "People thought they were seeing a craft in the sky. Definitely mass hallucination. What did you see from up here?"

"Just a bunch of people standing around a giant hexagram with a naked man in the middle of it. Told you it was a cult," Brenda said.

"Yeah, you were right, but it's more than that. They were all under the effects of mind-altering radio beams, their eyes dilated. Congressman Young was there, too, but with Nadine in an EMF-shielded hut." I smiled. "I fucking knew it! I told you it was a government plot! Are you absolutely sure you got it all on video? What about the drone video?"

"We got it," Brett said, "but you have to buy me another drone. If I hadn't flown it down to save your ass, you'd be getting butt raped by now."

"How far is the Jeep?" I asked. My pursuers couldn't be too far behind.

"Right where I left it, on the other side of the ridge to the west. Maybe half a klick. Follow me," Brett said, taking the lead.

We went down a hill through a thicket of trees, following a trail into a valley. Snow had been blown into the shaded ravine, so we stepped carefully over river stones and tree roots at the edge of the stream. A ghostly howl ripped from above, scaring the shit out of me.

"Did you hear that?"

"It's an owl," Brenda said.

Brett slipped on a rock and into the icy water. He reached out to me. "Help me up, bro, my leg is fucked."

I grabbed his hand and pulled him up. He grunted and threw his left arm over my shoulder. "Jesus, my leg is jacked. I can't walk." His two-hundred-pound body limped along beside me. We heard men yelling in the distance.

Brenda trailed behind. "If they catch us, they're going to fucking kill us, just like my aunt!"

"Not if they don't catch us. Keep going." To Brett, I said, "We might just need your crossbow."

Brett had the jeep covered in camouflage netting, snow, and spruce boughs. He leaned on the hood. "I can't feel my foot." I could see blood on his pants leg. He threw the keys to me. "You're going to have to drive."

Brenda and I cleared off the Jeep. I climbed into the driver's seat and got it started. Brett hobbled into the passenger seat, and Brenda climbed in back.

"Keep the lights off," Brett said, reaching over and toggling his secret all lights off switch. He handed me his night vision goggles. "Wear these."

I slid on the goggles, slammed the Jeep in gear, backed around, and headed down the ridge, going as fast and cautiously as possible on the snow-covered one-lane fire road.

Brett pulled up his blood-soaked pant leg. It looked like a compound fracture just above his ankle. "I'm going to need a hospital, soon." His voice quivered from the cold.

It had all been my idea, but we had the videos and three eye-witness testimonies. The mission had been worth it if we could get off the mountain and the video up on the Internet.

"We can't go back to the motel—or to Brenda's place," I said.

"Drop me at the hospital and get out of town," Brett said, tying a tourniquet with some rip cord he took from the glove box.

"I'm not about to just leave you there," I said. "What if they come for you at the hospital?"

"What choice do you have?"

"There's a light above us, following us," Brenda shouted.

"What do you mean a light?" I asked, my eyes on the glowing, pale green road. Had a government helicopter been called in? If they had infrared, they already had us in their sights.

Brett stuck his head out the window, looking behind us

and upwards. "Looks like a helicopter or something."

"Or something?" I asked. I glanced in the rear view to see for myself but was blinded by the brightness caused by the light amplifier in the night vision goggles.

"Watch out!" Brett shouted.

Several Sheriff's Department cruisers were ahead, blocking the way. I swerved out of instinct and drove us off-road and down a hill, the Jeep bouncing wildly as we barreled through the darkness.

"Fuck, dude!" Brett bellowed. "You're going to lose it!"

Tree branches and snow slammed into the windshield. I pumped the brakes to slow us down, only to lose control and slam into a tree. The airbags exploded, throwing me back into the seat. Brett screamed in pain.

I looked back at Brenda. "Are you okay?"

"Yes. No, I don't know."

Lights from police vehicles were approaching. Above, the bright light shone on us. I could hear the chugging blades of a helicopter. Next thing I knew, the police were at the Jeep and the lanky deputy I'd met on my second day in Missoula was pulling me from the vehicle.

"Get on the ground, punk!" he yelled.

Boot on my back, he slapped zip tie cuffs over my wrists and yelled at Brenda to stay put until another deputy came around and pulled her out. They hauled Brett out too, with him yelling in agony. The deputy led me up the hill and put me into his car. Brenda and Brett were getting into other cars. We took off down the road and eventually arrived at the Sheriff's Station where I was thrown into a solitary cell. The next morning, they led me out the back in handcuffs and loaded me into an ambulance.

"Where are you taking me?"

"To have your brain checked," said the deputy, as he slammed the door shut.

41

THE TRUTH

I was in a bed of molded plastic in a small, brightly lit room. Someone had dressed me in heather gray sweatpants and sweatshirt. I could see a drain in the middle of the vinyl floor. I smelled pungent Lysol. The door to the room, heavy with a small portal of a window, was open.

I'd been in the psychiatric hospital for less than twenty-four hours, its location unknown to me. They'd given me something that made me sleep. *Involuntary commitment for an evaluation*. But why? And why here? And where were Brett and Brenda? Brett must be in the hospital somewhere. Was Brenda in jail?

I threw my bare feet over the edge of the bed and slipped them into the pair of Salk SureGrip Terries. I padded out into the hall and advanced slowly to a nurse's station where I found two large men in white coats, one on a computer, the other flirting with a nurse.

"You are missing dinner," the nurse said. Why don't you go to the day room and eat something?"

"Can I use a phone?" I thought perhaps I could try to call someone for help, although I wasn't sure who.

She smiled and turned away. "Not now. It's dinnertime. Maybe later," she muttered.

"Can I leave?"

She chuckled. "No. You have to stay here. Go and eat."

"For how long?"

She sighed. "You'll need to talk to the psychiatrist."

"When can I do that?"

"On Monday, when she's in the office."

"What about my friends Brett and Brenda? Where are they?"

She shrugged. "I don't know."

"What hospital is this?"

"This is a military hospital," she said, sounding annoyed this time.

A Military psychiatric hospital? This couldn't be good. "For an evaluation? Why?"

"Talk to the psychiatrist. Now go eat."

Seeing I wasn't getting anywhere with her, I went to the day room where trays of food were arriving on carts. A few adults were sitting or pacing about. A large TV on the wall was tuned to CNN. A man with dark hair and an unshaven face, came up to me. He was Robert Shaw, the station manager at Channel 4.

"You're Ben Davenport from *Hot Reports*, Pulitzer-nominated investigative journalist."

"Yes, and you're Robert Shaw from Channel 4 in Missoula. Why are you here?"

He smiled. "Lots of journalists are here." He pointed across the room to an older man with greyed disheveled hair and a woman staring out a window. "James, over there, and so is Michele. She's from Channel Six in Billings."

I looked around the room. More than a third of the people there were reporters or journalists of some kind. "What's going on?"

He grinned. "We've apparently all lost our minds. Trying to report the truth can drive you crazy. Know what I mean? Thank God for Clozapine!"

"Do you know where we are? What hospital this is?"

"It's on a military base. I don't know. Maybe all the others were full." He leaned closer and whispered. "They are going to let me out tomorrow. Don't worry, you'll see the truth, too."

"What do you mean?" I asked, looking into his crazed eyes and seeing that he was no longer the same person I'd met before.

He chuckled. Something on the TV grabbed his attention. There was a special press briefing from the White House. I walked closer to the TV to listen. The President of the United States was speaking. "Fellow Americans, today we have entered into a new era of our understanding of the universe, and our place in it. For the last several days, the US Space Force, NASA, and others have been tracking alien signals in the vicinity of Earth. It turns out the signals were from intelligent life originating in a world far from Earth. We've received the message that they want to communicate with our government."

My jaw dropped. *This was it*: the official disclosure of alien contact and existence of extraterrestrial life that everyone had been waiting for. Was it true, or was this the false flag? The message on the bottom of the screen said that the stock markets had closed after losing nearly a quarter of the DOW's value.

The POTUS continued. "Americans have many questions tonight. Americans are asking: Who are these extraterrestrials? Where are they from? What do they want? Most importantly, are they a threat?

They come from Proxima Centuari B, a star system in the habitable Goldilocks Zone more than four light-years from Earth. Countless books and films have portrayed visitations to our planet by extraterrestrial beings from other worlds. But this is no fiction. We know from their communications and covert actions within our atmosphere that they may pose a serious threat. Make no mistake, the threat is real, but the extent of the danger is not fully known. I ask you to be calm and resolute, even in the face of this new and uncertain threat. We have already taken several immediate and necessary steps to prepare for what is before us. I signed several emergency executive orders just moments ago that are intended to provide the appropriate and necessary security."

I looked about the room. Half the patients were watching the screen, the other half were wandering dazed and out of it. I turned my attention back to the President.

"The first executive order is for a emergency funding to underwrite defense research and development to protect our world. I've also asked the Treasury Department to keep the markets closed over the next week. We'll also be implementing mandatory curfews in all communities across the United States. We've federalized and recalled the National Guard to assist with domestic order during this time."

Martial law—just what Daniel had said they would do.

"As a precaution, and until we know more, we are mandating that everyone wear masks and stand six feet apart to prevent any possible extraterrestrial viral transmissions."

Six feet apart. Dr. Trivedi had said the six-foot distance would be needed to calibrate the nanobots on a mass scale.

"We also know that the aliens are capable of telepathic communication. This means the ability to read and transmit information directly to the minds of others. While we have much to learn about this capability, I'm asking all Americans to make a conscious effort to not think about anything negative toward the Proximians or the government. In fact, make an effort to not think too much at all. It's okay not to think deeply. It's the right thing to do for your fellow citizen."

Did the leader of the free world just tell everyone to not think? What the hell is going on here? It's got to be mind control nanobots!

"You may wonder why we didn't warn the people of the Earth sooner. How could we have overlooked such a threat? We were aware of unidentified aerial objects in our atmosphere, but didn't know what they were, but now we do. I am joined tonight by several leaders whom I've asked to speak to you. I want full transparency about what we are doing to understand and mitigate the threat that contact with extraterrestrial life brings with it. I've appointed Daniel Byrne of the Proxima Foundation to be a special assistant."

"No fucking way!" I shouted. "You've got to be kidding me!"

"Mr. Byrne, working with Google, Apple, and other technology companies, has developed a special mobile app that will provide guidance and special updates for all citizens of the world. The app is free and will be automatically downloaded to all devices."

It's the iM4ET app. This can't be!

"Tonight, we are a nation and a world awakening to danger and called to defend our way of life, as we know it. What is at stake is not just America's freedom. This is the world's fight, civilization's fight, the fight of all who believe in our right to live and prosper on our planet. On behalf of the American people, I thank the world for its outpouring of support. God bless America."

The President stepped away and exited as Daniel Byrne stepped into his place, flanked by a Space Force four star and the Executive Director of NASA.

"Thank you, Mr. President," Daniel said. "It's an honor to be the liaison between our government and the Proximians."

"That son of a bitch! He's got them all conned! He's in on it!" I shouted.

Daniel continued. "Less than 48 hours ago, I made contact with the Proximians at the Proxima Foundation Ranch in Montana. They communicated to me there, including others with us, including the press, and we agreed to not report the event until we were certain it could be reported without retribution from the Proximians. Well, the Proximians want us to report it now. They agree that the press needs to report the facts of the situation, so we are going to show you some of that footage now, so people can see for themselves."

The camera zoomed out to capture the large flat panel display to the side of the podium. The video began with a distant shot of a large, triangular rainbow-colored craft descending and hovering above Daniel standing in middle of the hexagram. Two beings floated out, arms outstretched, and came to stand on their feet in front of Daniel. They stood facing each other until bare-assed Daniel bowed to them. After a few moments, Daniel looked up at one of the beings, nodded, and then the video went dark.

"Well, there you have it. Video of what happened at the ranch, witnessed by several dozen reporters, military leaders, and others."

I lost it. I pointed at the screen. "This is bullshit! I'm telling you, it's fake! This is a government plot! This is bullshit! I was there! This didn't happen!"

An anchor from one of the affiliate stations in Seattle began shouting.

Orderlies rushed into the day room and dragged me forcefully down the hall to a padded isolation room. They held me down until the nurse arrived with a large syringe.

I kept resisting. "Why are you doing this? Listen to me! What was just on TV was fake! I'm telling you, it's fake! I have proof! Just watch the videos we made!"

"That's enough, Mr. Davenport, you need to calm down," the nurse said while readying the syringe.

The orderlies held me face down on the padded vinyl floor, one with his knee on my back, the other keeping my legs from kicking.

"Just relax," the nurse said, moving closer. "this will calm you so that you can think more clearly. Doctor's orders."

"I am thinking clearly. I don't need any medication. I'd like to leave, please."

Unable to move, I felt the needle stick me in the ass.

The orderlies remained on top of me for a minute or so, then withdrew. I sat on the cushioned floor, my knees bent and my back to the wall, waiting for the noncompliant patient concoction to fully kick in. I stared at the chalky vinyl walls, the padding nullifying any sound I made. Above my head a single LED fixture pulsed pale light. I wondered what the pulsing was doing to my brain.

I was enraged. How dare they lock me up for calling bullshit to the government's fake alien invasion! It was obviously all orchestrated, and what of the other journalists locked up with me? I'd been witness to a secret government mind control operation, and when I'd resisted—when they realized that I wouldn't be fooled—they'd committed me to a psychiatric ward, no doubt replete with falsified documents. How many others like me were there out there with strength of mind who were locked up across the country? I'm not crazy, I'm the one who's rational. I had objective evidence, and my mind is clear. I cannot be fooled!

Desperation washed over me as the minutes passed. What comes next? How long would I be locked up in here? Would I survive this? Do I want to survive to live in a new reality of mass techno-psychological mind control? What an Orwellian nightmare!

I began bouncing my head repeatedly against the padded wall. I shouldn't have trusted Daniel or Marcus and *Hot Reports*. I have a master's in journalism from Northwestern and a Pulitzer nomination. I should have had the courage to do the podcast when I had the chance. Maybe it wouldn't have mattered. The government and the telecommunications monopoly would have just shut me down anyway, right? But I knew the truth.

Suddenly, I felt the familiar frequency in my ears, growing in amplitude with the pounding of my heart. Was the Clozapine kicking in, or was it the government's mind control rays? I closed my eyes and shuttered my ears with the palms of my shaking hands. Please, God, help me! Please help me resist this! Let me keep my clarity of mind! I want to know the truth! Don't let me be fooled!

With my eyes still shut, I looked up at the overhead LED and felt the artificial light passing through my eyelids, causing a warm, orange glow. I relaxed, and my mind's eye was viewing the high desert, the grass and sage shining in the tepid spring sun. I felt the warmth on my face and smelled the breeze. I was in Prescott Valley, Arizona, age ten. I was breathing and with every breath, the ringing in my ears faded. I heard the soft voice of my father. "Ben, my son, I have a lesson for you. Look at me." Excited, I opened my eyes to a pale-gray humanoid form in the center of the room, bathed in purple and silver light. It had a large head and dark, empty eyes. It spoke directly to my mind. "Truth is, and will always be, in the eye of the beholder."

THE END

ACKNOWLEDGMENTS

With deep gratitude, I wish to thank my family and friends for their support and encouragement while I wrote this book.

ABOUT THE AUTHOR

David D. Luxton, PhD., is Affiliate Associate Professor in the Department of Psychiatry and Behavioral Sciences at the University of Washington in Seattle, and a former research psychologist and health scientist with the US Department of Defense. Author of numerous scientific and policy-level publications, he consults widely on matters related to artificial intelligence, ethics, and psychological health. His previous books include *Artificial Intelligence in Behavioral and Mental Health Care*, *A Practitioner's Guide to Telemental Health*, and the novel *Behind The Machine*. He served in the United States Air Force and presently volunteers as a Preventive Medicine Officer with the Washington State Guard. He's also founder of the Wayfarer Records music label, and his recordings have been featured worldwide on radio, television, and in film. He lives by the Puget Sound in the Pacific Northwest, USA.

Learn more at www.davidluxton.com

Made in the USA
Las Vegas, NV
12 June 2021